**Also available from Sandra Owens
and Carina Press**

K-9 Defenders Series

*In His Protection
Her Delta Force Protector*

Operation K-9 Brothers Series

*Operation K-9 Brothers
Keeping Guard
Mountain Rescue*

Also by Sandra Owens

Blue Ridge Valley Series

*Just Jenny
All Autumn
Still Savannah
Caitlyn's Christmas Wish*

Dark Falls Series

*Dark Terror
Dark Memories*

Aces & Eights Series

*Jack of Hearts
King of Clubs
Ace of Spades
Queen of Diamonds*

K2 Team Series

*Crazy for Her
Someone Like Her
Falling for Her
Lost in Her
Only Her*

TO HOLD AND PROTECT

SANDRA OWENS

carina
press

carina press®

ISBN-13: 978-1-335-45850-6

To Hold and Protect

For questions and comments about the quality of this book,
please contact us at CustomerService@Harlequin.com.

Carina Press
22 Adelaide St. West, 41st Floor
Toronto, Ontario M5H 4E3, Canada
www.CarinaPress.com

Printed in U.S.A.

I'm dedicating this one to my husband because he's the inspiration for all my heroes.

TO HOLD AND PROTECT

Chapter One

"Arson," Parker told his brother, Marsville's police chief, as they walked through the house once the fire was out. It had been up for sale and was thankfully empty.

Tristan frowned. "That's three now."

"Yep." Parker kneeled next to Ember, his fire-accelerant detection dog, who'd alerted on several spots in the house. "Good girl." He held out his hand, and the red Labrador delicately took the treats from his palm. She was food motivated, the treats a reward for a job well done.

He'd collect samples to send to the lab, but he didn't need the results to know the accelerant was gasoline that had been poured on the floor. Gasoline burned downward and was the reason for the hole in the wood. It also formed a volatile air and vapor mixture above the origin of the fire that would then ignite. He looked up and noted the expected severe ceiling damage over this hot spot.

"So we got us a firebug," Tristan said. "What's the profile on an arsonist?"

Parker stood and stretched. "Young white male. Craves attention and power. Might get sexual gratification from the fire."

"Seriously?"

"Yeah, some do. But that profile doesn't mean our

firebug is a young white male. Could be older, could be a woman—although that's rare—or it could be kids. Statistically there are arrests in only about 10 percent of arson fires nationally."

"That's not encouraging."

"Nope. I'm going to collect samples, then head home. You and Skylar still on for dinner tonight?"

"Yeah, we'll be there."

"Great. See you then."

Although the fires could be unrelated, Parker doubted it. He hadn't pinpointed why yet, but these fires felt personal, like someone was…teasing him? No, *taunting* him. That was the word he was looking for.

He'd felt watched while his crew had been fighting the fire. As the fire chief, his responsibility was to direct the activities of his firefighters on the scene, and while he'd been doing that, the hairs on the back of his neck had stood up. He knew most everyone in Marsville at least by sight if not by name, and although he'd searched, he hadn't seen any strangers in the crowd who'd gathered to watch.

"Let's go home, Ember," he said after collecting his samples. They'd go to the lab tomorrow.

He made a stop at the station to drop off the samples. He was the chief of a small-town station located in the foothills of the Blue Ridge Mountains in North Carolina. The idea that they might have an arsonist working in Marsville was worrisome since the station operated with only a small crew, barely enough for the twenty-four-hours-on and forty-eight-off shifts. Normally that wasn't a problem, but it could become one if the arsonist kept starting fires at the rate he or she was going.

The two Marsville fire engines and their two ambulances were back in their bays, and his crew were in the kitchen, throwing something together for dinner. He poked his head in. "Good job out there today, people."

"Wanna join us, Chief?" Eric said. "Drummond's got plenty of pork chops on the grill."

"Sounds good but can't today. Next time." If he didn't get busy painting, he wouldn't have enough pieces ready for his upcoming New York show. Leaving his official fire chief's SUV in its bay, he and Ember got in his black-on-black Dodge Challenger Hellcat and headed home. Normally, he'd drive the SUV home since he was on call 24/7, but one of the city's motor pool mechanics was picking it up to take it in for service.

As he passed the house next door to his—which had been an empty eyesore even before Bob Landry had died—he noted a bright yellow VW Bug convertible in the driveway. Parker loved cool cars, but bright yellow was not a cool car color. His eyes were drawn to the woman on the porch and...his daughter? He slammed on the brakes.

"Sorry," he said when Ember gave him a dirty look from the passenger seat. He pulled in behind the VW. "Stay." He exited the car. "Everly Isabella Church, who gave you permission to leave the yard?"

"Uh-oh." Everly scooted next to the woman. "Daddy called me three names. That means he's mad at me." She sighed. "I probably won't get any pickles."

She had that right. The most effective punishment he could give his pickle-loving daughter was to take her pickles away. "Does Andrew know where you are?" Andrew, their everything—housekeeper, cook, and Everly's

manny—would blame himself for letting a willful little girl escape his watchful eye. He shouldn't, because
Parker himself had lost track of his sneaky daughter a
time or two.

"No." She hung her head, then lifted the same brown
eyes he saw every time he looked in a mirror. "I'm
sorry, Daddy. I just wanted to meet Miss Willow."

His baby girl had him wrapped around her little finger, and although he wanted nothing more than to scoop
her up and pepper kisses all over her face until she giggled, he didn't. She couldn't just go off on her own to
her heart's content. The world wasn't safe, and nothing meant more than making sure his reason for living
stayed safe. "Go home, Ev."

She peeked up at him through honey-colored bangs
that needed trimming. He needed to take her to get a
haircut, should have a week or two ago. "But, Daddy—"

"Now, Everly."

"Don't you think you're being a little harsh, Everly's
dad?" said the woman, Miss Willow he supposed, after
Everly ran from her yard to his.

"She's five years old. It's not safe for her to traipse
around the neighborhood by herself."

"I wasn't going to let anything happen to her." She
stood and held out her hand. "I'm Willow Landry."

Landry? A relative of Bob's then. Although he was
irritated with her because she was a stranger and how
could he know whether she'd let something happen to
his daughter, he couldn't bring himself to be rude and
ignore her outstretched hand.

Free spirit was his impression as he took in the straw
hat, flowery dress, and cowboy boots. Long, curly, strawberry blond hair, green eyes, a splash of freckles across

her nose, and…well, she was striking. Not that she was his type. He inwardly snorted. Like he even had a type anymore. He hadn't since bringing his baby girl home from France.

He put his hand around Willow's. His first thought was how small and soft hers was, his second was *here she is*, and a weird charge raced up his arm. *What the hell?* He snatched his hand away.

"Parker Church," he managed to say. "Gotta go."

"Nice meeting you," she called after him.

He waved his hand over his shoulder, refusing to look at her again, and reminded himself that she drove a bright yellow VW Bug. He could not be interested in a woman who drove a bright yellow anything, no matter how cute those freckles dotting her nose were.

Since he had a few hours until his family was getting together for a cookout, Parker left Everly under the watchful eye of her manny and closed himself inside his studio to paint. The studio was the first thing he'd spent money on when he'd sold enough paintings. He'd built it behind the house of horrors he'd grown up in. Now it was a house filled with love that he and his brothers had made their own.

Only his family and a few Marsville citizens knew he was the artist known as Park C. His dream as a boy had been to make enough money from his art to take care of his two older brothers. Well, he'd accomplished that beyond his wildest dreams. Not that Tristan and Kade didn't contribute their fair share, but yeah…his wildest dreams meant his bank account had surpassed anything he could have ever imagined.

The surprise was that he'd also ended up a fire chief,

making him the firefighter who painted. That amused him. After returning home from Paris, he'd signed on as a volunteer firefighter. The volunteer position became a paid one, and when the previous fire chief had retired last year, no one else had wanted the job.

At the time, one of his brothers was the police chief and the other was a Delta Force operator, so he'd decided he, too, should do his part to make the world a safer place. There might have also been a competitive impulse involved in that decision.

It was an odd combination of jobs, but that suited him. He knew himself, and if he did nothing but paint all day and into the night, he'd lose himself in what he thought of as his painting fog. He'd forget to eat, bathe, forget he had a daughter, brothers, forget that a world existed outside his studio. Having to go to the firehouse each day saved him from that. Strangely enough, his firefighter job turned out to be good for his art, too. Time away from his studio gave his creative mind time to rest and reenergize.

But the last thing he needed was an arsonist on the loose. He had a show in New York in a little over two months, and he still had five more pieces to paint. Although he was a fast painter, able to finish a canvas in a week between his time at the fire station and his daddy duties, he couldn't finish the final painting at the last minute since he needed to give it at least a week to dry and time to ship the canvases to New York.

Before he lost himself in a new piece, he went to Everly's space in the studio to see what she was painting. Even at five, his daughter was proving to be quite the little artist. She had more talent than he'd had at her age. Her favorite subjects were animals, and they had plenty of those for her inspiration. Her cat, Jellybean, was her favorite, and his brother Kade's dog came in second, probably because Duke was a clown. But Ember and Tristan's police dog, Fuzz, had their fair share of canvases.

She had an eye for the absurd, and her paintings always brought a smile to his face. In her current work, Jellybean was in attack mode, his rear in the air, his ears pinned back, and his eyes slitted as he prepared to attack Duke. She'd painted Duke with hearts hovering above his head and cartoon hearts in his eyes as he stared back at his favorite cat. She'd perfectly captured the relationship between the dog and cat. Duke loved Jellybean, and Jellybean lived to torture Duke.

As he did with each of her paintings, he added a tiny ladybug that she'd have to find. Once that was done, he returned to his easel. He'd already stretched the canvas and primed it so it would be ready for him to paint tonight.

He never knew what he was going to paint before he started. Sometimes it might be something he'd recently seen, and other times he had no idea where a piece came from. He never painted from a photo. He'd tried to once, a sunset he'd taken a picture of, and when he finished, he likened his effort to paint by numbers. For whatever reason, his art had to come straight from his imagination, and he often didn't realize exactly what he'd painted until he stepped back and looked at it.

After connecting his phone to the speakers, he selected one of his playlists, and with music blaring, he painted. When he came out of his creative fugue, he stepped back.

Standing in a field of cheerful sunflowers and wearing a flowery dress, cowboy boots, and a straw hat, a woman with strawberry blond hair, green eyes, and a splash of freckles across her nose smiled back at him.

"Well, hell."

Chapter Two

"Rude," Willow muttered as the black car backed out of her driveway, its powerful engine rumbling. The man's little girl was adorable, though.

Too bad he was grumpy because he sure was easy on the eyes. Most men looked silly with a ponytail—in her opinion anyway—but those few who could pull it off…well, it was sexy. And Parker Church definitely pulled off a ponytail. If she was honest with herself, the man checked off most of her boxes.

Tall. Check. Broad shoulders but not too big. Check. Narrow waist and lean hips. Check. Muscled but not too muscly. Check. Chocolate brown eyes and just the right amount of scruff on his face. Check. He did not get a check for being pleasant to be around, so that was something to keep him from being perfect.

He'd really be grouchy if he knew how much she'd learned about him from his chatty daughter. Everly had been a font of information. He was a famous artist—well, according to his daughter, but children tended to embellish things, so he'd probably sold a few paintings to friends or at a local arts and crafts festival. He was also a fireman, which supported her theory that he wasn't famous. Why would a famous artist be a fireman?

Everly had shared that she didn't have a mommy but wanted one, so he wasn't married. "My two uncles have girlfriends, and I'm going to be the flower girl when they get married," she'd said. "If my daddy had a girlfriend and they got married, I'd have a mommy," the sly girl had said, looking at her with innocence in her eyes that Willow didn't believe for a minute.

Willow smiled, wondering what the grouchy man would have to say about his daughter playing matchmaker. He'd probably need his mouth washed out with soap. As much as her new little friend wanted a mommy and seemed to be considering Willow for the job, Willow was off men for a while. *Thank you for that, Brady.* She'd take the little girl but not the father.

It was too bad Everly wouldn't be allowed to come over for visits. Not only had she enjoyed talking to the girl but spending time around children was beneficial to her job.

Speaking of said job, she needed to get to work if she was going to meet her deadline. She went inside to eat dinner before she lost herself in the story.

The house had been willed to her by an uncle she hadn't seen in years—her father's brother, and a man her father despised. The call from her uncle's lawyer had been a surprise and had come a few days after she'd ended a two-year relationship. Since Brady—the rat bastard cheater—owned the Cincinnati condo they lived in, she'd suddenly found herself homeless.

If that phone call had come before she'd caught her fiancé sticking his penis into her best friend, she would have put the house in Marsville up for sale without coming here. But in one night, she'd lost her future husband, her home, and her best friend of fourteen years.

Willow didn't get Ella's betrayal. Not in a million years. No matter how hot she thought a guy was, she never would touch her bestie's boyfriend. They'd both blamed it on too much alcohol, which in Willow's mind made it even worse.

They'd also denied it had happened before that night, but she knew Brady's tells, and the left side of his deceitful mouth had twitched, something it did when he was uncomfortable. He was lying through his twitchy mouth. Ella had refused to even look at her when she'd sworn it had never happened before.

If Brady and Ella had come to her and told her they were in love, it would have hurt, but she would have found it within herself to wish them the best. Well, she liked to think that was what she would have done.

To blame their cheating on too much booze was a cop-out. In a matter of seconds, she'd lost respect for the two people she'd loved most in the world. Funny that she thought she'd miss Brady more than she did. After she'd gotten over the initial shock and had a good cry, she'd realized she was more angry than hurt. That was a good thing.

Maybe it was because this was her second broken engagement that she didn't think it was the end of the world the way she had the first time around, like she was now immune from that kind of hurt. She'd loved Brady, but not in the all-consuming way she had Austin. When Austin had ended things a week before their wedding, he'd broken her. It had taken a long time before she could smile again. At least she and Brady hadn't set a wedding date, and she hadn't had to face the painful and embarrassing task of returning wedding gifts.

Because of Austin, she'd made a promise to herself.

Never again would she give a man the power to hurt her like that. She hated dating—had never signed up on a dating app—and everything involved in meeting new guys. She loathed the awkwardness of first dates, but she liked being in a relationship, and Brady had suited her...until recently.

The past few months Brady had been putting pressure on her to set a date, then getting irritated with her when she used her book deadline as an excuse to drag her feet. She wasn't sure why, since she had planned to marry him someday, but what was the rush? What she realized, now that he was out of her life, was that she'd loved him, but she hadn't been in love with him. Not the way she'd loved Austin. She wouldn't allow it. She also realized that her resolve to protect her heart hadn't been fair to Brady, and for that, she was sorry. Didn't excuse his cheating, though.

So, after a surprise phone call from an attorney when she was living in a hotel room with a semibroken heart and a looming deadline, wondering where to live, a house had landed in her lap. Since she could write from anywhere, she'd packed up her clothes, gotten into Sunshine—her yellow VW Beetle—and driven to Marsville.

Her first thought on entering the Victorian-style house was, boy, did it ever need a lot of work. There wasn't even a microwave, which was a necessity since she lived off microwavable meals when she was on deadline.

The first thing she'd done was order a microwave online since she didn't know where in Marsville to get one. Thankfully, it would arrive tomorrow. In the meantime, she was forced to cook dinner on an ancient stove that had only one functioning burner. Forget the oven. She'd taken one look inside and shuddered as she'd slammed the door closed. The kitchen was going to be the first room to remodel.

She hadn't gotten rich off her children's book sales, but she wasn't hurting either. She'd bought Sunshine with cash, and she planned to do most of the remodeling on the house herself to save on the costs. How hard could it be to tear up carpets and paint walls?

Her plan was to finish this book and the next one while she remodeled and then put the house up for sale. Then she'd buy a condo on an ocean somewhere. She just hadn't decided where yet. She didn't much care as long as she was living on the beach.

When the can of cream of mushroom soup was bubbly, she poured it in a bowl. After adding a handful of crackers and a peeled Mandarin orange to a paper plate, she put everything on a tray. She couldn't wait to have a working oven so she could bake her favorite cookies but with three store-bought oatmeal cookies and a glass of ice water, she was good to go. She carried the tray out the back door to the slate patio where she'd set up a small table and a lawn chair.

Her uncle had obviously never done anything with the backyard, and as she ate, her gaze roamed over the landscape. There was so much potential for a beautiful flower garden. If she was staying, she'd do it herself, even if it took a year or two to get it the way she wanted. But she wasn't, so she needed to find a landscaper who could make it attractive enough for when she put the house up for sale. She figured she could get that done fairly cheaply.

Sounds from next door filled the air. There was a tall

wooden fence, so she couldn't see her neighbor's yard, but that was Everly laughing, and it sounded like more than one dog barking. According to Everly, the family had three. There were male voices and more laughter.

Since she'd walked out on Brady two weeks ago, she hadn't taken the time to just sit like she was doing now, and hearing the family enjoying a beautiful spring evening, she was suddenly lonely. She'd gone from having a fiancé, friends, and a home to just her and a house that was going to be a money pit.

Maybe she should get a goldfish. At least she'd have something to talk to. Except she'd probably forget to feed it when she was on a deadline, and then she'd cry while she flushed it down the toilet. Finished with her dinner, she picked up her tray, and as she was going inside, she heard what sounded like Parker Church's voice and Everly giggling hysterically. Female voices were yelling cheerleader chants.

"Remember, curiosity killed the cat," she muttered, but after dropping the tray on the kitchen counter, she headed upstairs anyway.

One window in her bedroom looked down over her neighbor's yard. She pulled aside the edge of the ugliest curtain the world had ever seen, and dust swirled around her, making her sneeze. She mentally put *replace curtains* on her growing to-do list.

She fanned her hand in front of her face, clearing the dust. Then she peeked out the window and spied on her neighbors. What she saw confused her for a minute, but when she realized what they were doing, she laughed.

Three men—one was Parker, so she assumed the other two were his brothers since they favored Parker— were playing football in a backyard much larger than hers, using Everly as the football. One of the brothers held Everly against his hip as he dodged the other two while running toward an orange cone. When he reached it, he and Everly yelled, "Score!" Then he tossed Everly to Parker, and the scene was repeated, but in the opposite direction where there was another orange cone.

Two women—one blonde and one brunette—waving pompoms cheered them on, and three dogs raced around the yard, joining in the fun. Willow watched for a few minutes as Everly—a laughing human football—was tossed from one brother to the other.

She studied the two pretty women and wondered which one was with which brother. They were obviously friends, and having lost hers, she couldn't help feeling jealous and lonelier than ever. Her gaze returned to the men. Like him, Parker's brothers were big, strong, and good-looking, but it was Parker her gaze kept returning to.

As if he felt her eyes on him, he lifted his face and stared directly at her bedroom window. She jumped back. Had he seen her spying on them? No, it was impossible. Except for the slit she was peeking through, the curtains were closed.

Time to stop spying on her hot neighbor and get to work. This book wasn't going to write itself.

Chapter Three

"Everly asked Harper and me if we'd take her shopping for cowboy boots," Skylar said. "Said she wants some like Miss Willow."

"Who's Miss Willow?" Kade asked.

"New neighbor. Probably here to sell the house." Parker hoped so because that would mean she wasn't staying. She disturbed him.

After the football game, they'd grilled some hamburgers and were now sitting around the deck table, he and his brothers with a beer, and the girls enjoying a glass of wine. The three dogs were sacked out on the deck, tired from playing all afternoon. Kade and his girlfriend, Harper, had been out of town for a week and had returned yesterday afternoon. Everly was conked out on his lap, and he needed to wake her so he could get her bathed and into bed. He'd do that as soon as he finished his beer.

"What makes you think she's here to sell the house?" Tristan said. "I heard Bob's lawyer was trying to find the next of kin."

"Her name's Willow Landry, so she's obviously the next of kin. Her car has an Ohio tag, which is why I'm guessing she's here to sell the house."

"Oh, you met her?" Harper asked. "What's she like?"

He shrugged. "Didn't talk to her long." He didn't know why he was reluctant to talk about her other than the part where she disturbed him.

Skylar rolled her eyes. "Give us something. Young? Old? Pretty? Nice?"

"Yes, no, I guess, not sure."

Kade snorted.

He liked both his brothers' girlfriends. Skylar Morgan, soon to be Skylar Church, was the county sheriff. She and his oldest brother, Tristan, were made for each other. Took them a year to figure that out, with some misery thrown in there, but now they were very much in love.

Kade, who not long ago had been a Delta Force operator in the Army, now worked for Talon Security, as did Harper. He didn't talk much about what he did, but the reason for his recent trip had been to rescue two teenage girls who'd been kidnapped while on spring break in Mexico. Parker was proud of his other future sister-in-law. Harper had been put through hell by a deranged cop, and the experience had resulted in the job she did now for Talon, providing support for the women and children that Talon rescued.

He was happy for his brothers. If anyone deserved to be happy, it was them. He tried not to envy them, and even though he had no intention of falling in love again—been there, done that enough times that it was embarrassing—he did envy them a little. His problem was that he was a romantic at heart and fell in love too easily.

He'd truly believed he'd finally found *the one* in Everly's mother, but he couldn't have been more wrong. She'd cured him of loving the feeling of being in love. He didn't regret that time in his life, though, because he'd come away with a beautiful daughter.

"This girl needs her bath and bed." He'd put her straight to bed if she hadn't gotten so sweaty and dirty playing.

"How's the painting going?" Tristan asked. "You gonna be ready for your show?"

"I'm on schedule. As soon as I get Ev to bed, I'll paint for a while." He had no intention of putting the painting of Willow Landry in the show, so he still had five pieces to go, and that now had him a day behind the schedule he'd set.

"What's the theme of this one?" Kade asked.

"Scenes Through a Window."

Kade raised his brows. "All the paintings are scenes through a window?"

"Yep."

"Can we come see what you have so far?" Skylar asked.

"Not tonight. Maybe this weekend." He didn't want them coming in the studio because the painting of Willow was still on the easel, and he did not want the questions that would follow if they saw it. In fact, he needed to hide it before Everly saw it.

"We've all got our flights for your show and found a brownstone to rent that's big enough for all of us," Harper said. "It's going to be so cool to whisper to someone looking at one of your paintings that I know the artist." She grinned.

Skylar laughed. "You name-dropper you."

"You're going to do the same thing," Harper replied.

"True."

"Just remember my name's Park C. Tell them you know Parker Church and they'll yawn." He stood with Everly in his arms. "Enjoy your evening, people."

Ember followed him in and sat in the bathroom while he got Everly clean. The dog was more reserved than Tristan's dog, Fuzz, and especially Kade's dog, Duke. She was Parker's shadow during the day and had appointed herself Everly's nighttime guard, sleeping next to Ev's bed.

After Ev was clean and had her pajamas on, she chose a book. "This one tonight, Daddy."

It was her favorite, and she knew it by heart, so he couldn't cheat. But she'd be asleep before he reached the end. He got her under the covers, then he settled next to her and leaned back on the headboard. Worn out from their play and being a human football—one of her favorite games—she didn't even make it to page seven. He closed the book, then kissed his baby girl on her forehead. "Keep her safe for me," he told Ember.

His brothers and their ladies were still on the deck when he passed on the way to his studio, and he waved and kept going. As he often did, he paused inside the door as a deep sense of wonder rolled over him at what he'd achieved, and that he'd been able to build the perfect place for him and Everly to paint.

He'd included a lot of windows and skylights in the studio's design, and because he did much of his painting at night, he'd gone with the best lighting available. There was a mini kitchen, so he wouldn't have to make trips to the house for something to drink or eat, a bathroom with a shower, a daybed for catnaps, a large screen TV—which he rarely turned on unless he wanted to catch the news—and the best sound system money could buy, since he needed music when he painted.

After locking the door behind him so there would be no surprise visitors, he walked to the easel. The painting hadn't miraculously morphed overnight into a scene through a window. It was still Willow Landry standing in a field of brilliant yellow sunflowers with a mysterious smile on her face.

What was up with that smile, anyway? She hadn't smiled at him like that. He should paint over the canvas, but he couldn't bring himself to do it. Nor could he bring himself to put *Willow in Sunflowers* aside and get to work on an art showpiece.

Eff him. He'd gone and named the piece. Now he had to finish it. Since he couldn't move on until the painting was done, and he really needed to get on the art show pieces, he turned on his music full blast and got busy.

He finished as the black night was turning to dawn gray. Coming out of his fog, he studied the painting. "Pretty damn good," he murmured. Too bad no one would ever see it.

When he'd built the studio, he'd included a fireproof room for storing his art, and he carried the painting there and left it to dry. That done, he returned to the house. It was too close to having to get Everly up for kindergarten to try to sleep, so he made a pot of coffee. It wouldn't be the first time he'd painted through the night and then changed his painter's hat for his fire chief's hat without sleep in between. If it was quiet at the station, he'd catch a few winks.

After feeding his chatty morning-person daughter— she sure didn't get that from him—breakfast, he got her dressed, then loaded her and Ember in the Hellcat. As he passed the subject of his renegade painting, he jerked the wheel to the left when Everly yelled, "Daddy!"

Double eff him. He'd almost taken out a neighbor's mailbox because his attention was distracted. "Sorry, baby girl." Willow Landry—her hair in a ponytail and wearing a tank top, denim shorts that barely covered her ass cheeks, and cowboy boots—was in her front yard trying to push a lawn mower through grass that Parker couldn't remember the last time had been cut. Bob had never been the best at yard maintenance, or much of anything actually.

After dropping Everly at kindergarten, he glanced at Ember, sitting in her place on the passenger seat. "You sleep good last night? Because I didn't. Gotta tell you, that woman needs to get out of my head."

He should turn the car toward the firehouse, but he drove back to his street instead. The lawn mower was parked in the middle of the yard and only about two strips of grass had been mowed. The offensive yellow car was gone. He glanced in the rearview mirror, and not seeing the Beetle driving down the street, he pulled into her driveway. With a quick check, he discovered the lawn mower's gas tank was empty.

He got back in his car and called his captain. "Morning, Greg. Everything quiet?"

"Quieter than Mrs. Jefferson's library."

Parker chuckled. She was retired now, but when Mrs. Jefferson was the school librarian, you did not talk if you valued your ears. She could sneak up behind you and twist your earlobe before you knew she was there.

"Great. I'll be there in about an hour. I have something I need to take care of this morning. Call if you need me."

"Will do, Chief."

He drove to his house, put Ember inside, then got out the riding lawn mower and attached the bagger. Considering that it would take Miss Landry all day or more to push that little mower through knee-high grass, cutting it for her was the neighborly thing to do. Added advantage, he wouldn't have to see her doing it in those tiny shorts.

And listen up, Park C. You will not paint her wearing those shorts.

Chapter Four

Foothills General Store wasn't like any she'd ever been in. She was here to buy a gas can to fill the lawn mower, but paint samples sidetracked her. The place fascinated her with its scarred wooden floors that creaked as she walked on them, the baskets of hardware, oversize jars of hard candies, a selection of fudge—she bought several flavors—beef jerky, salves, homemade soaps, and more. She ended up spending an hour in the store and planned to go back and explore it more.

Before returning home, she walked around the town a little, looking in the windows and familiarizing herself with the stores and what was available. A clothing store, Fanny's Place, had some really cute clothes in the window. She'd have to check that out next time she was in town.

She was delighted to discover the bakery, and it was going to be one of her regular stops while she lived here. Cookies were her writing fuel. When her energy flagged after a few hours on her laptop, a cookie and coffee break perked her right back up. She usually baked her favorite, oatmeal chocolate cherry, but without a working oven she'd have to rely on the bakery.

The town itself was adorable and unique, with its

multicolored awnings and pots of spring flowers. Each store had a different color awning, and many of the doors were painted to match the store's awning. She took out her phone and snapped pictures to send her sister.

Her successful CEO sister didn't understand why Willow was in a small town in the South called Marsville. As far as Cynthia was concerned, a big city was where the opportunities were. She also didn't understand why Willow wanted to write children's books. Bottom line, her older sister didn't understand her at all.

They were too different to be close, but Cynthia was her sister, so Willow made an effort to maintain a relationship. When she'd told Cynthia the wedding was off, she had lied and said that ending things was a mutual agreement between her and Brady. If Cynthia knew the real reason, that Brady had cheated, Cynthia would have said, "I told you so," even though Cynthia had not told her any such thing. Her sister was judgmental.

Cynthia was ten years older, so that was another divide between them. Too much of an age difference to have much in common. Even so, Cynthia had told her to move to Chicago—and that had been said in the form of an order—that she could stay in the spare bedroom in Cynthia's downtown condo. Willow would set up housing in a tent before she moved in with her sister and be bossed around and criticized for everything from her career choice to her taste in clothes, especially the cowboy boots she favored.

No, thanks. Marsville was the perfect place to crash for a bit while she licked her wounds, wrote her books, and looked for condos for sale on a beach. She gave herself six months to finish the two books and get Uncle

Bob's—well, now her—house remodeled and sold. It was a good plan.

Returning home, she pulled into her driveway. Huh? Who mowed her grass? Willow sat in Sunshine and stared at the yard. Whoever had mowed it had even bagged the clippings.

She picked up her bag of goodies from the general store, along with the cup of iced mocha coffee, the bags of assorted muffins and cookies from Sweet Tooth Bakery, and exited the car.

Unless Uncle Bob had a lawn maintenance provider, which she doubted, considering the grass had been two feet tall, someone had mowed it for her. She glanced at the house next door. It had to be one of the Church brothers who'd done her a kindness, but which one? She couldn't imagine the grouchy one doing her a favor, so it had to be one of his brothers.

She took the new gas can she'd filled to the garage, then carried her purchases inside. That done, she returned to the bakery. Another bag of assorted cookies and a yummy-looking chocolate cake in her possession, she drove past her house, instead turning into her neighbor's driveway. She fished the notepad and pen she always carried in her purse for when a book or plot idea struck, wrote a thank-you note without specifying a name since she didn't know who to thank, and then she walked to the door with the cake and cookies.

The outside of the Victorian-style house was beautiful, and she took a moment to imagine how her Victorian would look when the remodel was finished. This house was bigger than hers—three stories instead of her two—and was painted pale gray, the trim and front door a deep burgundy, and the windowsills white. She stepped onto a wide porch that stretched across the front. Green ferns hung in baskets between each post, and on the left side was a swing with a blue seat cushion and blue and burgundy pillows. She eyed the swing with envy, wishing she had one. What a perfect place to sit with her laptop and write on a beautiful day. Maybe they'd let her borrow it occasionally.

According to Everly, she and her dad, one uncle and his girlfriend lived here with the third brother and his girlfriend spending some nights here. It was an interesting family, for sure. She pushed the doorbell, and a few moments later a young man opened the door.

"You must be Andrew," she said. Her little font of information had told her all about their housekeeper slash cook slash manny. It had cracked Willow up hearing the word *manny* out of Everly's mouth.

"Yes, ma'am," he said. "I don't know you."

She smiled, charmed by his directness. "I'm Willow Landry, the new next-door neighbor. Um, someone mowed my yard this morning, and I'm pretty sure it was one of the brothers."

"Parker."

"Oh, okay." *Well, there you go surprising me, Mr. Grouchy.* "So, that was a really nice thing to do, and I just wanted to drop off this cake and cookies as a thank-you."

"He's not here."

"No problem. How about I just leave them with you?" She held the cake box with the bag of cookies sitting on top out to him. "He can share the goodies with you and the family."

Andrew eyed the box. "I like cake."

"Well, you tell him he better give you some." As he

took the box and bag from her, she got a glimpse of the inside and gasped. "Wow, that chandelier is gorgeous. And those stairs! Wow." The foyer floor was black-and-white marble squares, and a massive crystal chandelier hung from the third-story ceiling between two curving staircases, one on each wall.

Andrew lifted his gaze to the chandelier. "Parker designed it because he's an artist."

Mmm, maybe her arts-and-crafts artist theory was a little skewed. "It's really beautiful. Is the whole house as amazing?" She badly wanted a tour.

"It didn't used to be, but now it is."

Well, that didn't tell her much. "I'd love to see the rest." Maybe she could get ideas for what to do with her money pit.

"I'm not allowed to let strangers in, and I don't know you."

"No, you don't, and you're absolutely right not to let a stranger in." She smiled as she stepped back. "You have a nice day, Andrew."

Uncle Bob's house—she was having trouble thinking of it as hers—was similar, as were the other Victorian style houses on the street, all built about sixty years ago. Most that she'd driven by had been updated, but a few like hers showed their age. What she wouldn't give to see what had been done to Parker's house. She could use some inspiration and ideas on what to do with hers.

Besides the difference in sizes, hers had a small yard, whereas the Church house, from what she could see from her bedroom window, sat on at least an acre. Beyond the four-car garage and the separate building with all the windows and skylights, she could see the corner of what she thought was a barn and in the far back a pond. She was glad she didn't have that much land to deal with.

She returned home and parked Sunshine in the drive-way, wishing the garage wasn't crammed full of junk so she could get the car in. Maybe she should start on getting the garage cleared out first. But she needed a working kitchen. So, that first, then the garage. As she jogged up the steps to the porch, she changed her mind. A porch swing first, then the kitchen.

For the rest of the afternoon, she wrote. She was a middle-grade children's book author and had sixteen books in print worldwide. The book she was working on was the first of three in a new fantasy series, and she was having a blast with it.

Her phone chimed, and she blinked, wondering why the room was dark except for the light from her moni-tor. Okay, it was nighttime. Huh. That tended to happen when she lost herself in a story. She read the last few lines she'd written as she answered her phone.

"Hey," she said, expecting it to be her agent, who'd texted that she would call tonight.

"Willow, how are you?"

"Great." She disconnected. Should have checked the screen before answering. Why was Brady calling? Her phone chimed again. She let it go to voice mail. A min-ute later, he called again. "Jeez, Brady," she sighed as she answered.

"Don't hang up, Willow."

"Will if I want to. Why are you calling?"

"You had some clothes in the dryer that you forgot. Tell me where you are, and I'll bring them to you."

"Throw them away."

"I miss you."

She laughed. "Yeah, I noticed how much you thought of me when I caught you sticking it to Ella."

"That was a mistake. Come on, where are you staying? We can talk."

"None of your business, and if you want to talk, go talk to Ella."

"I'm not seeing her. Please, Willow. I love you, and I really miss you."

"Should have thought of that before your so-called mistake." She sighed. "Truthfully, you and Ella did us a favor. Getting married would have been a mistake. I'm not in love with you, Brady. Go find a woman who can be."

"You don't mean that."

"I do, and I wish you the best." She disconnected before he could reply, then she deleted his contact information and blocked his number. She should be sad, right? But she wasn't, and any lingering regret or doubt that she'd done the right thing by leaving disappeared. Hearing his voice hadn't sent longing through her or made her want to cry. She wasn't even angry with him anymore.

She celebrated the-freedom-from-anger-revelation-yay(!) by going online and ordering a porch swing, a pretty seat cushion for it, and pillows.

Chapter Five

"Miss Willow brought you a cake and cookies," Andrew said as soon as Parker and Ember walked into the kitchen on arriving home from the fire station. "She said I could have some."

"Why?" A cake box and white bag with the Sweet Tooth logo on them sat on the counter.

Andrew looked from him to the cake box. "It's okay. I don't have to have any."

"That's not what I meant." He put his hand on Andrew's shoulder. "Of course you can have some, but why did she bring me a cake and cookies?"

"Because you mowed her yard."

How did she know that? And did that mean he had to thank her now? His intention was to ignore her disturbing existence. He had a possible arsonist to catch and an art show to get ready for that he was a few days behind on because of her. She was a distraction he didn't need.

Everly ran into the kitchen, followed by Jellybean and Kade's dog, Duke. If Duke was downstairs, it meant that he'd been locked out of Kade's third-floor quarters, something that only happened when his brother and Harper were having playtime.

The last time he'd had some playtime had been four

months ago, at a conference for fire chiefs in Atlanta, and that one he'd ended up regretting. As the fire chief, he didn't need a reputation as a player. That left him with out-of-town conferences and his art shows in other cities for a hookup, but his enthusiasm for random bed partners had soured after Atlanta. As for dating, he might consider that after Everly went off to college.

There was still Asheville. The woman who lived there couldn't care less that months might pass before he called to say he was in town, but Andrea always welcomed him when he did. It might be time for another Asheville trip.

"Daddy! You're home!"

His daughter ran at him, and he opened his arms for her to jump into. This precious girl was his life, the only female he needed. "Hey, ladybug. What's cooking?" He nibbled on her neck. Her giggly laughter would put a hyena to shame. God, he loved his baby girl.

"What's that?"

He followed her gaze. "That would be a cake."

"What kind?"

"Don't know. Let's see." Still holding her, he lifted the lid. Anything from Sweet Tooth was going to be good, but their chocolate cake was food from heaven.

"I want some, Daddy."

"You know the rule. No dessert before dinner." He glanced at Andrew. "What's on the menu tonight?"

"It's Tuesday," Andrew said as if puzzled why Parker was asking that question.

"Right. Taco Tuesday." He would have known that if a certain new neighbor wasn't messing with his brain cells. "Cake after dinner, baby girl."

"Did you buy us a cake, Daddy?" she asked.

"Miss Willow did," Andrew said.

"Miss Willow!" Everly yelled, clapping her hands. "I love her."

"She's nice," Andrew said.

"Ev, inside voice, please. What did you learn in school today?" That was an effort to distract his daughter from effusing over Miss Willow.

"Daddy, did you know we need trees to breathe?"

"Wow, really?" Aaand she was off. He nodded at all the right places as he carried her to their rooms on the first floor. He left her in her bedroom to play with Ember, Duke, and Jellybean while he showered the day away.

After dinner, Kade took Harper and Duke out for a ride. "And ice cream," Kade whispered so Everly wouldn't hear.

As he and Everly walked to their studio, her tiny hand in his, he glanced at the second-floor window of the Landry house, where a light shone around the edges of the curtain. Was that her bedroom? He'd thought he'd seen the curtain move when they'd been playing football with Everly and had wondered if she was watching them.

Get your mind off her bedroom.

"Daddy, I'm going to paint Miss Willow a picture, and we can take it to her."

"What are you going to paint for her?" He'd get Harper to go over with Everly when she finished the painting because he was not.

"I have to think about it. I know! We can go ask her what her favorite thing is."

They were not going to ask her…anything. "If you're painting a gift for her, it needs to be a surprise." He opened the door to the studio to let her and Ember in. "After you, my lady."

She giggled. "You're silly, Daddy."

"Yep, that's me. Silly Daddy. You ready to start a new canvas?"

"No. I have to finish Duke and Jellybean."

"Better get to it. You have an hour, then it's bath and story time." He wouldn't start a new canvas until after she was in bed, otherwise he'd lose track of time and paint right past her bedtime and she'd paint right along with him.

Ember went to the bed Parker had placed near his easel. She was the only animal allowed in the studio. Duke had gotten in once and the result had been a dog with a coat of many colors, a ruined half-finished painting, and a colorful floor. Ember was content being near him and having a rawhide to chew on. Eventually, she'd go to sleep.

He got his brushes and oils ready, and because he needed to actually sleep at some point, he set an alarm for midnight. It was something he had to do to keep from coming out of his painting fog and seeing the sun shining through the windows.

"Daddy, I found the ladybug!"

He smiled. "Yeah? Where'd she put this one?" He had her convinced that there was a ladybug fairy who came while she was sleeping and added a ladybug to her paintings.

"It's on Jellybean's ear. Come see."

An alert blared from his phone as he walked toward her to see the magical ladybug, and his little girl sighed, knowing what that meant.

"Daddy has to go, Ev."

Another even bigger sigh. "I know."

He picked her up. If he didn't carry her back to the house, she'd go at the speed of a snail. Ember, having learned that the sound of his alert tone meant it was time to go to work, was at the door, her body vibrating with eagerness as she waited for it to open.

Andrew had gone home after cleaning up the kitchen from dinner, but Parker had set him up to also get alerts. He lived with his parents three miles away and would be here in minutes to stay with Everly, even if Kade and Harper were home, since they, too, could be called away without notice.

Honestly, they'd be lost without Andrew. He wasn't blood, but he was a valued member of the family. Just don't try to help him with anything that he considered a part of his job. He could get testy.

As soon as Parker was able to hand Everly over to Andrew, he and Ember headed for the address of the fire. Since his official SUV was being serviced, he'd put his fire chief's jacket and helmet in the Hellcat's trunk.

The fire was at another vacant house, this one on the opposite side of town. Greg Greenlander, his captain, was standing in the front yard when Parker arrived. His firefighters already had the fire out, and were inside, looking for hot spots.

"Stay," he told Ember after cracking the windows a few inches. He stopped next to Greg. "Doesn't look like a total loss."

"We got lucky. A neighbor was out walking his dog and saw someone climb out a bedroom window and run through the backyard. Since he knew the residents were out of town, he called the police and was waiting on the sidewalk for an officer to arrive. A few minutes after he made the call, he saw flames through the living room window and called Dispatch again, so we got here before it had a chance to go full-blown."

"Is he around?" A cluster of spectators were huddled together under a streetlight.

"Across the street, two houses to the right. Name's Les Hardy. He didn't want to stick around. I told him you'd want to talk to him tonight, so he's waiting for you."

"You know the drill. As soon as the hot spots are cold, seal the doors so no one can go in."

"On it, Chief."

Parker returned to his car and opened the passenger door. He picked up the leash from the floor and clipped it on Ember's collar. "Time to go to work." If anyone had the odor of any kind of accelerant on them, she'd alert.

First, he went to the cluster of people. "Good evening. Did anyone see anything suspicious?" His gaze scanned over the faces, his artist eye memorizing their features. As he studied them, the hair on the back of his neck wasn't standing up, and he didn't feel like he was being watched as he had during the last fire.

"I didn't see anything," one man said. "Heard the sirens and came out to see what was going on."

One of the women nodded. "Same here. Can I pet your dog?"

"Sure, but she's shy, so be gentle." Ember didn't particularly like strangers touching her, but knowing it came with the job, she tolerated it. While they'd been talking, she'd sniffed each of the five people in the group and hadn't alerted.

"Do you all live on this street?" They confirmed they did. Since there was nothing to be learned here, he excused himself. When he knocked on Les Hardy's door, a dog barked on the other side. A man opened the door only enough to see out but keep the dog in.

"Mr. Hardy?"

"Yes. Are you the fire chief?"

"I am. Would you mind stepping outside for a few minutes to talk to me? I have my dog with me."

Hardy glanced down at Ember, sitting quietly next to Parker's leg. "Sure." He slipped out and almost closed the door on his barking dog's nose. "Wish mine was as well-behaved."

"Ember is a working dog, so she's been extensively trained."

"Cool."

"My captain said you saw someone come out a window shortly before you noticed a fire?" While they were talking, Ember had sniffed him, then lost interest.

"Yes. Gotta tell you, wasn't expecting that. This is a nice neighborhood. We've never had any problems."

"Can you describe the person?"

"Wish I could. They didn't look my way. He jumped out the window and ran away."

"He? So you're sure it was a man?"

"Well, no. I guess I just assumed it was."

"Height? Weight? What kind of clothes?"

"It's only a guess, but medium height and thin. The clothes were all black. Oh, I did notice one thing. The person had a ponytail like you."

"Hair color?"

"Again, it was dark, but I think brown."

It wasn't the best description, but better than they had before tonight. "You notice any kind of container, like a gas can?"

"No, didn't see anything like that."

Parker handed him a card. "If you think of anything else, call me. You did good tonight, Mr. Hardy."

"Hope you catch the bastard. The Marstons are in Florida for a funeral. They didn't need this."

"Have you contacted them?"

"Talked to them while I was waiting for you."

"I'm going to do a walk-through shortly. Tell them they can call me tomorrow at the number on the card if they want to know the damage."

"Thanks. I'll do that."

"So, the house wasn't for sale or abandoned," he told Ember as they walked back to the Marston house. Did the arsonist know the family was away, and if so, how? That made four now, and the first one people lived in.

A few hours later, he arrived home tired and smelling like smoke. Ember had only alerted on one spot, the sofa. An empty Mason jar smelling of gasoline was sitting on the coffee table. Hundred to one the arsonist hadn't meant to leave it behind. He could only hope that it had fingerprints on it.

He was sorry the Marstons would come home to the damage, but at least now he had a description, slim though it was, and maybe fingerprints. Tristan and Skylar had already sent out alerts to their officers to be on the lookout for a thin dark-haired man with a ponytail.

So much for his art show schedule, though. More late nights in his studio than he'd planned for were in his near future. Too tired to care, he showered, then fell facedown on his bed. There was always tomorrow.

Fifteen minutes later, he sighed. It was bugging him how the arsonist had known the owners were away, and he could make an educated guess on that. Until he proved his theory, he wasn't going to be able to sleep.

Getting out of bed, he got his laptop. Miss Mabel, the town's eccentric matriarch, had a Marsville Community social media page where the residents were free to post. Bringing the page up, he scanned through the posts.

Sure enough, Emily Marston had posted, asking for prayers because her husband's brother was in intensive care, not expected to live. The next day, she posted that he'd died, and the family was going to Florida for the funeral. When would people learn not to advertise that they were going to be out of town and their house would be empty? That was like offering burglars free access to the candy store.

It was a page he'd keep his eyes on now, and he clicked on getting all notifications of new posts. If anyone else posted they were going to be out of town, the arsonist was going to have a surprise waiting for him in the form of him and his brothers.

Chapter Six

Willow heard bells. She tilted her head, listening, but the bells were gone. If this house was haunted, she was outta here. She lifted the sledgehammer she'd bought this morning at her favorite general store, where she'd wasted another hour perusing the aisles. Of course, she'd come home with more than the sledgehammer, things not on her list, like fudge and some sweet-smelling soaps. For the sake of her bank account, she needed to limit her visits to Foothills General Store.

"Okay, let's do this." She brought the sledgehammer down on the kitchen cabinet with as much strength as she could muster. A piece of the cabinet door flew off, almost hitting her in the face. "Well, that was fun."

There were those bells again. Oh, the doorbell maybe? They didn't sound like a typical doorbell, but better that than the bell-ringing ghost she was imagining. A contractor was supposed to stop by to give her an estimate on the kitchen, but that was later this afternoon. She dropped the sledgehammer on the floor and went to the front door, hoping there were people there.

"Oh, thank goodness, not a ghost," she said after opening the door and seeing Everly there with the two women who'd been cheerleading the football game.

"Were you expecting a ghost?" the brunette said, amusement dancing in her eyes.

"No. Just my imagination getting away from me. Happens all the time." They must think she was nuts.

"Miss Willow, I brought you a present!"

"Really, a present?" It had been a week since she'd seen her chatty little friend, and she'd thought she might never see Everly again thanks to Grumpy Pants. That had made her sad. "I'm so happy to see you."

Everly held out what looked like the back of a canvas. "I painted it."

"Can we come inside?" the blonde asked.

"Oh, of course. Sorry, I'm obviously a terrible hostess." Had she used the word *hostess* ever in her life before now? Um...no. She got sidetracked by that for a good ten seconds before realizing two women and a little girl—with a present for her no less—were still standing on her porch waiting to be invited in while she stood in front of them, blocking their way.

Her mother was right—her head spent the majority of the time in the clouds. She stepped back. "Please excuse the mess. I'm remodeling." She looked around at the furniture her uncle had probably bought forty or so years ago when he'd moved into the house. She'd pushed it all up against one wall until the dumpster arrived.

"I'm Skylar," the blonde said. "I'm engaged to Tristan, Parker's oldest brother."

"She's also the sheriff, so stay on her good side," the brunette said. "I'm Harper, girlfriend to the middle brother, Kade."

"They'll be engaged any day now," Skylar said. "Kade said he's just waiting for her to propose to him."

Harper jerked her gaze to Skylar. "He said that?"

"Yep. So you going to propose? It needs to be romantic. Reserve a suite at the hotel on the lake. I know someone at their restaurant who can set you up with a candlelight dinner on the balcony. I can see it now, you dropping to a knee and—"

Harper put her hand over Skylar's mouth. "I am not dropping to a knee."

"But he'd love that."

Everly took Willow's hand and pulled her to the dining room, which was also a mess. "They do that all the time, Miss Willow. You want to see my present?"

Willow glanced back at the two women and they both grinned at her. Ah, they were letting Everly have the stage. She kneeled, lowering herself to eye level with the girl. "I sure do want to see."

Everly's smile was beautiful. "I painted it for you."

She turned the painting around, and Willow was floored at seeing it. "You painted this?" No way a five-year-old painted this.

"You don't like it?"

"Oh, sweetie, I love it. It's amazing." She held the canvas out. In it, she was sitting on the steps of her porch wearing the clothes Everly had first seen her in— her floppy hat, flowery dress, and cowboy boots—and was that what her smile looked like, as if she was having the best day of her life?

"You painted this?" she stupidly said again. She was having trouble believing it. It wasn't the work of a mature artist, but it really was incredible, considering Everly's age.

"Hard to believe, isn't it?" Skylar said as she and Harper joined them.

Willow nodded. "It's beautiful, Everly. I love it so much."

"I'll paint you another one. What's your favorite thing in the whole world?"

"Cookies, but you don't have to paint me another one."

Harper chuckled. "If she wants to paint you something, you won't be able to stop her. She's like her dad that way. Just go with it."

"My daddy likes you," Everly said.

That sounded more hopeful than true, but the only thing she could think to say was, "I like your daddy, too."

Everly's eyes brightened, and Willow wished she could take back the words. She already knew the girl wanted a mommy and she was afraid that she was being considered as a possible contender.

"Now you've gone and done it," Skylar said, laughter in her voice.

Willow stood. "I didn't mean to."

"Everly, honey, why don't you go find the perfect wall for the painting, and if it's okay with Miss Willow, we'll hang it up."

"I'll find the best place, Aunt Skylar."

"I think someone's playing matchmaker," Harper said after Everly was out of the room.

"Not going to happen." But she hadn't discouraged the girl, had she?

The two women laughed.

"I mean, she was telling me that she was going to be a flower girl when the two of you got married, and if her daddy was dating someone, they could get married, too."

"Well, look out," Harper said. "When she gets an idea in her head, there's no talking her out of it."

"I'm afraid she's going to be disappointed if she's set her sights on me. Parker doesn't even like me, so I'm the last woman he'd want to date. Not that I want to date him." Even if he was the sexiest man she'd ever seen.

"Well, that's interesting." Skylar glanced at Harper. "Don't you think so?"

Harper nodded. "Very interesting."

"What, that I don't want to date him?"

Skylar shook her head. "No, that you think he doesn't like you. What makes you say that?"

"I've only met him once, and it was obvious. He was rude."

Two pairs of eyebrows shot up and the women looked at each other. "Parker's never rude," Harper said. "He's actually very sweet."

"Coulda fooled me."

"So interesting," Harper said.

"Yep." Skylar grinned. "We're cooking out tomorrow night. You have to come have dinner with us."

A conspiratorial grin crossed Harper's face. "Oh, yeah."

Willow didn't trust either one of those grins. They had *trouble* written all over them. "I don't know. I'm on deadline, and—"

Everly ran to her. "Please come eat with us, Miss Willow."

How was she supposed to say no to that hopeful face? "I'd love to have dinner with you, Everly."

"Yay! I found where to hang your picture. Wanna see?"

"Sure."

"What kind of deadline are you on?" Harper asked as they followed Everly to the living room.

"I'm a children's book author. Middle grade."

"What does that mean?" Skylar said.

"Middle grade is ages eight to twelve."

"That's cool," Harper said.

Everly stopped in front of the painting she'd propped against the wall. "Here, Miss Willow."

She'd chosen the space between two living room windows. "That's perfect, Everly. Tomorrow I'll go buy a hook so I can hang it up."

"My daddy can do it. I'll tell him to when he comes home."

"Oh, that's okay. I'll do it first thing in the morning." She glanced at the two women, not sure which one had chuckled, but they both appeared highly amused.

"So, what was all the banging we heard?" Skylar asked.

Grateful for the change of subject, Willow said, "It's demo day. I'm starting with the kitchen. I figure I can save money by doing that myself. I've asked two contractors for estimates to do an entire remodel."

"Who's giving you estimates?"

"Buddy Napier is coming by this afternoon to take a look, and Franklin Hodges is stopping by tomorrow."

Skylar wrinkled her nose at the last name. "Go with Buddy. He's good and reliable. Franklin does good work when he's sober, which unfortunately isn't often."

"Thanks for the heads-up. I'll call and cancel his coming by."

"We're headed to the Kitchen for lunch. Want to come?"

"Your kitchen?"

Skylar chuckled. "That's what it sounded like, but no. Katie's Corner Kitchen. Everyone just calls it the Kitchen."

"Ah. Well, thanks for the invite, but I have cabinets to demolish today."

"Okay, but dinner tomorrow night," Harper said. "Come over around five and we'll have a glass of wine while the guys grill."

"Looking forward to it. What can I bring?"

"Chocolate cake!" Everly said rather loudly.

"You got it."

They left, and she got busy smashing cabinets and counters—attempting to, anyway—until Buddy Napier arrived. She liked the older man, and he had some good suggestions for her house remodel. He promised to get back to her in a few days with an estimate, but unless it was outrageous, she already knew she was going to hire him.

The dumpster had arrived, and she was hauling pieces of cabinets out to it when her porch swing was delivered. She'd bought the necessary hardware at her favorite general store after watching a video on hanging a porch swing, and she wanted it up. She was sure she could manage it.

Chapter Seven

What the devil was she doing? Parker stopped the SUV in front of Willow's house. The woman was standing on the top of a stepladder, the end of a long chain in her hand as she tried to pull up the swing attached to it. He rolled his eyes. She was going to fall, break a leg, then his EMTs were going to have to come tend to her.

She glanced at his car as he backed up to park in her driveway, narrowed her eyes at him when he exited the car, then looked away, dismissing him. Annoyed by that, and then annoyed that he was annoyed, because that was what he wanted, right? He sure planned to ignore her.

Although that was going to be difficult if she kept wearing shorts that showed off her long legs. She was missing the straw hat, but the cowboy boots were on her feet. She grunted with the effort to pull the chain up to the hook.

"You sure the hooks are in a support beam?" he said as he took the chain from her. She rolled her eyes, and he almost chuckled, thinking that he'd rolled his eyes at her only a minute ago.

"I'm sure."

"Okay, move out of the way."

She saluted him. "Yes, sir."

He suppressed another chuckle. She was a feisty one. Her mass of curly hair was pulled back in a high ponytail, and he had the urge to tug on it like a twelve-year-old boy tormenting a girl he liked because he didn't know how else to flirt with her. And that was the thing—he truly didn't have that skill anymore. He'd forgotten how to flirt somewhere around the time he'd held a red-faced newborn in his arms and had dedicated his life to her.

Not that he hadn't had girlfriends. He'd loved four girls in high school, one each year. He'd started on the love path when he was six and decided he was going to marry Lina Peterman. She was the cutest thing with her missing two front teeth. But it had been in France when he'd lost his heart for the last time, and he had no intention of ever recovering it. His romantic soul was cured of wanting to be in love.

He had his daughter, his brothers, his art, and a second job he loved. What else did he need? Sure, he liked sex as much as the next person, but he could go months without thinking much about it. Mostly because he stayed busy. It was Willow's fault he had sex on the brain lately, and he'd call Andrea soon and make a trip to Asheville.

Even if he did want to be in a relationship, he wouldn't unless the woman absolutely loved his girl, and Everly loved the woman. And even then, he'd be hesitant because if things didn't work out, Everly—who loved as easily as he once had—would be hurt, and that was unacceptable. It had worried him that she didn't have a female role model in her life, but now that Skylar and Harper were in the picture, that was no longer a concern.

So, any thoughts—and there had been—of pursuing something with free-spirited Willow Landry were just that, thoughts. No matter how intriguing and striking she was. Besides, she drove a yellow car, and just no.

"You don't have to do that," he said when Willow tried to help by lifting the end of the swing. "I got it."

She threw her hands up and stepped back. "Fine, Mr. Muscles."

He wished she'd stop being amusing. After securing the end of the chain to the hook, he moved to the other side and slipped the chain on that hook. "All done, and a thank-you cake isn't necessary."

"Can I just tell you thank you then, or is that for-bidden?"

He almost smiled. "Not forbidden, and you're wel-come." He'd reached the porch steps when the swing crashed to the floor. She screamed, and he raised his brows. "I'm going to go out on a limb here and say those hooks were *not* screwed into a support beam."

"Anyone ever tell you that you're funny?"

He pretended to think about it for a few seconds. "Hmm, not that I can recall."

"Now, there's a surprise."

A chuckle escaped before he could stop it, and he coughed to cover the sound. When she put a foot on the stepladder, presumably to unscrew the hook, he sighed. "Stand back." She continued to the next step, and he shook his head. Stubborn girl. He put his hands on her waist, picked her up, and set her on her feet away from the stepladder.

"Hey, what are you doing?"

Damn hands didn't want to let her go. "Keeping you from breaking your neck." He turned his back on her and squeezed his eyes shut. As soon as he fixed her swing, he'd go to work and not think a single thought of Miss Willow in her shorts and cowboy boots. And when he drove by her house, which unfortunately he had to because they were on a dead-end street, he'd keep his face forward, his eyes on the road, and he would not even glance at her house. The next time he did, he'd probably see her on the roof trying to lay tile or repair a leak.

Fifteen minutes later, he had the screws secured in a support beam, the swing hung, a somewhat pissy thank-you from her, which amused him and then because it did, made him pissy.

"Oh, you have your dog with you," she said from behind him as he neared his car.

He stilled. "Yep," he said, not turning around so he wouldn't have to look at her and those long legs. Well, that didn't work because she moved ahead of him, stopping at the open window of his car.

"What's its name?"

"Ember."

"A girl doggie?"

"Yes, a girl *doggie*." Ember thought highly of herself, and he doubted she appreciated being called a doggie.

"Can I pet her?"

No, but you can pet me. "Stop it."

"Pardon?" She frowned at him. "Are you okay?"

"Just peachy. Yes, you can pet her. She's shy, so she won't react to you." And then his dog went and made a liar out of him.

"You're such a pretty girl, yes, you are," Willow said,

sticking her face through the open window and laughing when Ember tried to lick her chin.

Parker scowled at his dog. Ember never greeted him with licks. *Traitor.*

"Are you on the way to work, and does she go with you?"

"Yes and yes. She's a working dog."

"Oh, like a Dalmatian that rides on a fire truck, just without the spots?"

He swallowed a laugh. Again. "No, she's an accelerant detection dog."

"Meaning?"

"What it sounds like. She alerts on accelerants if they were used to start a fire."

"Oh, that's cool." She gave Ember a last scratch behind the ears, then turned and leaned back against the car door. "What made you want to be a fireman?"

"Firefighter. We don't call ourselves firemen." She was a chatty thing.

"Sorry. Didn't mean to insult you. I'll have to remember that if I ever have a *firefighter* character in one of my books." She smirked.

Even her smirks were cute, and that had him scowling again. Why was he standing here chitchatting with her when his plan was to avoid her? "Need to go." Before he asked her what books, because now he was curious.

"Oh, okay. Well, I'll see you tomorrow."

Not if he could help it.

The next day, Parker and his brothers got a group text from the girls that a cookout was on for tonight. He called Tristan. "Have I forgotten a birthday or something?"

"I was wondering the same thing. Let me call Kade, see if he knows what's up."

"Okay. Let me know if I have to go buy a present for some reason or other." He knew it wasn't his or one of his brother's birthdays, but maybe Skylar or Harper? No, not Skylar. Tristan would have known that.

Tristan called back five minutes later. "He doesn't know anything either, other than it's not Harper's birthday. And it's not Skye's. Guess it's a no-reason cookout."

"We just had one of those, and I don't have time for another no-reason cookout. I need to be in the studio."

"Well, you tell Skye and Harper that."

"Nope, I'm scared of them when they put their heads together. I guess I have to eat, but that's it. No chatting over a beer or two."

"Understood."

He couldn't shake the feeling that those two women were up to something, and when he arrived home at the end of the day, he found out just what. Willow Landry was sitting at the table on the back deck with Skylar and Harper, a glass of wine in front of each of them. His daughter was sitting on Willow's lap eating a pickle. All of them were laughing.

The only thing different about her from the first time he saw her was the floppy straw hat was missing, but the flowery dress and cowboy boots were there. Her hair was down, the long strawberry curls framing her face. His fingers itched to paint her laughing like that. He glanced with longing at his studio. Unfortunately, if he locked himself up in there, his future sisters-in-law would come drag him out. He took a mental snapshot of her and all that hair and stored it away for later.

"Hey," she said when she noticed him, waving her fingers at him. Ember trotted over to her new friend and Willow smiled. "There's my pretty girl."

His brothers' women had ambushed him, and he scowled at them. Both looked back at him with fake innocence on their faces. Tristan and Kade came out, carrying a bucket of beer on ice and a plate of cheeses, crackers, grapes, and pickles. Tristan slid into the seat next to Skylar, and Kade sat next to Harper. That left only the chair next to Willow.

"You gonna join us or stand guard," Kade said with a smirk on his face.

"Daddy! Come sit next to me and Miss Willow."

"Sure." What else could he say? Definitely not what he wanted to, that Willow Landry disturbed him, thus he didn't want to be anywhere near her.

Everly hopped from Willow's lap to his. "Guess what, Daddy?"

"What, ladybug?"

She leaned over the arm of his chair toward Willow. "Daddy calls me ladybug because the ladybug fairy sneaks in the studio when I'm not there and paints a ladybug on my pictures."

"Wow, that's so cool."

"Yes! You want to come see?"

"I'd love to see the ladybugs."

"Not now, Ev." He didn't need Willow in his space. He didn't need to be smelling her flowery scent either—lavender maybe, which suited her. "What were you going to say? Guess what?"

"Oh, I almost forgot. Miss Willow brought a chocolate cake for dessert."

His gaze shot to Willow's, and when she smirked,

her message was clear. *You can't tell me what to do.* He bit the inside of his cheek to keep from laughing. He didn't want to be amused by her.

"Daddy, we need to go hang up my picture."

"What picture's that?"

She sighed, sounding as if he somehow wasn't keeping up. "You know, the one I painted for her. I found the best place for it, didn't I, Miss Willow?"

"You sure did, but I can hang it up tomorrow after I get a hook for it."

"Daddy has lots of hooks." She leaned her head back and looked up at him. "Right, Daddy?"

As much as he wanted to lie and say he didn't have any hooks, he'd made a promise he'd never lie to his daughter. "Right. I'll give her one before she goes home."

Everly shook her head. "No, we can hang it for her."

"I think Miss Willow wants to hang up your picture herself." He stared hard at Willow, mentally urging her to agree.

Chapter Eight

Willow sweetly smiled at the man who didn't want any part of hanging a hook for her. "That's so lovely of you to offer, and yes, I'd adore it if you'd hang a hook for me." She sighed (a bit dramatically). "If I did it, it'd probably fall off the wall…you know, kind of like my swing fell down." She was pouring it on, but it was so amusing to rattle his cage and get that scowl that was on his face now.

He was confusing. She didn't know why he didn't like her, being the nice person she was. It wasn't her fault his daughter had found her way over to her house, if that was what his problem was. The rest of his family was great, though. Everly was precious, his brothers funny and nice, and she could see herself being friends with Skylar and Harper. She could use a girlfriend or two after her bestie betrayed her.

Everly reached over and patted her hand. "My daddy won't let it fall down. You want a pickle?"

"Um…" Before she could say she'd pass on a pickle, Everly handed her one, then took another one for herself.

"Aunt Skylar, Miss Harper, you can have a pickle, too. I can't call Miss Harper aunt yet because she doesn't have a ring. When she does, then I can. My uncles don't like pickles, but my daddy will eat one with me sometimes." She peered at her father. "Right, Daddy?"

"Right. Now how about you use your ears for a little while, okay?"

"Okay." She sent a sigh Willow's way. "That means I have to stop talking and listen."

Willow wanted to laugh when Everly gave another sigh, a big one this time. The little girl was just too cute. She glanced at Parker over Everly's head to see he was looking at her, and she could swear his lips had almost twitched when he met her gaze.

His saving grace was his love for his daughter, evident in the way his eyes and smile softened when he looked at her. She wondered where Everly's mother was. The little girl had said she wanted a mommy, which made Willow think her birth mother had died. Maybe that was why Parker was grouchy…or that he really wasn't grouchy but grieving.

If she was right, then her heart went out to him. It had broken her when Austin walked away, but he was still on this earth, and because he was, buried deep was the awareness that he might decide he'd made a mistake and would come back to her someday.

For a long time after he left, there had been the hope that would happen. That hope had faded over time, and now it was just an awareness of the possibility. She was over him…believed she was. Hoped she was. Sometimes, when she let herself imagine Austin appearing out of the blue and telling her he'd made a mistake, she wondered what she'd do. Take him back or not? She didn't know. But the death of someone you loved? Knowing there would never be a chance to see them again, hold them, love them? How did you get over that? Was Parker's grouchiness a front for his grief?

She crunched on her pickle while thinking about this new insight and stealing glances at the man as he studiously ignored her in return. What was his problem with her specifically? The more she was around him and the more he scowled at her, the more he fascinated her. She wanted to solve the puzzle of Parker Church.

Oh, that's not good. I don't need to be fascinated by any man.

"Willow writes children's books," Skylar said. "How cool is that?"

Everyone's gazes landed on her…well, except for the man who was pretending she didn't exist. "It really is pretty cool, especially when I get a letter or an email from a kid who wants me to know how much he or she loves my stories. A few days ago, I got one from a boy who said he used to hate to read but now he loves reading my books. He wanted to know if I could write faster. Made my day."

"What kind of stories do you write?" Tristan asked.

"My target audience is ages eight to twelve. My current series, the one I'm working on, *The Magic Quill*, is fantasy."

"What's it about?" Harper asked.

"There are five friends, two boys and three girls. In the first book, Bri goes with her mother to an antique store. While her mom is browsing, Bri finds a quill, and—"

"What's a quill?" Everly said.

"It's what people a long time ago used to write with. Here, I'll show you." She picked up her phone from the table, and when she had a picture of a quill on the screen, she showed it to Everly.

Everly's eyebrows scrunched together as she sat forward and stared at the photo. "How do you write with a feather?"

"Tell you what. I have one that I'll show you one day."

"Now?"

Parker pulled his daughter back against his chest. "Not now, Ev. Let Miss Willow finish telling us about her story."

"Tomorrow?"

Willow smiled. She loved children's curiosity. "Sure." She glanced at Parker. "If your dad says it's okay for you to come over." That got narrowed eyes from Parker, and she wanted to laugh.

"Can I, Daddy? Please."

"We'll see."

The old *we'll see*, meaning not if he could help it. If he only knew how stubborn she was. She'd make a friend out of him or die trying. "Anyway, when Bri finds the quill, she just has to have it, and her mom buys it for her. Turns out it's a magic quill. Bri's having a hard time with something, and the quill helps her on a journey of discovery in *Bri and the Lost Ring*. At the end of Bri's story, she gives the quill to her friend Griffin, who's being bullied, and the magic quill will help him, and so on to the next child in the series."

"That's so fascinating," Harper said. "Now I want to read them."

Next to her, Kade smiled at his girlfriend. "Creative minds are fascinating. I've never understood where Parker's paintings come from. Neither Tristan nor I have a creative bone in our body. No one in our family did as far as I know."

"Our aunt was an artist," Parker said.

Tristan's eyes widened. "Say what now?"

"Huh?" Kade grunted.

By the way Parker was frowning as if he hadn't meant to say that, the reaction of his brothers, and how Skylar and Harper glanced at each other, this news was something big. Willow's intrinsic curiosity wanted to know what the story was, because there was one here.

Parker shifted his gaze to hers. "You want to go hang that hook now?"

There was pleading in his eyes that she couldn't refuse. "Sure."

While they'd been talking, and probably bored with the conversation, Everly had scooted off her father's lap and had lain down on the deck in the middle of the three dogs. Willow glanced down at her to see the little girl was asleep with the dogs wrapped around her as if protecting her. An idea for a scene in one of her magic quill books formed in her mind, and she took a mental picture.

Parker stood. "I have to get a hook. Be right back."

"Did you know that?" Tristan asked Kade after Parker went to the building with all the windows and skylights.

"I did not. How could we not know that?"

Tristan shrugged. "I never saw her paint."

"About the only thing I saw of her was her back as she closed herself up in her rooms as soon as we got home from school," Kade said. He glanced at Willow. "Sorry for the bit of family drama, but that was a bomb Parker dropped."

"No problem. I'll just go wait for Parker at home so you guys feel free to talk. Tell Parker to come on over."

"You're coming back, right?" Skylar said. "The guys are going to start the grill soon."

"Oh, sure. See you in a few." Although she'd love to stay and learn more about the family, especially Parker, she was an outsider. Whatever that bomb that Parker had dropped meant, she knew they wouldn't feel comfortable talking about it in front of her.

She was a writer, and people's personal stories interested her, often spurring her imagination. She sensed that the Church brothers had an interesting story to tell. Obviously, they didn't like the aunt, but where was their mother, their father? She'd love to know why Parker knew something about their aunt that his brothers didn't. And more than ever, she wanted to see Parker's art.

Parker arrived a few minutes behind her, and she showed him the spot Everly had picked out. "Your daughter's quite the artist, especially for her age."

"Yep." He'd brought a picture hook that adhered to the wall and a level.

"I was just going to hammer a nail in the wall." She wasn't, but she had a feeling that would get her the look he was giving her right now—disdain and almost an eye roll—and she hadn't been able to resist. She'd never before had a desire to rile a man up like this, yet she thought he needed riling up.

"Done," he said after hanging Everly's painting on the hook.

Willow stepped back and admired it. "Perfect. It's my first piece of art. When she's famous and her paintings are selling for millions, I'll be able to look at this and remember the sweetest little girl I ever knew."

For a few seconds, his eyes softened, then he tore his gaze away from hers. "You don't have to come back to the house if you don't want."

"Reading between the lines, something I'm pretty good at, you don't want me to, right?"

"It's not you."

She laughed. "Man, is that ever an overused line." It was almost as if he was afraid of her, and somehow, she was going to find out why. "I'll send my excuse to miss dinner back with you on three conditions."

Wariness crept into his eyes. "Those would be what?"

"That you let me be friends with Everly—" she shook her head when he opened his mouth, to protest, she was sure, and he snapped it closed "—and you let her come over tomorrow so I can show her my quill. I don't want to disappoint her. That you show me some of your paintings, and that you give me a tour of your house." She threw her arms out at the mess she'd inherited. "I need to get this place ready to sell, and I don't have a clue what I'm doing. On top of that, I'm on a deadline, so the faster I figure out what to do with it, the better."

"What's the hurry?"

"I need to sell it so I can move to the beach."

"You're leaving?"

"As soon as the house is sold, and that won't happen in the condition it's in."

His gaze scanned the room. "You need a contractor."

"Got one. Buddy Napier."

"He's good."

"That's what Skylar said, but I'm doing as much of it myself as possible, so it'll take a little longer. I'm demolishing the kitchen right now, and that's not as easy as they make it look on those DIY shows. Then I have to do the bathrooms." Turning away from her, he strode into the kitchen, and she followed him.

"Haven't gotten much done, yeah?"

She put her hands on her hips. "These cabinets don't come down easily."

"That's because they're thick oak, not like the flimsy cabinets they're putting in houses today." He picked up the sledgehammer she'd left on the floor, lifted it over his head, and with one downward sling, took down the cabinet next to the one that her muscles still hurt from demolishing.

"Um…feel free to keep going." There was that almost twitch of his lips again. One day she was going to make that mouth full-on twitch. She stood to the side, amazed at how fast he demolished the rest of the cabinets, and as he did, the muscles in his back, shoulders, and arms expanded and flexed. She brushed her fingers across her mouth to make sure she wasn't drooling.

As soon as he finished, he dropped the sledgehammer. "Gotta go." He looked down at the floor, then lifted his gaze to somewhere over her shoulder. "You can come back over if you want. You should."

Oh, she did want, but she wanted him to meet her conditions even more. "So, my conditions?"

"Agreed to. After she gets home from school, Andrew will bring her over and stay while she's here."

"Andrew's welcome to stay." He didn't really know her, and she respected that he wouldn't just agree to send Everly over without someone he trusted.

"No on seeing my paintings, but I'll give you a tour of our house."

"Nope, I want all my conditions met." She hadn't had this much fun since…she wasn't even sure since when. He'd never admit it, but she sensed that he was enjoying their sparring as much as she was. "Forget it. I'll come back with you. When I left, they were talking about the bomb you dropped that your aunt was an artist. What was that about?"

Chapter Nine

"It was about nothing," Parker said, and even to his own ears, it sounded like he'd growled the words. This woman with her questions and conditions. And why was he even negotiating with her? Well, why was he even asking that question, because he did know the answer. Going toe to toe with her stirred his blood.

She made him say things he'd never intended to say. Not that it was exactly her fault that he'd let that little nugget about his aunt slip out, but it wouldn't have if they hadn't been having that creative minds conversation, which had happened because of her. That was a secret he'd kept all these years, even though his aunt demanding he not tell his brothers about the time he spent with her had forced him to divide his loyalty between her and them. It was one reason he'd stopped talking for years unless he had to…too afraid the secret would slip out.

He'd wanted to tell his brothers their aunt wasn't as bad as they thought in some ways and worse than they could imagine in others. She'd been so mean and spiteful to them, that no matter what he said, they'd always hate her. He didn't blame them.

As an adult he could look back and see how their aunt

had manipulated him, and now he wished he'd told them everything. They'd deserved his loyalty, not her. That was something he still felt guilty about, and one of the reasons he'd fled to France as soon as he graduated. He'd been drowning under the press of her thumb and her secrets, secrets that left him feeling dirty.

She'd died three years after he'd left home, and even though he'd shared a love of art with Aunt Francine, all he'd felt was relief that she was gone. All the lies and secrets would be buried with her. His brothers had arranged a funeral but only because the town expected it. Left to them, there would have been no mention of her passing, no pretending she was going to be missed. As for him, he'd refused to come home for the service.

"Well?"

"Well, what?" His gaze roamed over her face. He'd gotten her freckles wrong on his painting. He needed to go to his studio.

"My conditions. Are we agreed? And why are you staring at my nose?"

"I wasn't." He totally was, but he wasn't about to admit he was counting and memorizing the placement of her freckles. "Fine, I agree." He'd only said that to distract her from his staring at her, but he should have negotiated. Only agreed to Everly spending time with her and a tour of the house.

He wasn't sure why he didn't want her in his studio, other than it seemed too personal. That didn't make a lot of sense. He wasn't an artist who had to work in secret, and he let his family, including Skylar and Harper, in anytime they wanted.

"When?" she asked.

"Your tour of the house?"

"And your studio."

He was hoping she'd forget that. "Sunday." He didn't go to the station on Sundays unless there was a fire or a serious accident. "Listen, come back for dinner." He didn't want to be around her…there was that disturbance thing going on, but he was a jerk for making her think she wasn't welcome. "You don't have to miss dinner."

"Honestly, I have a deadline looming and need to get some words on paper. But thanks."

"If you're sure."

She smiled. "I am."

"Okay. Everly gets home from school around two. After she has her pickle and changes clothes, Andrew will bring her over."

"I guess I'll see you Sunday then. I tend to stay up half the night writing, so I'm not a morning person. After lunch work for my tour?"

"Sure. One o'clock works." She didn't say anything to that, and the silence that fell was awkward. "Okay, I'm going now."

"Okay."

He almost said okay to her okay but managed to keep his mouth shut. He'd been smoother than this when flirting with his first serious girlfriend when he was fourteen. Not that he was flirting with Willow.

If he didn't have a show coming up and was running out of time, he'd help with the rest of the demolition because the faster she could get the house ready to sell, the faster she would leave for the beach.

As much as he wanted to deny it, he was attracted to her, and the last woman he'd been attracted to had come close to destroying him. If not for the baby she'd given him, he wasn't sure he would have recovered from her treachery.

He was sure he never would have picked up a brush and painted again if not for his daughter. Because of Everly, he'd had a reason to face each day, a reason he *had* to. He'd smiled again because of her and had found his way back to his art because of her. But never again would he make himself vulnerable to a woman.

"The kebabs are on the grill. Where's Willow?" Harper said when he returned home.

"Isn't coming back. Said something about a deadline and that she needed to write."

She looked at Skylar and some kind of message passed between them. Harper shifted her gaze back to him. "Not buying it."

"Nope, me either. He said something to keep her from coming back." Skylar nailed him with a stare that made him feel like he should confess all his sins. "What'd you do, Parker?"

Made her feel unwelcome because he was an ass.

"I want to talk about you knowing our aunt was an artist." Kade glanced at Tristan. "You, too, right?"

"Yup."

Four pairs of eyes stared at him, waiting for him to answer all their questions. These people were his family, and he loved them and would die for them, but he had no answers for them, not any he was willing to divulge.

He turned his back on them, went inside the house, made two PBJ sandwiches, put two pickles in a baggie, some chips in another one, and grabbed two root beers. After putting dinner for him and Everly in a plastic bag, he walked back outside, scooped his sleeping daughter up, and went to his studio. Without a word to his brothers and future sisters. He couldn't deal with them or answer their questions right now. Maybe never.

This turmoil going on inside him like a Cat 5 hurricane was all Willow's fault. Everything had been fine before she showed up. He had his life distributed into manageable compartments. He was first a father, then he did his job as a firefighter, and he painted. He spent time with his brothers without worrying about spilling secrets. He welcomed the women his brothers had fallen in love with to the family with open arms.

His life was going along without any drama, just the way he wanted. He'd had a lifetime's worth of drama in France, and all he wanted was to have each day pretty much like the last. Love his little girl, go to the firehouse, paint, drink a few beers with his brothers while talking about much of nothing…rinse, repeat.

Now a woman who had his artist fingers itching to get her freckles right had turned his ordered life topsy-turvy. He had feelings. He loved his baby girl more than he thought he could possibly love anyone. He loved his brothers, even though they were sometimes assholes. He was learning to love his future sisters. He was passionate about his art, and he was a damn good fire chief.

He had everything he needed. He was happy. Not over-the-moon happy. *Content* was probably a better word. But he was satisfied with the life he'd carved out after a woman without an honest bone in her body had done a number on him.

He did not want to be repainting freckles. But that was exactly what he did after lowering Everly to the daybed and telling Ember to watch over her. It didn't take long to get the freckles right, and now he could get to work on paintings for his show. But first, he needed to wake Everly up and get her to eat some dinner. He grabbed the blanket from the daybed, spread it on the floor, and set up a picnic.

Two hours later, he had his girl fed, bathed, a story read, and put to bed with Ember sleeping at her feet, guarding her. After a trip to the attic and avoiding his family, he slipped out to the studio, hoping to get some painting done before his brothers showed up with their questions.

"Shoulda locked the door," he said when they walked in. He'd expected them sooner, but they'd given him a few hours to himself.

Tristan snorted. "You do know a lock won't keep Kade out."

"Why I didn't bother. You could pretend I didn't say anything about Aunt Francine." Knowing this was a conversation he couldn't avoid, he slid his brushes into a plastic baggie so they wouldn't dry out.

"Too late," Tristan said. "Cat's out of the bag."

"That's Harper and Skylar," Kade said as he studied the painting.

"Very good, brother. I would be a poor artist if you didn't recognize your girlfriend's face."

Parker eyed the canvas. The two women were standing in front of a window looking out at a winter wonderland. The ground was covered in snow, as were the evergreen branches. A flock of cardinals perched in one of the trees, the red birds and the green branches the only colors in the landscape outside the window. Inside, a fire burned in the fireplace, the mantel was decorated for Christmas, and Jellybean was curled up on a rug in front of the fire. Skylar wore a red sweater to contrast with her blond hair, and Harper's sweater was a summer sky blue, a color that complemented her highlighted brown hair.

"I call dibs on it," Kade said.

Tristan shook his head. "It goes over the fireplace."

"Y'all can flip a coin or arm wrestle for it." He'd known they'd both want it. It would go in the show but wouldn't be for sale. "I don't suppose you two will go away and let me paint?"

"Nope," they said in unison.

"Was afraid of that." He knew how they were going to react, the reason he'd never told them what he was about to. Why had he opened his damn mouth?

Chapter Ten

Parker needed fortifying for this conversation. He walked to the mini kitchen and took down a bottle of whiskey from the cabinet. After pouring the liquor into three glasses, he handed his brothers theirs, then took the last one for himself. He moved to the wall, leaned back against it, and then slid down to sit on the floor. Kade sat next to him, and Tristan settled on the daybed.

"That comment about our aunt slipped out," he said. "I never had any intention to tell you any of this."

"Was it that big of a deal?" Tristan asked.

"Yeah, but only because Aunt Francine made it one." He'd been four, the baby, when their mother dumped them on their aunt. He remembered staring out the window for hours on end, watching for Mom to come back. She never did.

"If she was an artist, how come we never saw her paint?" Kade said. "I can't remember ever seeing anything she painted."

"Because she didn't. She sketched. There's a box of her sketch pads in the attic."

Tristan, the brother who'd raised him and Kade, frowned. "Why was that a secret?"

"Because…" He closed his eyes. He'd never wanted to have this conversation.

Kade's hand landed on his leg. "Parker, you can tell us anything."

He knew that, and he should have told them when it was happening. He opened his eyes and spilled his secret. "Our aunt only sketched male nudes."

Tristan, who'd just taken a drink of his whiskey, choked. "Say what now?"

"Jesus," Kade said.

"Wait a minute." Tristan leaned forward, his eyes on Parker, as suspicion dawned in them. "What male nudes?"

Parker pressed his head back against the wall. *Here it comes.* Their reaction and the reason he hadn't told his brothers what had been going on under their noses. Even as a young boy, he'd understood that if he told them, they would have gone ballistic, and then where would they have ended up? Because of him, they would have had no place to live.

"Parker, what male nudes?" said the man who'd made himself responsible for his two younger brothers at an age when the only thing he should have been worrying about was if the girl he was crushing on liked him, too, and would he make the football team.

"Any male who caught her attention."

Tristan's eyes narrowed to slits. "Including you?"

"Yep, including me."

"I'm going to dig her up and crush her fucking bones to pieces," Kade said, venom dripping in his words, his deadly voice sounding like the warrior he was.

Tristan stood, grabbed the whiskey, and topped each

of them off. "I might have to get drunk for this. Start at the beginning."

Parker took a healthy swallow of the whiskey, welcoming the burn as it traveled down his throat. "The beginning…okay. A few weeks after we were dumped here and you both were at school, she came into my room. Back then, she was so mean to us that she scared me. She caught me drawing a picture of our mother. I was going to give it to her when she came back for us."

"Shit," Kade muttered. "We shouldn't have let you think that woman gave a damn about us enough to come back."

"Kade," Tristan cautioned. "Let him finish without commentary."

"Sorry, baby brother." Kade gave him a noogie, something he used to do to annoy Parker.

Parker slapped his hand away. "Are you ever going to grow up?"

"Probably not, but sorry. Tell us everything."

"Everything. Well, she praised the drawing, and from that day on, she was nicer to me, but only when you two weren't around. I'd show her my drawings, and she'd show me how to do something better. I think she felt like we shared an artist soul or some such shit. I liked her being nicer and even at that age, I sensed that it was a secret, that if I told you two that she was being nice to me, she would stop."

"That's probably true," Tristan said. "It had to be a heavy secret for you to bear, but I'm glad to know that she was nice to you, especially as young as you were. Did you have to pose for her?"

His brother was trying to sound as if he wasn't furious, but there was rage in his voice. "No, she never asked me to. As far as I know, no man posed for her. I don't know why sketching male nudes consumed her, but they did. There's a whole box of them in the attic."

"You weren't a man," Kade growled.

"No, I wasn't, and I never found another boy in her sketchbooks that she drew naked. Honestly, her sketches of me look pretty innocent. Like she wanted to capture the beauty of a boy's body." He had to believe it was that simple. "If you're willing to look, there's a sketchbook under that pillow next to you, Tris. Maybe you two can tell me if you see them the same way I do."

For years after discovering his aunt's sketches, he'd agonized over what they meant. Although she'd never asked him to pose for her, they were all of moments he recognized. Like the first one his brothers would see when they opened the sketch pad. It would have been shortly after they arrived at their aunt's home, so he would have been around four. He was standing next to the bathtub, his hair wet, and water dripping down his skinny chest. Two hands were in the drawing, holding a towel out for him to step into. If someone saw it and didn't know the circumstances, they would think the hands belonged to the boy's mother.

There was nothing sexual about the sketch, about any of them. At least, he'd never thought so. Some were actually poignant. But they'd confused him, and discovering them had set in motion the course of his life, one of the reasons he'd fled to France. Looking back, and with a better understanding of art, he could say that he'd probably overreacted by running away.

As an adult and an artist, looking at the sketches she'd done of him, he didn't know what to think about them. Had she wanted to capture the innocence of a boy, and that was all they were? On the other hand, he'd never ever sketch Everly nude no matter how innocent the drawing might be.

Tristan slipped his hand under the pillow and pulled out the sketchbook. He stared at it, then at Parker. "I feel like I'll vomit if I open this."

"Then don't." He wanted his brothers' assurances that the way he saw the sketches was right, but he understood if he was asking too much. If they saw them as sexual drawings, he was the one who would puke his guts up.

"I think I have to, that you need me to."

Gratitude filled his heart that his brother understood. He sat silent as Tristan turned the pages. No expression showed on Tristan's face as he looked at the drawings, and Parker forced himself to wait. It wasn't easy.

When Tristan finished, he handed the sketch pad to Kade, and still nothing showed on his face, nor did he speak. Parker finished off his whiskey, thought about refilling his glass.

Kade had only turned a few pages when he closed the sketch pad. "I've seen enough."

"In the last drawing, it looks like you were around seven or eight?" Tristan said.

"That's my guess. I think that's about the time she stopped sketching me." Thank God. Why wouldn't he say the sketches weren't sexual? Were they?

In France, he'd taken art classes on drawing the human body, and they'd had nude models, both male and female. After the first few classes, he'd gotten over the weirdness of having a naked person in front of him. When he'd returned, he'd found the sketchbooks that had sent him fleeing to France hidden in the attic. He'd

gone through all of them, and he recognized her drawings for what they were—a study of the male body,
much like those lessons he'd taken. Was it still weird?
Yes, but none of her sketches felt sexual, not the ones
of him or the other men.

"I'm not an artist," Tristan said, "so I don't see things
through yours or our aunt's eyes, but although she was
obviously fascinated by the male body, I don't feel anything sexual about them."

"Still sick as fuck," Kade said.

"Well, she was a strange duck," Tristan said, then
snorted at the unintentional rhyme.

The three of them looked at each other, then burst
out laughing. Their reaction probably had as much to
do with the whiskey consumed as it did with Tristan's
rhyme.

"After I came home from France, I expected that one
of you would have found her sketch pads after she died.
When nothing was said about them, I thought she'd destroyed them, but to be sure, I searched the attic. I was
hoping she'd burned them to a crisp."

"That's an excellent idea." Kade stood. "Let's do it."

"Now?"

Kade reached down and pulled him up. "No better
time."

"You know what…you're right. You and Tristan go
start a fire, and I'll bring the box down." He grabbed
the whiskey bottle and handed it to Kade. "Can't have
a bonfire without the booze."

As he passed the theater room, the sound of a movie
playing caught his attention, and he peeked in. Skylar
and Harper were kicked back on the recliners, bowls of

popcorn in their laps, watching *Pretty Woman*, a movie they'd seen a half a dozen times at least.

If he hadn't run Willow off, she'd probably be in there watching it with them, and a stab of guilt hit him. It wouldn't kill him to be nicer to her. Wasn't her fault she disturbed him. Without bothering them, he headed to the attic.

The box was in the back corner, shoved under an old desk. It had taken him a while to find it, and as he'd sat on the dusty floor, and as he flipped through her sketchbooks, emotions had warred within him. A part of him hated her for how she'd treated his brothers—and him when they were home—but there was another part that held a sort of...fondness, he guessed was the right word.

Why she'd showed him a side of herself that no one else was allowed to see, he'd never know. She'd taught him how to draw hands, the part of a body he'd had the most trouble with. She'd taught him about colors and shading. But in all the years she'd secretly been nice to him and taught him about art, he'd never known she'd been sketching him.

He learned about the other men when he started high school. She showed him a few of her drawings, asking his opinion. He was scandalized in the beginning, but she told him there was no shame in the human body, that her sketches were art. To prove it, she took down her art books in the library that was off-limits to him and his brothers, and showed him paintings of nudes—both male and female—by famous artists. He never thought to ask her why she didn't draw female nudes.

Then during his senior year of high school, he filled up his sketch pad and knew his aunt had a supply of blank ones. She'd gone to the grocery store, and not wanting to wait for her to come home so he could ask for one, he went into her room—a place he was banned from, but she'd never know—to get a new one.

He could be in and out before she got home, and she'd never miss one from the stack. A sketch pad with his name on it was on her desk, and curious, he flipped it open. His heart dropped to his stomach at seeing the drawing of him as a younger boy...nude. "What?" he whispered as if afraid she'd hear him, catch him. As he flipped through the pages of sketches of him naked, bile rose in his throat, and he ran out of his aunt's room.

The next time she left the house, he searched for and found more sketch pads filled with nudes of him, going back to when he and his brothers were brought to live with her. As far as he could determine, the one of him getting out of the bathtub was the first one she'd sketched.

Sick in his stomach, feeling betrayed and violated, he fled his aunt's room without a new sketch pad. Instead, he spent the next few days applying for a passport, creating a portfolio, and filling out an application to send to an art school in France...as far away from his aunt as he could think to get.

If he'd known then he'd be betrayed again—and in the worst possible way—in France because he was the boy who couldn't help falling in love, he still would have gone for one reason. Everly. His treasure and reason for living.

He hefted the box and carried it to where his brothers had rolled a barrel to the middle of the yard and had a blazing fire going. In between passing the whiskey around, they took turns tossing sketch pads into the fire. The pages caught fire, the edges turned black, and then curled before turning to ashes and floating away. It was liberating.

"A naked man broke into a church," Kade said. "The police chased him around and finally caught him by the organ." He passed the whiskey bottle to Parker.

"Don't laugh. Don't encourage him," Tristan said.

"Seriously, Kade?" Parker said, then laughed so hard he tripped over his feet. He blamed the whiskey for his feet misbehaving, but he was liberated, and wasn't that something?

Chapter Eleven

What was that racket? Willow peeked out her spy-on-the-neighbors bedroom window. A fire was burning in a barrel in the middle of the backyard, and the three brothers stood around it, passing a bottle around, tossing what looked like notebooks into the fire, and laughing themselves silly.

They were drunk, had to be. She watched them for a few minutes…well, her gaze was mostly on Parker. He'd pulled off the band holding his ponytail, and his hair was loose. What would it feel like to comb her fingers through it? Was it as soft and silky as it looked?

"Stop it," she hissed. She was on a time-out from men. No thinking about how soft Parker's hair was. She dropped the curtain back in place. She needed to write, not waste time fantasizing about a sexy grouch's hair.

A few hours later, she reached her minimum word count for the day, but was on a roll and kept going until her eyes began to burn. It was getting late, and she had a busy day tomorrow, so she logged off her laptop. She wished she hadn't signed up for the book fair and signing in Charlotte, but her travel schedule had been booked at the beginning of the year, before she'd broken up with her fiancé and inherited a house that was going to drain her savings account dry to get it ready to sell.

Fortunately, Charlotte was a little under a two-hour drive, so she'd go tomorrow afternoon, do the book signing the next day on Saturday, and come home that evening, back in time for her tour of the Church house and to see Parker's art. She wasn't about to miss that.

Everly was supposed to come for a visit tomorrow afternoon, and although Willow had planned to leave for Charlotte earlier, she'd wait to go until after her time with the little girl. Something else she was looking forward to.

She yawned, stretched her arms over her head, and wiggled her fingers. It had gotten quiet next door, and she went to the window. The fire was out, and the brothers were gone from the yard, but lights were on in what she now knew was Parker's studio. The windows didn't have any coverings, but the only thing visible from her angle was a daybed and what appeared to be a small kitchen.

Was he in there, painting? And so what if he was? What did it matter to her? She dropped the curtain, determined to stop thinking about Mr. Grouchy Pants.

Bells chimed a little after two, and Willow went to the door, expecting to find Andrew and Everly on the other side. Instead, there stood Grouchy Pants wearing a paint-stained navy blue T-shirt with the Marsville Fire Department logo on the chest, and his little girl perched on his hip.

Be still my heart.

A few awkward seconds passed while she stared at

him, and he stared back. Then his brows lifted at the same time Everly yelled, "Miss Willow! I'm here."

Willow shook herself out of her that-was-about-the-hottest-thing-she'd-ever-seen trance. "So you are." She glanced up at Parker. "I thought Andrew was bringing her over."

"As you can see, I'm not Andrew." He smiled... freaking smiled at her. "One eager ladybug delivered as promised." He set Everly down, then slid a canvas tote off his shoulder. "She brought art supplies so she can draw with you. I'll be back in an hour to pick her up." After handing Willow the tote, he leaned down and kissed Everly on the cheek. "You be good, okay?"

Everly rolled her eyes, which, in a five-year-old, Willow thought was the cutest thing. "I'm always good, Daddy."

"That's debatable. You two have fun." He took a step back, then stopped. "I should give you my phone number in case you want to send her home earlier."

"I won't, but probably a good idea." She gave him her number.

"Okay, I just texted you, so you'll have mine."

Her phone was on the dining room table, and she heard it chime with a text message. "Got it."

"Well, have fun." A lopsided smile appeared on his face. "I said that already, didn't I?"

She wanted to say, "Who are you, and what did you do with Mr. Grouchy Pants?" Instead, she said, "You can never wish too much fun on anyone."

"Guess not." His eyes connected with hers, and she could swear the air crackled around them. What was that about? He lowered his gaze to his daughter. "Love you, ladybug." With that said, he left.

"Do you like my daddy?" Everly asked as they watched Parker jog across the yard.

"Of course." She was still processing that he'd smiled at her, an honest-to-goodness real one and not a fake one. What was up with that? Also, he'd left Everly with her without him or Andrew supervising. Did that mean he trusted her now?

Not sure where Everly was going with her question, Willow said, "Let's go inside. We can have some cookies and juice while we draw."

"Yes! And you can tell me a story. I love stories, Miss Willow. Do you write good ones?"

"I like to think so. Why don't you get your drawing stuff set up on the dining room table while I get our snack?"

"What do you want to draw, Miss Willow? I only brought my colored pencils because it's too messy to bring my paints. Daddy only lets me paint in the studio. What story are you going to tell me? Does it have a princess in it? And pickles!"

This girl and her exuberance were delightful. "I have an idea. What if I tell you a story and you draw it?" Since she couldn't draw worth beans.

"Oooooh, yes!" Everly clapped her hands. "You have good ideas, Miss Willow."

"I try. So, do you want a princess story or a magic dragon one?"

Everly pressed a finger to her lips and lifted her gaze to the ceiling. After a few seconds of thinking, she threw her hands out. "I thought I wanted a princess one, but a magic dragon one is better. Do you have a picture of a dragon for my inspiration?"

Willow grinned. How many five-year-olds even

knew what *inspiration* meant, much less how to use it in a sentence? She could fall in love with this little girl. "Here, I'll find one on my phone for you."

"He's green," Everly said when Willow showed her a photo of a dragon. "Can mine be pink 'cause she's a girl dragon?"

"She can be whatever color you want her to be. Do you know what an illustrator is?" When Everly shook her head, Willow said, "An illustrator is an artist who draws pictures to go with a story. Like in some of your books where there's pictures that go with the story. An author tells the story, and the illustrator draws the pictures that go in the book. That's us. I'm the author, and you're my illustrator."

"Is it like a job? My daddy has a job. I want a job."

"Yes, it's a job. So, this is how it works. I'll start telling our dragon story, and as soon as you feel inspired, you start drawing. Okay?"

Everly opened a sketch pad, arranged her colored pencils to her liking, then gave Willow a thumbs-up. "Ready!"

It was beyond adorable how the sweet girl talked in exclamation points and yelled half her conversations. An idea sprouted of a girl who was cursed by…well, who she was cursed by Willow would figure out later, but she was cursed to yell everything she said, and the magic quill would somehow help her talk normally so the other kids would stop making fun of her.

Willow had never had a muse, but she thought she'd found her first one. Parker better not decide she couldn't spend time with Everly, or he'd have an epic battle on his hands.

"I said I was ready, Miss Willow. You can start our

story now." Everly raised her brows in a perfect imitation of how her father had as he'd stood on the porch, delivering his daughter.

Instead of peppering kisses all over the cutest little girl in the world's face, and instead of laughing in delight with that little girl, Willow solemnly nodded as she turned on her phone's recorder. "All right, this is Serafina the pink dragon's story." She changed her voice to the one she used when reading her books to preteens. "Serafina the dragon was pink. You might think that was a good thing since pink is such a pretty color, but in the dragon world, if you were pink, you were a weak dragon. All her life, Serafina had been laughed at, and that especially hurt her because a dragon tournament—"

"What's a tournament?"

"A contest. In our story, the dragons are playing games in the tournament, and the prize is a treasure chest of gold and shiny stones like diamonds, rubies, and emeralds. Did you know dragons love treasures, and the shinier the gold and gems are, the happier they are? Serafina was told she couldn't help her family try to win the treasure because she was pink and weak."

Everly's eyes widened. "Girls aren't weak. My daddy said girls are strong, that I can be as strong as I want to."

Heaven help her. She didn't need to be seeing Parker as an awesome man and a daddy who said cool things like that. "Your daddy's right, and Serafina's daddy told her the same thing."

Everly had started drawing, and as a pink dragon with a pink bow holding a lock of hair straight up emerged, Willow looked on with awe. Did Parker even realize his daughter was a prodigy? When Everly finished sketching Serafina, she flipped a page on the sketch pad and drew a mighty midnight blue dragon.

"That's the daddy dragon," Everly said. "He's really strong, but Serafina's strong, too."

"Yes, she is, and she has a secret plan to help her family win the treasure."

Everly lifted wide eyes to her. "Oooh, a secret. You can tell me, Miss Willow. I promise I won't tell anyone."

"Okay, but for Serafina's plan to work, no one else can know. On the morning of the tournament, the four dragon families gather on the field, all of them hoping to win the treasure. In the first contest, the dragons have to fly as fast as they can to the top of a mountain. A gold ribbon's tied to a tree branch, and the first dragon to reach it, take it from the tree, and fly back to the field with the ribbon is the winner."

"Wait." Everly held up a finger. "I need to draw that."

Willow smiled at the way Everly's tongue stuck out the side of her mouth as she concentrated on drawing the scene. While she drew her dragon families, Willow watched the story coming alive right in front of her eyes. Would Parker let her send the finished story and his daughter's illustrations to her agent? She had a feeling that Courtney could sell it just based on the art.

"Okay, you can tell me more now." Everly turned to a new blank page.

"Well, since pink dragons aren't allowed to be in the contest because they're thought to be so weak that they can never win, Serafina paints herself purple. When she flies onto the field and joins her family, her father knows right away the purple dragon is Serafina, and he winks at her."

"But no one else knows?"

"Right, only her daddy."

"Daddies are smart, Miss Willow."

"They sure are. Well, it takes all day to play the different dragon contests, and who do you think wins the treasure for her family?"

"Serafina!" Everly dropped her pencil and clapped her hands. "I love that story so much."

"And I love your illustrations so much. Your daddy will be here soon to get you. Maybe you can finish working on the drawings for the story at home?"

"Okay. But did Serafina stay purple?"

"Nope. After she wins the treasure, she flies into the lake and washes the purple paint away. The dragon families are surprised and amazed that a pink dragon is so strong that she won, and from then on, pink dragons can enter the tournaments."

"Oh, goody. Do you have any pickles? I like them better than cookies."

"I'm sorry, I don't." But she'd keep them on hand from now on. The bells chimed.

"What was that?" Everly looked up at the ceiling.

"My doorbell. I think it's your daddy." She put her hand on Everly's shoulder when she started to get up. "I'll go see." At confirming it was Parker through the peephole, she opened the door. "Good timing. We just finished our story."

"I have a favor to ask. Can you keep Everly for a little longer? I've been called in, and normally Andrew watches her if none of us are home, but he went with his parents to Asheville for the night."

"Sure. We're having fun." A fire department SUV was in the driveway, the engine idling, and Ember was in the front passenger seat. "Is there a fire?"

"Yeah. Can I come in and talk to Everly for a sec?"

"Of course." She stepped aside, and when he passed by her, she got a whiff of something spicy, and she leaned forward and inhaled as she followed him. He glanced back at her and frowned.

Busted. But who could blame her? The man smelled delicious. The kind of deliciousness that made a girl want to bury her nose against his neck and breathe him in.

"Daddy!" Everly shouted at seeing him. "Guess what? Miss Willow's writing a story, and I'm ill...illa..." She looked at Willow and scrunched her nose.

"Illustrating."

"Yes! You know what that means, Daddy?"

"I do. Are you having fun with Miss Willow?"

"Oh, yes! I drew pictures for her dragon story. Want to see?"

"I sure do, but it'll have to be when I get back from work. Brought you something to hold you over until I get home." He set a jar of pickles on the table.

"Yay! Miss Willow doesn't have any pickles."

"Which I'll correct immediately." Who would have guessed a five-year-old preferred pickles over cookies?

"I have to go, ladybug. You're going to stay with Miss Willow until Skylar picks you up."

"Yippie!"

He kissed his daughter's cheek, and then Willow walked to the door with him. "We're having a blast, so she's fine until Skylar gets here." It would mean a delay in leaving for Charlotte, but she could go early in the morning if necessary.

"Thanks, I really appreciate it."

"Like I said, we're having fun. Your daughter's delightful." And unbelievably talented. She wanted to talk to him about showing her agent their story and illustrations, but now wasn't the time.

"That she is." He nodded at her, then jogged to his car.

And her daddy is one fine-looking man. Even though she was on a Man Hiatus, her eyes still worked. "Stay safe," she whispered as he drove away.

Chapter Twelve

After a lecture on the danger of fires and a warning of what would happen if they did it again, Parker turned the two tween brothers over to their father. The twin boys had stolen a few cigarettes and a book of matches from their father, and hiding in the woods behind their house, they'd ignited a wildfire when one of them had tossed a cigarette aside without putting it out first. It hadn't rained for over a month, which hadn't helped.

The good news, it wasn't arson. Maybe their firebug had moved on. One could hope. Parker returned to his crew, who had the fire contained and were close to putting it out. Thankfully the boys had run to their father and confessed as soon as they realized they'd started a fire, otherwise it could have been much worse.

His captain joined him. "The boys in a lot of trouble?"

"Their father wasn't happy. Said they were grounded for the rest of their life."

Greg chuckled. "I sneaked a cigarette from my dad when I was twelve. Smoked it and then barfed my guts up. Cured me of ever wanting to smoke."

"Never had the desire to even try." And if he had, and

Tristan had caught him, he would have been grounded for a month.

"We'll finish up here in an hour or so if you want to head out, boss."

The back of Parker's neck prickled, and he scanned the area. "Notice any strangers around tonight?"

"No, why?"

"Just getting a weird feeling, like we're being watched." And not for the first time.

"Huh." Greg gaze darted around them. "I haven't seen anyone suspicious."

"Probably my imagination, but keep an eye out."

"You thinking our arsonist is hanging around?"

"Maybe. I'm going to take a look." He walked the perimeter of the fire with Ember at his side. A little over halfway around the circle he was walking, Ember stopped. She looked up at him, then headed toward a nearby stand of trees.

"What is it, girl?" He let her take the lead as he followed her. When she stopped, sat, and peered up at him the way she did when alerting to an accelerant, he paused next to her. "You find something?"

The woods were thick, blocking out the sun. He took his flashlight and shined it on the ground ahead of them. The low brush was flattened, evidence that someone had stood there. Parker turned and, no surprise, he could see his firefighters as they battled the last of the fire the boys had started. The arsonist had watched them from here.

The strong smell of gasoline permeated the air, and he rubbed a finger over leaves that were wet. He brought his finger to his nose and sniffed. Gasoline.

"He was here. Good job, Ember." He rewarded her

with a few treats. "What's that?" He focused the light on what had caught his attention. Thumbtacked to a tree was a picture…a Polaroid. Who even had a Polaroid camera anymore? His gaze narrowed in on the photo. It was a photo of the first fire.

"Shit." Parker didn't doubt for a second that the arsonist had left it for him to find. That was probably the reason for the gasoline, to make sure Ember would lead him here. His feeling that he was being watched hadn't been his imagination. He didn't have any rubber gloves on him, and he didn't want to get his crew stirred up yet, so he called Tristan.

"I need you and one of your CSI people," he said when his brother answered. He gave Tristan his location.

"That's out of the city limits, so you need Skye."

"Right." The sheriff and police departments shared crime scene technicians since both departments were small, but Tris was correct—this was Skylar's territory. "Did Skylar pick up Everly from Willow, do you know?"

"She did."

"Then you need to relieve her so she can come out here. This fire was started by some boys smoking cigarettes, but our arsonist was here."

"Hell. I'm headed home now. She'll meet up with you in thirty or so. As soon as we hang up, I'll get a CSI headed your way."

The CSI arrived ahead of Skylar. "Good afternoon, Maurisa."

"Chief. What you got here?"

"A little gift from a firebug." He stood back with Ember while Maurisa collected and bagged the Polaroid and a few of the gas-soaked leaves. When Skylar arrived, he told her what he'd found.

"He, or she, if that's the case, is taunting you," Skylar said after she studied the photo Maurisa had bagged.

"Yeah, I had that feeling by the third fire. Since a female arsonist is rare, for ease of conversation let's go with a male unless we learn differently. There's a message on the back." It read, *In fire, there is beauty. There is purity. I see you, Parker. See me.* "I don't like this at all."

"Don't blame you." Skylar handed the photo to the CSI, then put her hand on his arm and walked him away from the interested ears of the CSI. "He's making it personal to you."

"I know, and you can't imagine how much I wish otherwise."

"Have you fired anyone, interviewed anyone you didn't hire, had an argument with anyone?"

"No, none of those. Our man either has a scanner or he followed me or the firetrucks here." His money was on a scanner.

"Well, someone's out to get your attention, so think hard on who in your past would do something like this."

Only one name came to mind, but he immediately discarded the mere idea of it. He'd agreed to all of Simone's demands, so she didn't have any reason to travel here from France and cause trouble. Did she?

His eyes gritty and burning, Parker glanced at the large clock on the studio wall. Three in the morning was a good reason for gritty eyes. He should go to bed, but his mind was chaos. So much had happened in the last twenty-four hours that there was no way he'd be able to sleep.

Finally confessing his secret to his brothers had been cleansing, and maybe it was a bit overly dramatic, but he felt like his sins had been washed away. He'd carried the weight of the secret he'd shared with his aunt for so long that, unburdened of it now, the crushing weight gone, he wouldn't be surprised if he floated away.

Too bad he wasn't going to be able to enjoy this new contentment thanks to an arsonist who apparently was targeting him for some reason. He'd thought hard about anyone he knew who might have it out for him. Not a single name came to mind. Yet, something nagged at the back of his mind.

He shrugged as he stepped back to see what he'd created in his painting fog. Whatever was nagging at his mind would come to him, or it wouldn't. He ran a critical eye over the canvas. It needed more work, but the bones were there.

A boy, his face hidden in shadows, his shoulders sagging as if the weight of the world rested on his back, leaned on the windowsill of a dark room as he looked out at a raging storm. The clouds were dark and angry, and lightning streaked down from the sky. In the distance, though, a golden ray of sunlight parted the black and purple clouds, shining down a ray of hope that the boy lifted a hand toward, as if reaching for that hope.

Parker set down his brush and considered a title for the painting. One word came to mind.

Liberated.

No one but him would understand the title of the painting, no one would know it was a self-portrait from a time when he was a confused boy. And because no one would understand the significance of the painting, it would go in the show, but it wouldn't be for sale. How many were not for sale now? Lawrence, the gallery owner, wasn't going to be happy about the no-sales.

He cleaned his brushes, then turned off the studio lights before going out. Bed called, but his feet took a detour. By the time he'd made it home it was dark, and Willow's yellow car hadn't been in the driveway. Had she gone on a date? He told himself he was just being a good neighbor by making sure she was safely home. When he reached his front yard, he stilled and frowned. Her car still wasn't in the driveway.

Not his business if she'd gone on a date and wasn't spending the night in her own bed. It irritated him that the thought of her with some other man bothered him. He didn't know why he cared. Exhausted, he went inside his house, showered, and then crashed facedown on his bed. He was in that hazy in-between of wakefulness and sleep when his eyes snapped open.

Two years ago, he'd sold a painting at a New York show, the only one he'd ever done of a fire. The scene was from a wildfire, and he'd managed to catch the power and yes, the beauty of a fire, and the horror of it.

He'd never forget that day. It had been a dry late summer, and wildfires were popping up all over. This one had been particularly brutal, refusing to be contained. He and his crew were clearing brush to create a fire line when a mama bear and her cub raced out of the flames. Once cleared of the fire, the mama bear stopped, stood on her hind legs as she turned back to face the fire, and emitted a hair-raising cry.

"She's got another cub in there," someone on the line said.

A gasp escaped past Parker's lips when the mama growled at the cub, and then disappeared back into the flames. The cub whined as it paced, but it didn't follow its mother. The growl from mama must have been a warning to stay put. A few minutes passed, then the mother bear emerged with a second cub dangling from her mouth.

She dropped it to the ground, and it didn't move. Parker held his breath, wishing he could do something to help as the mother licked her cub, trying to revive it. After what felt like hours but was only minutes, the rescued cub made a kind of coughing noise. As soon as the cub was up and moving, the bear family ran toward them. The line crew parted, and the bears raced past them as if they didn't exist.

Compelled to paint what he'd witnessed, Parker had included the painting in a show. He'd titled it *Escaping the Fire*. Even though it was only his second New York art show, the turnout had been impressive, considering he was a newly discovered artist. He didn't like crowds, but he understood the importance of mingling so everyone attending could talk to him. There'd been one man he'd taken an instant dislike to.

Parker closed his eyes and visualized the man, tried to remember his name.

Before Parker knew he didn't like the man, and was doing his mingling thing, he'd walked up to the guy as he stared at the painting. "That was a day I'll never forget." He told the man about seeing the mama bear go back into the fire to rescue her cub.

"What would have been amazing was if she'd come out of the fire with her fur in flames," the man said. "Imagine how beautiful that would have been."

Struck speechless, Parker took a step away. He needed to go mingle somewhere else.

The man grabbed his arm. "Don't pretend seeing something like that wouldn't give you a thrill. You and I understand the power of a fire, the beauty of it. This painting is proof of that."

He tried to avoid the guy after that, but every time he turned around, the man was in his face. The guy followed him around, interrupted when Parker was trying to talk to other people. He wanted to buy *Escaping the Fire*, but said the price was too high and Parker should give him a deal on it since they both understood the beauty of the fire.

"You'll have to talk to the gallery owner," Parker said, wanting the man to leave him alone. "He sets the prices."

"You're the artist, you can tell him you want to give me a deal on it."

"Sorry, but according to my contract, I can't do that." It was a lie, but something inside him didn't want the man to have the painting.

He'd thought he was rid of the man, but a little later the guy returned, and he was furious that the painting had a Sold tag on it. Parker didn't know who'd bought it, but bless them. He'd give it away before letting the man have it...what the hell was his name?

Parker sat up, swung his legs over the side of the bed, and turned on his lamp. Kade had still been in the Army and was on a mission, so he hadn't been able to come to the show, but Tristan had been there. Parker grabbed his cell phone and called his brother.

"Another fire?" Tristan said on answering.

"No, but—"

"Then why are you calling me at four in the morning?"

"You remember that dude at my second New York show that I had to get you to run interference on when he wouldn't leave me alone?"

"Yeah. Why?"

"Do you remember his name?"

"No. Again, why?"

"It's possible he's our arsonist."

Chapter Thirteen

Willow groaned when her alarm went off. "Five more minutes," she mumbled as she punched the snooze button. Thirty minutes and three snoozes later, she resisted hitting the button a fourth time and dragged her tired butt out of bed.

After a shower and her second cup of coffee, she started to feel normal again. The book fair had been a success, and although she'd intended to drive home as soon as it was over, a group of her author friends guilted her into going out to dinner with them. Her plan to leave for Marsville as soon as they finished dinner was hijacked when they talked her into going to a bar where a friend's band was playing.

Since she was driving home as soon as she could escape, she'd nursed a beer until midnight, when she'd hugged her friends and then left for home. She should have booked a room and stayed overnight in Charlotte, and she would have if not for the promised tour of Parker's studio and house.

She hadn't left because of Parker, since men were on her no-no list for a while. Nope, the studio and house tour were the reasons she hadn't stayed to spend more time with the friends she only got to see at book signings and author conferences.

What should she wear for her grand tour?

At precisely one o'clock, Willow rang the Church brothers' doorbell.

The door opened, and Everly grinned up at her. "Look, Miss Willow. I got cowboy boots, too!"

Well, just go and melt my heart, sweet girl. "I see that. And they're pink. I want pink cowboy boots, too."

"Aunt Skylar and my almost Aunt Harper took me shopping yesterday. I can tell you where you can get pink ones." She formed an O with her mouth and clapped. "I know! I can take you shopping to get pink boots, Miss Willow." She looked behind her. "Daddy, I need to take Miss Willow to the boot store."

Parker walked up behind his daughter and put his hands on her shoulders. "Not today, kiddo. Miss Willow is here to get a tour of the house and see our studio."

"She could see it better with pink boots."

"No doubt, but—" Parker's gaze slid over her sundress, then down to her feet "—her brown boots will have to do for today. Where's your manners, ladybug? Are you going to invite Miss Willow in or make her stand on the porch?"

"I have manners." Everly took her hand and pulled her inside. "See."

"So I see. Why don't you go out to the studio and finish getting your illustrations ready to show Miss Willow? We'll be there shortly."

"Okay, but hurry. I'm so excited to show her what I drew."

"Yes, ma'am."

"Before you go, Everly, I brought you a present." She handed the little girl a small gift bag, something she'd seen in a bookstore in Charlotte and had thought of Everly.

"I love presents." She wasted no time digging into the tissue, and when she pulled the gift out, her eyes widened. "Is this mine?" Willow nodded. "Oh, thank you! I wanted a quill so bad. Is it magic?"

"No, quills are only magic in stories. I got it for you so you could say you have one."

"It's pretty, but I'd like it better if it was magic."

"Everly," Parker said with a reprimanding tone.

She gave her father a defiant look. "You said always tell the truth."

Willow swallowed a laugh, both at the little girl's statement and Parker's sigh. "I wish it was a magic quill, too, sweetie."

"Go to the studio and get ready to show Miss Willow what you've been working on." Parker gave his daughter a push. "Sorry about that," he said after Everly left.

"Nothing to be sorry about. I want a magic quill, too."

"Don't we all?" He stuffed his hands in his pockets. "So, a tour. You're obviously in the foyer."

"Andrew said you designed the chandelier. It's beautiful."

"Thanks." He walked to a door behind the staircase on the right, and she followed him. "This is the library."

She stepped inside the room. "Oh. My. God." On all four walls were built-in floor-to-ceiling shelves filled with books. "You can just leave me in here for the rest of my life."

He chuckled. "Sure. I'll just throw food in once a day."

"Who's the booklover? Have you read them all?" She wandered to one of the shelves and skimmed the titles.

"Our aunt, and no, I haven't read any of them. Tristan and Kade are determined to work their way through them." He muttered something.

"Pardon?"

"Nothing."

"*Out of spite.* Isn't that what you just said?"

"Didn't mean to let that slip out."

"Well, you did, and now I have to know what you meant. Nosy person here." That was her author brain at work, needing to know the story, and there was one.

He blew out a breath. "We lived with our aunt after our mother…" He frowned. "Growing up, we weren't allowed in this room, couldn't touch, much less read her books."

"That's horrible. As a children's author, I'm appalled. Every child should be encouraged to read." And after their mother…what? Had she died? No wonder he was moody if he'd lost both his mother and his wife.

"Not going to argue that."

"So your brothers are reading their way through this amazing library to spite your aunt? I take that to mean she's no longer in the picture?"

"Correct."

"You don't sound sad about that."

"Correct." He walked out.

Mmm. Touchy subject, apparently. She trailed behind him to another room, her mind churning with a thousand questions. Because any talk of his aunt turned him prickly, her questions wouldn't be asked. She sure was curious, though.

"This is my future sisters-in-law's favorite room." He waved a hand for her to walk in ahead of him.

"Wow. I can see why. This is amazing." She'd just walked into one of those ornate theaters of old, including red velvet drapes and chandeliers. The only modern things were the black leather recliners instead of theater seats. Maybe the ladies would invite her over one day to watch a movie with them.

When they walked back into the foyer, he pointed up. "Kade and Harper have the top floor, and Everly and I are down here." He pointed to a hallway between the two stairs. "Tristan and Skylar have a loft downtown, but they also spend time here. They have the second floor."

"It's cool that you each have a floor."

"Keeps us from getting on each other's nerves."

From the little she'd been around them—and from her spying on them out her bedroom window—the brothers seemed to get along great. Better than her and Cynthia.

"This is obviously the dining room," he said, leading her through another door.

Her gaze was drawn to a beautiful painting of a sunset over the mountains, and she went over to it. At seeing the artist's signature on the bottom, she gasped. "Are you kidding me? You have a Park C painting?" Her mom had one that she'd spent a fortune on, and Willow had told her mother, "You can leave everything else to Cynthia if you designate this as mine in your will."

The painting she coveted was titled *Hummingbirds*. The colors in it were brilliant shades of blues, greens, yellows, and purples, each hummingbird one of those colors. One tiny hummingbird was perched on a feeder, his little chest puffed out as if defending the sugar water from the invaders helicoptering around him. She'd give anything to know how the artist had made the colors iridescent, or how they looked so real, as if you could touch them and feel their soft feathers.

She loved hummingbirds, and thinking of her mother's painting reminded her that she needed to hang some sugar water feeders on her porch so that when she sat in her new swing, she could watch them.

"Either you're rich or you bought this before anyone knew who Park C was." When Parker didn't answer, she glanced back at him. He stood with his hands stuffed in his pockets again and had an odd look on his face.

He snorted, then walked out a door at the back of the dining room.

"Huh?" she muttered. She gave the Park C painting one last loving look, then followed him…into a kitchen that had her jaw dropping. "Okay, wow!"

She'd wanted this tour to get ideas for remodeling her house, but she'd need buckets full of money to make it look like this one. The first thing that caught her eye were the granite countertops. She'd never seen granite in those colors, a swirl of grays, blues, and purples. One entire wall was windows that framed the Blue Ridge Mountains in the distance.

"You want something to drink?"

"I'm good, thanks."

"That was thoughtful to give Everly a quill, even if it's not magic."

She chuckled. "Yeah, she was disappointed about that. I saw it in a bookstore in Charlotte yesterday and thought of her."

"You were in Charlotte?"

"Yes. I had a book fair and signing. Drove over Friday night." Something flashed in his eyes, as if he liked hearing that. She couldn't imagine why it mattered.

A large orange-and-white cat strolled in. "Well, hello. Who are you?"

"That's Everly's cat Jellybean."

"Aren't you a pretty thing. Girl or boy?"

"Boy. A very spoiled boy."

The cat purred when she scratched around his ears. "Does he get along with Ember? Where is Ember, anyway?"

"They're friends, and she's in the studio with Ev. Speaking of, we should go out there before one impatient little girl comes searching for us."

"I'm looking forward to seeing your studio." And seeing for herself what kind of artist he was. She hoped he was good so she wouldn't have to lie and say his paintings were great. "Before we go, I wanted to run something by you. Your daughter is unbelievably talented."

"She is."

"Her illustrations for the story we wrote are amazing, and I'd like to send the story and her illustrations to my agent."

"No."

"But—"

"No."

"Why not?"

"I have my reasons." He walked out the back door.

All righty then. Grouchy Pants was back.

Chapter Fourteen

Why had he told her all that crap about his aunt? And what was she thinking, wanting to put a five-year-old child in the public's view? Especially the daughter of Park C. That was a big fat no. Of course, she didn't know he was Park C, but she would in a few minutes. Despite himself, he was curious to see her reaction when she learned who he was.

He'd never set out to be famous, had never dreamed it was possible. All he'd wanted was to be able to pay the bills with his art. He'd been discovered in France and had been making a name for himself when Simone had almost destroyed him. He'd lost any desire to paint. His mentor had encouraged him to put her betrayal behind him and to pick up a brush again.

"Son, you have too much talent to let that bitch take that away from you," Benoit had said. But she had.

Benoit called once a week, even after Parker returned to America, begging him to paint. Then, because his baby girl had brought joy back into his life, the need to paint returned. He reinvented himself, and Park C had picked up a brush and painted. The day Parker told Benoit that he was painting again, the old man had been so happy that he'd cried.

Benoit had called a friend of his who owned an art gallery in New York City and raved about a new up-and-coming artist on the scene. As a favor to Benoit, the gallery owner asked to see some of Parker's work. Next thing Parker knew, he had a New York show.

As for Simone, he'd made the best trade of his life. By his caving to her blackmail and agreeing not to prosecute her, she'd given him Everly. After handing their two-day-old baby over to him, she'd walked away without a backward glance. There was a constant worry he tried to keep buried that someday she'd show up and want to see her daughter. He prayed that never happened, and he didn't know what he'd do if it did.

Simone and Everly were the reasons he'd never have a serious relationship again. Simone had taught him that he couldn't trust his judgment when it came to women. As for Ev, if he brought a woman into their lives and it didn't work out, she'd be crushed. He'd die before he'd allow his baby girl to be hurt.

He wanted to be in love, and that was the hardest thing to deal with, accepting that it would never happen for him. He was a one-woman man, always had been. As soon as he'd discovered the wonder of girls, he'd wanted that special one. Someone who loved him. Someone who looked at him as if he hung the moon for her. Because he would have.

Thanks to Everly, his brothers, and now their women, there were people in his life who cared about him. He was lonely, though. A minor problem he could live with. If a wild child with strawberry hair and freckles got his blood stirred up, he'd ignore the attraction he felt toward her. He was used to ignoring the things he longed for. When those longings threatened to overwhelm him, all he had to do was think of his daughter to remind himself the path he'd chosen for himself after she'd entered his life was the right one.

"So, this is your studio?" Willow said when he opened the door.

"Yep." She was seconds from discovering who he was, and he almost slammed the door closed to keep her out. Until she'd seen his painting in the dining room and gushed over Park C, he hadn't cared about showing her his studio. It hadn't occurred to him that she'd know who Park C was. Would it change how she saw him? But why was he even wondering that, since he didn't care what she thought of him. Okay, maybe he cared a little, he just didn't want to.

"Miss Willow!" Everly shouted as soon as they walked in. "Come see my illustrations for our story."

Willow's gaze scanned the room, and Parker's gaze was on her. Knowing he'd bring her in here, he'd locked up all his canvases except for the one he was working on, which was about half finished. Maybe she wouldn't realize who he was. She saw his easel and took a step toward it.

"Miss Willow!"

Parker chuckled at the impatience in his daughter's voice. "You better go look at her work, Miss Willow." He followed her to Everly's worktable. Her sundress was sleeveless and dipped down past her shoulder blades in the back. In his mind, he mixed the colors that would re-create on canvas the creamy white of her arms and shoulders. Was her skin as soft as it looked, her hair as silky?

He would drape her in emerald green silk that matched her eyes and paint her from the back as she

looked over her shoulder at her lover, her green eyes
darkened and shimmering with desire. Her strawberry
blond hair would be wild and tangled and her lips would
be swollen and damp from her lover's kisses. She'd be
standing in front of a window with panes and pale blue
distressed wood, and the moonlight would cast a sil-
very light over her. The silk she was draped in would
be billowing from the breeze flowing through the open
window. Her lover would be a mere shadow in the painting, a faceless man watching her as he sat in a wooden
hardback chair. Behind him would be a small bed, the
pure white satin covers mussed from the man making
love to her.

The man was him. He blinked at that thought. No,
it would never be him, but his fingers twitched with
the need to paint the image in his mind. *Willow in the
Moonlight.*

Ah, hell. He'd titled it, wouldn't be able not to paint
it now. It wouldn't be a piece for his show, and he didn't
have time for detours. Detour he would, though, probably starting tonight. He'd just have to paint faster on
the show pieces. Of the five he'd needed to reach his
goal, two were finished, the one on the easel was halfway there, and then two to go. He could manage it if he
didn't get any more Willow inspirations and the arsonist didn't keep interrupting his schedule.

"These are amazing," Willow said as she bent over
the table where Everly had her drawings spread out.

Parker brought his mind back to their conversation.
Everly had refused to show him her finished illustrations before Miss Willow saw them. As he studied them
now, the word *prodigy* came to mind, and he didn't like
it. He wanted a normal life for his daughter, not some

phenomenon that the public would put under a microscope the way Simone had been as a child. The adoration, the scrutiny, and the public's erroneous belief that she belonged to the world had, in the end, done irreparable damage to a woman who came to crave the attention and to believe anything was hers for the taking, no matter who it hurt.

Over his dead body would he allow the same thing to happen to Everly. He was profoundly thankful that Simone wasn't aware of Everly's talent, because being her mother wouldn't stop her from exploiting Everly to her benefit. That was another reason he wouldn't allow his daughter's name to become public. If Simone ever got a whiff of Everly's talent, she'd be on their doorstep demanding custody of his baby girl. And Everly *was* his. All Simone had done was birthed her. End of story.

"Can we make a book, Miss Willow? Your story and my pictures?"

Willow lifted her gaze to his, her brows raised.

He shook his head. "No," he mouthed. He put his hand on his daughter's shoulder. "Did you show Miss Willow what you're painting now?"

"Oh!" Everly jumped up from her chair. "Come over here and look, Miss Willow." She took Willow's hand, taking her to her easel.

Parker picked up one of Everly's illustrations. A dainty pink dragon with a pink bow in her hair and pink dangling earrings—he smiled at that little touch—crouched over a treasure chest of gems, a triumphant smirk on her face. Damn, she was good. When she was at the age that Simone couldn't take her away, he would tell her the story of Parker, Simone, and Everly. After that, he'd support whatever she decided to do. Put her art out in the world or not if that was what she wanted. Until then, he'd do what was best for his daughter.

"...and the ladybug fairy comes in while I'm sleeping and draws a ladybug in my pieces."

He'd missed the beginning of their conversation, but he smiled at the part he was hearing. When would the day come when she'd realize there wasn't a Santa or a ladybug fairy? He hoped never. He set the illustration down with the others. Everly's sixth birthday was in two weeks. Maybe for a present he'd get with Willow and have a book made of their story, just for the two of them. His baby girl would go bananas over that. He'd do it if Willow promised not to tell anyone about Ev.

Tristan and Skylar walked in, and he met them at the door. Tristan glanced over at Willow and Everly. "They seem to be getting along."

"Like two peas in a pod." A part of him was happy about that because there was nothing he loved more than seeing Everly happy. The other part wanted to drag his daughter away and wipe her memory of ever knowing a cowboy-boot-wearing, free-spirited woman. But it was good for Everly to know someone like that, right? He felt like he was damned if he did and damned if he didn't.

Skylar drifted away to join Willow and Everly, and instantly the three of them had their heads together. He resented how easily Willow fit in with the people he loved when he was determined to ignore her. They liked her, so they'd find ways to bring her into the family, which would make it next to impossible to pretend she didn't exist. Painting her wasn't helping either.

"You got that drawing ready for me?" Tristan asked.

Parker tore his gaze away from studying the way

Willow's hair curled around her neck and shoulders. "Yeah. Let me get it." He walked to the other side of the room to get the sketch, and when he returned, Tristan had joined the women and Skylar was gushing over Everly's illustrations. He'd drawn two pictures of the man he remembered from the show, one with the short hair he'd had at the time, and another with a pony-tail. When he handed the sketch to his brother, Willow glanced at it.

"Can I see that?" she said. After examining it, she handed it back. "I might have seen this man. Who is he?"

"Let me see." Everly reached for the sketch.

Parker's first reaction was to snatch it away, to not let ugliness touch his daughter, but what if she saw him at some point? "If you ever see that man, you need to come tell me right away. Or one of your uncles or aunts."

"Okay," she said, then, the photo forgotten, she turned back to her illustrations.

There hadn't been any fingerprints on the Polaroid or mason jar, and he'd called the gallery owner, hoping to get a name but had not lucked out there. Lawrence hadn't even remembered the man and hadn't saved the security camera videos from back then. They needed to find out how and where Willow had seen him, but he didn't want to talk about the man anymore in front of Everly. It was enough that she'd seen his picture and knew to tell someone if she ever saw him, and he hoped to God that she never did. He glanced at Skylar. His future sister-in-law was good at reading people, and she nodded.

"Everly, your uncle and I are spending the night here, but I need to get a few things from our loft. Want to go with me? We'll make a stop for ice cream on the way back."

"Yes! I want ice cream so bad. Miss Willow, you want to come with us?"

Parker gave a slight shake of his head.

"I can't tonight, sweetie, but next time. Okay?"

"Promise?"

"Cross my heart." She made an X over her chest.

"Where and when did you see this man?" Parker asked Willow after Skylar and Everly left.

"I'm not sure it was the man in your sketch, but it could be. He was walking on the side of the road a few miles outside of town."

"What road did you come in on?" Tristan asked.

"It was after I turned off 221 onto that road that eventually becomes Main Street."

"Mackel Lane, named after the Mackel family, the town's founders," Tristan said. "What did you notice about him? Clothes, height, weight, anything unusual?"

"Nothing unusual. He had on a yellow T-shirt. I remember thinking his shirt matched my car, and that was why I noticed him. Oh, he had a backpack that had what looked like a rolled-up tent attached to the bottom. The only other thing I remember about him was that he had a ponytail like in your sketch. What'd he do?"

"If it's the man we're looking for, he's an arsonist," Parker said.

"Oh. That's not good."

Parker glanced at the sketch. "What about height and weight?"

She shrugged. "I'm not good at guessing things like that. I'd have to say average maybe?"

"If he's camping out, that's going to make it even

harder to find him." Tristan tapped the sketch. "I need to get this copied and distributed to my officers and Skye's deputies. You have time to show Parker where you saw him?"

She nodded. "Sure."

And that was how Parker found himself spending more time with the woman he'd planned to ignore.

Chapter Fifteen

Willow had never put much thought into cars. She'd bought Sunshine because she'd wanted a reliable vehicle that would last a long time, and Volkswagens were known to last practically forever. Plus, it was a fun little car to drive, and it was a convertible, something that had been a must-have for living at the beach. Yellow was such a happy color, and she was going to love zipping around her beach town in Sunshine with the top down.

"What kind of car is this?" she asked as Parker drove them to where she'd seen the man walking alongside the road.

"A Dodge Challenger Hellcat."

Of course, a sexy car would have to have a cool name. Although she didn't know much about cars, this one was powerful. She could hear it in the rumble of the engine—it sounded absolutely wicked—and she could feel the automobile's power as Parker accelerated.

"I'm guessing you like cars?" she said.

"Yep."

The man was exasperating. For the past ten minutes since they'd left his house, all she'd gotten out of him was only enough words to answer her questions. She wished he didn't fascinate her. The last thing she needed on her Man Hiatus was a fascinating man she was insanely curious about…one who lived next door, which meant she couldn't avoid him. It didn't help that she found him even sexier than his ridiculously sexy car.

"There!" she said when they reached the spot she'd seen the man. "I remember because of that weird-looking tree stump. I noticed him, then got distracted at seeing a stump with a face that looked like a goat. I meant to come back and take a picture, but then I forgot about it." After seeing the money pit she'd inherited, the last thing on her mind had been goat-faced stumps.

"You can get one now." He stopped the car in front of a dirt driveway next to the stump. "Old Man Earl lives up there. After lightning hit the tree and killed it, he carved the stump in honor of Billy."

She got out her phone and clicked on the camera icon. "Who's Billy?"

"His goat."

Humor laced his voice, and amusement lit his eyes, and as she looked at him, all she could think was that Mr. Grouchy Pants maybe wasn't so grouchy after all, and that she liked him…when he wasn't being grouchy. She liked him a lot, if she was being honest with herself, and she always tried to be that. And in the spirit of being honest with herself, she was attracted to him. Maybe more attracted than she'd been with any man since Austin.

Question, am I going to do anything about that?

The answer was that she didn't have one. And when she was faced with that dilemma, she didn't do anything while she made a list of the pros and cons, and then thought about it some more. So that was what she'd do.

"Billy the Goat." She grinned. "So original."

He grinned back, and that sparkle of amusement was still in his eyes. "Billy's name not so much, but Old Man Earl is an original. I need to ask him if he's seen anything, so prepare yourself to meet Billy the Goat because where Earl is, Billy is. Word of warning, though, Billy loves to eat dresses and will have you naked before you know it if you don't pay attention to what he's doing."

When he said "naked" and his gaze slid over her, she almost groaned at the way his eyes changed from amusement to heat.

Stop it. Just stop. Man Hiatus, remember?

"Gotcha. Beware of Billy the Goat."

He drove down the dirt lane, slowing to a crawl because of the potholes. His jaw clenched, and she kept the grin off her face at realizing it was killing him to drive his precious car down a dusty road dotted with holes, some big enough that the Hellcat's body dipped when a tire fell in one.

They came to a stop in front of a red barn, and she glanced around. "Where's his house?"

"He converted the loft in the barn into living space. It's actually not bad. He's got a living room, bedroom, bath, and kitchen. No different than living in an apartment. Since he uses the original ladder to get to the loft, he built a lift so he can get Billy up and down."

"Billy lives up there with him?"

"Like I said, where Earl is, Billy is." He pointed to an ancient, rusted truck that looked abandoned. "That's his truck, and if you peek in the window, you'll see that Billy has eaten the seats, the lining, and most of the dash. Earl sits on a board to drive it."

She laughed. "That's hilarious. I need to incorporate a truck-eating goat in one of my stories."

An old man wearing overalls and carrying what appeared to be a rug ambled out of the barn. Sure enough, a black-and-white goat trotted next to him. Parker lowered his window as Earl approached. "Afternoon, Earl, Billy."

At hearing her chuckle when he greeted Billy, Parker glanced at her and winked, and whoa! She'd been winked at before, but a man's wink had never made her heart flutter. Before she could examine that, Earl draped the rug over Parker's door. The goat stood on his hind legs, put his front hooves on the rug, and peered in at them. This was one of the most bizarre things she'd ever experienced, and she was loving every minute of it.

Parker scratched Billy's nose. "You hanging in there, Billy?"

"He was off his feed a little yesterday, but he's feeling better today," Earl said.

"Glad to hear it. Earl, I'd like you to meet Willow Landry. She's Bob Landry's niece and inherited his house."

Earl put his head next to Billy's and dipped his chin at her. "Pleased as punch to meet ya, Miss Willow. You sure are a pretty lady."

"Why thank you, Earl." Willow pegged him to be in his late sixties, early seventies, and there was a kindness in his eyes that made her instantly like him.

"Y'all wanna come in? I got me some sweet tea baking in the sun that should be 'bout done. I won't let Billy eat on your dress, Miss Willow."

"Thanks, but we're going to have to pass on that today," Parker said. "Have you seen any strangers around lately, particularly a man with a ponytail like mine and walking around with a backpack."

"Cain't say as I have. Why? He done somethin' bad?"

"Maybe. We have someone starting fires in the area, so keep an eye out for anything suspicious. If you do see a man with a ponytail and backpack, you call me, the chief, or the sheriff right away, okay?"

"I surely will. He comes around here starting a fire, he'll get some buckshot in his bottom." Earl shifted his gaze to her. "Pardon my language, Miss Willow."

"No problem." She was utterly charmed by the man.

"Well, we need to get going. You need a ride from the jail next week, give me a call." Parker pried Billy's mouth from the sleeve of his T-shirt. "Sorry, bud, but you don't get to eat my clothes today."

"I'll do that, but the sheriff or chief will probably show up when it's time to go." Earl pulled Billy away from the car, picked up the rug, and ambled back to the barn.

"If that goat ever dies on him, Earl will probably dig a hole and put himself in the ground right next to Billy," Parker said as he backed up to turn the car around.

"He's adorable."

"Billy?"

That freaking grin of his. It did things to her stomach that she wasn't sure she was ready for. "No, silly. I assume there's no Mrs. Earl?"

"No, she died a while back."

"What was that about giving him a ride from the jail?"

"Three times a year, Earl gets a drunk on. On the anniversary of his wife's death, the anniversary of his best friend getting killed when standing next to him during Desert Storm, and on the anniversary he killed a man."

"What? He killed someone?"

"Yeah. For a long time, everyone knew the reason for his drunk on the date his wife died. It was only recently he finally told Skylar the reasons for the other two times. He has a soft spot for her, so I guess that's why he unburdened to her. She asked if she could tell me, Tristan, and Kade, and he said she could."

"I can't see him killing someone. He seems too gentle."

Parker glanced at her. "He really is. The man he killed was a second cousin he caught raping his wife not long after they got married. On the anniversary of each of those events, he rides his lawn mower to Beam Me Up, gets his drunk on, then calls Dispatch and tells them he's ready to go to jail. He spends one night in a cell, his penance, I guess. The best part of that story is Billy. The goat rides on the hood of the mower to the bar, spends the night in the cell with Earl, and the next morning one of us takes them back to the bar where his riding mower is so he and Billy can ride it home."

"That's both hilarious and sad at the same time."

"Yeah, it is."

They were back on Main Street and would be at their houses in another ten minutes, and since he seemed to be in a good mood now, she'd ask him one more time to consider letting her send her story and Everly's illustrations to her agent. Seeing her drawings in a published book would thrill Everly to no end.

"I still can't get over Everly's illustrations. They're amazing for her age. When did you know she had talent?"

"When she was around two. I'd take her into the studio with me and put her down on a pallet next to my easel. One day, she said, 'Me, Daddy' when I was painting. I thought she wanted me to pick her up, so I did, and she reached for my paintbrush. Curious, I set up a new canvas, put a brush in her hands, and held my palette of paints in front of her. She painted an abstract that wasn't great, but the colors she chose were complementary colors of the same brightness and hue. I thought it was a fluke, so the next day, I gave her another blank canvas. On that one, she painted another abstract, but in perfect contrasting colors."

"That's amazing. When did she start painting actual things?" Talent was one thing. She'd always been a talented writer, but would she ever write a book that the entire world wanted to read? No, and she was good with that. She'd found her niche, and she was happy. But Everly's talent transcended anything normal.

"I don't remember exactly, but around three."

"Have you ever heard of someone that young—"

"There are numerous children who have shown that kind of artistic talent at very early ages. One little girl was only two when her art was selling for thousands. Ev's not a freak."

She hadn't meant to, but she'd obviously hit a nerve. "Of course she isn't, but you have to admit that talent oozes out of her fingertips. I wish you'd let me send her illustrations to—"

"No."

"Even if there's interest, and I think there will be, you won't have to agree to anything. We could just test the water."

"No."

"Why not? You're really adamant with that no. Is there a reason you won't even consider it?"

For the rest of the way home, he didn't say anything,

and she wanted to shake the reason out of him because there must be one. They reached her house, and he turned into her driveway and stopped. He tapped a finger on the steering wheel as he stared out the windshield, and she had the impression he was debating with himself.

He sighed as if giving in to something he didn't want to do. "I need to tell you a story."

Chapter Sixteen

Later that night, after he got Everly to bed, Parker walked over to Willow's with Ember at his side. He'd told her he'd come back later tonight because he wanted some time to think about what he was going to say. To decide if he even was going to tell her about the worst time in his life and the way his ex-fiancée had played him.

He didn't know Willow, not really, and what if, thinking she was doing a good thing, she took it on herself to send her agent his daughter's illustrations despite his telling her no? Throughout the afternoon and early evening, he'd almost texted her and called off going to see her. But, as much as he resented that she'd put him in this position, he'd share his story with her if it kept her from doing something behind his back. For his little girl, he'd bare his soul.

Ember had picked up on his tension and hadn't wanted to go to bed with Everly, a first since she'd started sleeping in his daughter's room. Everly had refused to go to her room without Ember, so the sneaky dog had escaped as soon as Ev was asleep and had returned to Parker's side.

He'd texted Willow that he was on his way, and when he reached her porch, she was sitting in her new swing.

His artist eye soaked up the picture in front of him. She wore a white sundress dotted with yellow daises and had a yellow shawl wrapped around her shoulders. Her hair was loose and curling around her face and neck, and instead of her favored cowboy boots, white flip-flops were on her feet. His gaze caught for a moment on her toenails. Lime green shouldn't look that sexy. She'd strung fairy lights since he'd last been here, and colorful flowers in pots were scattered around. Two hummingbird feeders hung at the edge of the porch's ceiling.

As if his artist mind had found a new muse, he longed to set his easel up here on her porch and paint. *Willow*... He shut that thought right down. He was not titling another nonexistent Willow piece that he'd have to paint.

"You brought Ember," Willow said. "Hey, pretty girl. Come give me some love." Tail wagging, his dog rushed to her. "You're just the sweetest thing." The two of them acted as if they were best friends who hadn't seen each other in years. Other than him and his family, Ember only tolerated others, so this affection she'd shown toward Willow from the start was surprising.

Willow glanced up at him, then patted the seat next to her. "Come sit."

Next to her where he could feel her body heat and smell her lavender scent? No. He moved to the railing near the swing and leaned back against it. "I'm good here."

"Suit yourself. Is Everly home by herself? We could go sit on your deck if you want."

"Kade and Harper are there." She showed more concern for his daughter than Everly's own mother ever had. His worry that she'd ever do anything that would hurt Everly eased, especially if she understood why Ev's art couldn't go out into the world. He had to tell her.

She picked up one of the bottles of beer from the table next to her and held it out. "Isn't this the brand you drink?"

It was. She'd apparently paid attention when at his house, and something warm unfurled in his chest that she'd bothered to notice. He took the beer from her. "Thanks."

"Welcome." She picked up a second one and brought the bottle to her lips.

His gaze arrested on her mouth wrapped around that bottle, and he almost groaned. He needed to tell her his story, then get the hell away before he decided it would be a good idea to learn how his mouth felt against hers, how she tasted. That couldn't happen because he was afraid if he kissed her, he wouldn't want to stop.

"About Everly's illustrations—"

She held up a hand as she stood. "Wait. I'll be right back."

He blew out a breath after she disappeared inside. This wasn't going the way he'd imagined. He wasn't supposed to come over here, see a new Willow painting in his mind, find her feet sexy, and wonder what she tasted like. Maybe he should leave, just hope that she wouldn't do anything behind his back with those illustrations. Before he could decide whether to go or stay, she came back out carrying an afghan. She folded it, then set it on the floor.

"Here you go, Ember, a nice soft bed for you while your daddy and I talk."

This woman. She apparently had the ability of bewitching anyone and everything in her orbit. Everly loved her, his family was well on the way to loving her, and his dog thought she was better than cheese, which was saying something. Ember curled up at her feet, then licked them, giving her a dog thank-you.

Willow toed off one of her flip-flops, and then as she swung, she kneaded Ember's back with her sexy toes. His dog sighed in ecstasy. Parker had never thought to wish for someone to massage his back with their feet, but he found himself envious of his dog. It was ridiculous.

"So, you were saying?"

He tore his gaze away from her lime-green toenails. He would not go back to his studio and see if he could re-create that color. "Yeah." He took a healthy swallow of his beer, wishing he was anywhere but here, telling his story. He also wished that he probably wouldn't go to his studio later tonight and experiment with mixing colors to make lime green. He was ridiculous.

"If I just told you that it was important Everly's illustrations didn't go out in the world, would you be satisfied with that?"

She tilted her head, and he could see the wheels turning. A few moments passed, then she said, "Her illustrations or her name attached to them?"

Ding. Ding. Ding. Give the woman a prize. "Her name."

"If that's all you feel comfortable telling me, then I'll be satisfied. You know why?"

All he was capable of doing was shaking his head.

"Because you love that little girl with every fiber of your being, and you're standing on my porch prepared to tell me something you don't want to if it means keeping her safe. I have to respect that."

She was a writer. Was she like him and her creative mind could see things others couldn't...like she could see right into his heart where the most precious thing in his world lived, his little girl? Understand the fear always inside him of losing his baby if her talent was put out there for the world to see? It seemed she could.

"If my ex finds out about our daughter's talent, she'll show up on my doorstep, demanding custody, and then she'd exploit that talent to her benefit." *Shut up, mouth!* Willow had as much as agreed that she wouldn't do anything with Everly's illustrations, so why was he talking?

"So her mother didn't die, and she would do that?"

"Without hesitation, despite what that might do to Everly. Why'd you think my ex was dead?" There had been times when he'd wished it, then had felt like the lowest human being on earth for those thoughts.

"I guess because I couldn't imagine that precious girl's mother not being a part of her life if she was around, and Everly never talks about her, so I just assumed. Please, come sit." She scooted over, giving him plenty of room.

He sat. He didn't know why. It wasn't a smart thing to do, but Willow Landry apparently had superpowers that had men and dogs doing her bidding. Her superpower also included getting him to talk.

"No one knows this, well, not in this country, and that includes my brothers, so I'm trusting you here."

"I would never betray your trust."

He hadn't thought Simone would either, and look how that had turned out. He picked at the label on the bottle. "I left for France a week after I graduated high school. Paris." He glanced at her. "That's where all the starving artists go, right?"

"So I hear."

"What's that smile for?"

"The first day when Everly came over, she told me that you were a fireman and an artist. I figured it was a hobby and that you probably sold some art to family and friends, and maybe at local arts and crafts festivals. I was way off base, I think."

That had him smiling, too. "A bit." Tristan had interrupted them on her studio tour, and they'd left before she had a chance to see the piece on his easel. She would have realized from even that half-finished piece that art wasn't just his hobby.

"Sorry for interrupting. Go on with your story."

He let his mind drift to the day that would change his life forever. "I met Simone Marchand in an art class in Paris. The next day when I arrived, she'd moved her easel next to mine."

"Was she any good?"

"Extremely so, but she was lazy. There were things I learned about her much later that I wished I'd known then, but my impression at the time was that she had talent but lacked ambition. That for her, art was just a hobby."

"Did that bother you?"

"It seemed a shame that she was wasting her talent, but it didn't bother me at all. Art is a personal thing, and if it's a hobby someone enjoys and that's all they want from it, that's great. Anyway, she let me know that she was interested in me, and we started seeing each other. A month after we met, we moved in together."

"Did you love her?"

He stared down at the toes she still had in Ember's fur. "I loved who I thought she was. You know what they say about hindsight. Simone is a narcissist and self-ish to the extreme, something she was an expert at hiding. Once my eyes were opened and I could see her for what she was, I realized the signs had been there, but I hadn't wanted to see them. She's very good at pretending to be what she thinks you want."

"What happened?"

"She found out she was pregnant. It wasn't planned, but we were happy. Well, I was, and I thought she was. I wanted to get married, but she kept making excuses, then weird things started happening. One of my paintings disappeared, then another. It had to be her taking them, right? When I asked her about them, she accused me of not trusting her.

"I thought her crying and mood swings were a pregnant woman hormonal thing, so I tried even harder to make her happy. She was carrying my baby, you know. Around the time she was five months, personal stuff went missing. A shirt she'd given me for Christmas, several sketchbooks of my drawings, a silver bracelet I'd bought after selling my first piece, even a chair we'd bought together." He shrugged. "It reached a point I couldn't keep ignoring things disappearing, and we had an epic battle over it."

"What was her explanation?"

He set his empty beer bottle on the floor. "She refused to explain anything. She would disappear for hours at a time, and then one night, she didn't even bother to come home. When she returned the next day, we had a fight that lasted for days."

"You don't know where she went?"

"Not then. Some more of my art went missing." He glanced at her. "I was losing it, Willow. I didn't know what to do. If she hadn't been pregnant, I would have walked away, but I just couldn't do that. I'd felt my baby kick, had the sonogram, and knew we were having a little girl." Although they hadn't planned for Simone to get pregnant, the minute he knew they were having a baby, he was all in. He'd held that sonogram in his hand, stared at it, and fallen instantly in love.

"Of course you couldn't walk away from your child. What happened then?"

"I decided I needed to find out what was going on, so I followed her one night."

She put her hand on his arm. "I don't blame you. In your place, I would have done the same thing."

Her hand was warm and calming, and when she took it away, he wanted to snatch it back. "Long story short, she was seeing another man. I followed her to an apartment, and he was standing outside, waiting for her. They kissed, then disappeared inside. I knocked on the door, and when the guy opened it, I barged in. Guess what I saw?"

"Your chair and your art?"

"And you didn't even need three guesses. My art was stacked against the living room wall. What followed wasn't pretty. Some really nasty things were said by all of us. Then she said…" This part still made his heart beat against his chest in rage. "She said she was putting the baby up for adoption. Turned out the man, Julian, was her first love, and she'd never gotten over him. They didn't want the baby because it wasn't his."

"Don't get angry for me asking this, but was it—"

"My baby? I asked the same thing, and she swore it was, that she'd gotten back with Julian after she found out she was pregnant. After a lot of heated words, we agreed to make a trade. She'd have the baby and give it to me if she could have all my art and I didn't call the police."

"Dear God. I can't wrap my mind around that."

"Tell me about it." He pushed his feet against the floor, making them swing. "There were things I learned later when I went to my teacher, who became a good friend and mentor, and explained why I didn't have any art for the show he'd scheduled for his students. Benoit knew Simone's background and told me he'd been concerned when I started seeing her but hadn't said anything because it wasn't his place to put his nose in someone else's business.

"Simone Marchand had been a child prodigy and spoiled by her parents because they'd basked in her notoriety. Then when she was a teenager, she was all about partying and had gotten into drugs. She eventually cleaned up and was trying to paint again, but Benoit said her heart wasn't in it."

"Why'd she want your art?"

He gave a bitter laugh. "To pawn it off as her own."

"You're kidding me."

"I wish I was. Benoit wanted to expose her, but I wouldn't let him. I'd made a deal with her, and I kept it. For Everly, I'd do it all over again. I did have a DNA test done after she was born even though I knew for certain she was mine the minute they put her in my arms. It was insurance in case Simone and Julian popped up some day and tried to claim she was his."

"You're afraid of that happening, and that's why you don't want anyone to know how good Everly is."

It wasn't a question, and he was relieved she got it. "If Simone so much as suspected how talented Ev is, she'd be on my doorstep demanding custody. And then she'd exploit Everly to her benefit, maybe even claim Everly's art was hers." He stared into her eyes, wanting her to understand the only important thing. "I can't let that happen."

"Of course you can't. She's never tried to see her, never called and asked how she's doing?"

"Not once. She handed our baby over to me and walked away without a glance back."

"Good. That woman may have given birth, but she's not entitled to be called a mother. Why haven't you told your brothers about this?"

He shrugged. "A few reasons, one being that I was embarrassed. My brothers were always protective of me, and they didn't want me to go to France. They believed I was too young and sheltered to be taking off like that." They were right, but they hadn't known why he'd had to go.

"Ah, you didn't want to admit you should have listened to them?"

"Something like that. Also, Kade was in the Army by then and one scary dude. If he'd known what Simone did…well, I don't want to imagine what he would have done. Likely make her disappear without a trace. Even now, if he knew, I wouldn't put it past him to find a way to punish her. Tristan would probably help him. She kept her end of the bargain, and the last thing I want is for my brothers to stir things up."

"I don't approve of violence or revenge, but in this case, I think I'd cheer them on." She moved closer to him. "Can I hug you?"

Chapter Seventeen

If there was ever a man who needed a hug, it was Parker Church. He stilled, and she thought he was going to refuse, then he nodded. She pulled her knees under her, wrapped her arms around his shoulders, and rested her head against his chest. At first he was so stiff that she might as well be hugging a statue, but then his body relaxed and he brought his hand to her lower back. The heat from his palm seeped through the thin material of her sundress and warmed her skin.

He wasn't hugging her back exactly, but when he let out a soft sigh, she smiled to herself, pleased that she was giving him what he needed after he'd shared his heart-wrenching story. She couldn't wrap her mind around how anyone could do the things that woman had. How did you walk away from your child without a backward glance?

Something grew inside her that wanted to build a protective wall around Parker and Everly and guard them from the evil witch. He rested his head on top of hers, and although she was in an awkward position, she didn't move because he needed this from her, her strength and understanding. He'd said he hadn't told his brothers any of this, and she was honored that he'd shared his story with her, even if it was only because he needed her to know his reason for refusing her. But it also meant that, until now, he'd carried the burden of what had happened to him alone. He needed a friend, and she was going to be that for him.

"You smell good, like spring flowers and lavender," he murmured as he nuzzled his nose in her hair.

She smiled against his chest. "You smell pretty good yourself." His scent was an enticing combination of spice, soap, and a hint of paint. He was fit, a man with broad shoulders and hard muscles that her hands wanted to explore. When his thumb made circles over her sundress, the compassion that had inspired the hug changed to desire that started as a small flutter in her belly but grew as she inhaled his scent and soaked in the heat from his body.

"Willow."

That was all, just a rasp of her name, but she heard the longing in it, a longing that was growing inside her, too. She lifted her head and their eyes locked on each other. As if pulled by invisible strings, she leaned toward him until their mouths were touching. As soon as she felt his lips, she froze. What was she doing?

He made a sound deep in his throat as he finished what she'd started, and his mouth took possession of hers. He wrapped his arm around her and pressed his fingers into her hip. His other hand cupped the side of her face, and his palm cradling her cheek felt intimate, the kind of thing a lover would do. None of her boyfriends had touched her like that, not even Austin, who'd claimed to love her with all his heart until he didn't anymore.

Parker slid the tip of his tongue over her lips, seeking entrance, and she forgot all about Austin and old boyfriends as she opened her mouth, inviting him in. She was still on her knees, and when she moved to try and get more comfortable, he pulled her onto his lap without breaking the kiss.

She didn't know how long they kissed. Time seemed irrelevant. Nothing mattered except this man and this moment. She'd never been kissed so thoroughly or so passionately, and she wanted more. She needed more. Based on his arousal that she felt against her bottom, he wanted more, too. She broke the kiss.

"Do you want to come inside?"

He stared at her for a moment, then his gaze fell to her mouth. "I want to, but not tonight."

"Oh, okay." She shouldn't be this disappointed. Not only was she just getting to know him, but she was on a vacation from men. Or she was supposed to be, but one could change vacation plans, right? She tried not to feel rejected as she scooted off his lap.

"Hey." He put his hand on her arm. "I'm not saying no, just not tonight. We both need to think about the wisdom of doing this and the consequences."

"Consequences?" As far as she could see, the consequences would be good for both of them. From the passion of their kisses, she was sure they'd be good together, might even set the bed on fire if the heat that had ignited between them was any indication.

"Yes. I have Everly to think about. I can't date you—"

"I'm not asking you to."

He leaned his head back against the swing and closed his eyes. "You're planning to leave after the house is sold, right?"

"That's my plan. I've always wanted to live on the

beach. I don't know where yet, but I'm going to use the money I get from selling this house to buy a condo right on the sand."

He opened his eyes and looked at her. "My daughter wants a mommy, and it would only take the slightest hint there was something between us that would have her setting her sights on you. If she knew we were dating, she'd be picking out her flower girl dress. When it didn't happen, she'd be crushed, and that doesn't work for me. If we had a one-night hookup or a fling until you leave, it would have to be a secret. Would you be good with that?"

Would she? She understood what he was saying, but how would that work? "I—"

He put his finger on her lips. "Don't answer now. Think about it, and we'll talk tomorrow." He leaned over, kissed her forehead, then stood. "Good night, Willow." He snapped his fingers, and Ember jumped up from her bed and followed him off the porch.

"Good night," she whispered to his retreating back.

The next morning, after a sleepless night, Willow still hadn't decided if she was willing to be a man's secret. She couldn't argue with Parker's reasoning—she respected his need to protect his daughter—and she really had no desire to start dating yet, but being a secret felt wrong. He'd said they would talk today, and she assumed that would happen sometime tonight after he put Everly to bed.

In the meantime, her contractor was here, and work on the house was finally starting. She'd caved on doing any more of the demolition herself. Handling a sledgehammer just wasn't in her wheelhouse. Besides, if she didn't get busy writing, she'd miss her deadline for the first time.

Because of the noise from the workers inside her house, she'd set herself up on her porch swing to write. She'd spent most of the morning distracted thanks to Parker's question. She normally wouldn't agree to be someone's secret fling, but she understood why he didn't want Everly thinking there was something between them. She had no more desire to confuse or hurt that precious little girl than Parker did. Besides, they wouldn't be hurting anyone.

And the thing was, there *was* something between them...lust. She'd never fallen in lust before, and it was both exciting and intriguing. To have an affair with a man like Parker had moved to the top of her bucket list overnight. She didn't care if she was shallow for wanting to be skin to skin with a man as mouthwatering as him. Neither Austin nor Brady had rocked a body like Parker's, and she wanted her hands on those muscles of his.

Her uptight mother and sister would have a conniption if they found out she was considering his condition, but her hippy, poetry-writing father would smile and say, "Do what makes you happy, sweetheart."

"Gah!" What to do? Maybe she should just flip a coin. Heads yes, tails no.

Well, she had the rest of the day to decide, and words weren't getting on the page while she stared off into space. She'd promised her agent she'd send her the first ten chapters by next week, and if she didn't get busy, that wasn't going to happen.

She managed to push Parker to the back of her mind and lose herself in *Bri and the Lost Ring*. When her stomach growled, she glanced at the time on her laptop. It was past lunchtime, and she loved when she got so into the story that the day got away from her. Buddy Napier and his crew were still working inside, so she decided to take a break and go into town to get some lunch.

Since coming to Marsville, she'd not tried Katie's Corner Kitchen and it was time. She found a parking space beside an ancient turquoise Cadillac. Much to her mother's chagrin, her dad drove a gold classic Caddy, so she got out her phone and took some photos to send to him.

"Why are you taking pictures of my car, girl? Are you a spy?"

Startled, Willow yelped and spun around. An elderly woman leaning on a cane was scowling at her. "Um, no, of course I'm not a spy. I was just admiring your car."

"I don't recognize you," the woman said as she squinted her eyes at Willow. "Who are you?"

"That's probably because…" Her gaze shifted to the man walking toward them, the very man who was the reason for her sleepless night. He had on his dark blue T-shirt with the Marsville Fire Department logo on the chest, and he was looking mighty fine.

"Miss Mabel, how's my favorite lady this fine day?" Parker said, then winked at Willow.

"Parker Church, just the man I wanted to see. Those hoodlums at the community center didn't turn off the lights when they left."

"When would that be?"

"Last night."

"Ah, those hoodlums. That would have been the Silver Belles Wine and Romance Book Club. I'll be sure and have a word with the scoundrels."

Willow snickered, getting a glare from Miss Mabel before the woman turned her attention back to Parker. "See that you do. You built the community center, so I hold you responsible for the goings-on there." Miss Mabel huffed. "Romance books. A waste of one's time." She scowled at Willow again. "Now, missy, you were going to tell me who you are and why you're spying on me."

Parker built their community center? She didn't think Miss Mabel meant with his own hands, so did that mean he funded it? On a firefighter's salary? Although, considerable money had been invested in the remodeling of his house, so maybe the brothers had received a big inheritance from their aunt.

"Girl." Miss Mabel tapped her cane on the sidewalk. "I asked you a question."

"Oh, sorry. I'm—"

Parker stepped next to her. "Miss Mabel, I'd like to introduce you to Willow Landry, Bob Landry's niece. She inherited his house. Willow, this is Miss Mabel Mackel. Her family founded Marsville, and her nephew Luther is our mayor."

"It's a pleasure to meet you, Miss Mabel." Not really.

"Your uncle was a waste of space. Let's hope that doesn't run in the family."

Well, yes, you old bat, it runs in the family. We're all a complete waste of space. "I didn't know my uncle very—"

"You'll deal with that silly book club, I trust," Miss Mabel said to Parker, cutting Willow off and dismissing her.

"Yes, ma'am. And may I say you look lovely today,

Miss Mabel. That dress is very pretty. Orange is your color."

"This old thing? You're a silver-tongued devil, Parker Church." She patted his arm. "You're my favorite Church brother."

The lady clearly ate up his praise, and Willow managed not to roll her eyes. The woman should never wear orange. It clashed with her blue hair, the kind of bluish silver some older women's hair turned from too much product. After Miss Mabel headed down the sidewalk, Willow shook her head and grinned at him. "Favorite brother, huh?"

"She says the same thing to Tristan and Kade. Her favorite Church brother is the one who happens to be talking to her and telling her how pretty she looks."

"Well, for such a little thing, she scares the daylights out of me."

"You and the rest of the town. Where you headed?"

"Katie's Corner Kitchen. Since my kitchen is demolished, I decided to take a break and give the diner a try for lunch."

"It's just the Kitchen to locals. I'm headed there myself to meet my brothers. You should join us."

"Okay." He'd gone from Mr. Grouchy Pants to Mr. Sweetie Pants, and when first meeting him, she hadn't expected to like him, but she did. A lot. It was a nice surprise.

"Have you eaten here before?"

"I haven't. Is it good?"

"Yep. Kade swears Katie's burgers are the best he's ever had, Tristan alternates between a hamburger and a melted ham and cheese sub. Katie has several healthy things on the menu, and those are what I go for. You'll like whatever you decide on."

He opened the door, and as she entered ahead of him, he put his hand on her lower back. "They're at the back table."

She headed that way, disappointed when he dropped his hand. That was the moment she knew what her decision would be. She wanted his hands on her, wanted to feel his fingers dance over her skin, wanted more of his amazing kisses. There was nothing wrong with having a secret affair if the two people involved were agreeable and understood what it was and was not. She'd leave for the beach as soon as the house was finished and sold, which was good because they'd have an expiration date.

"I found a stray," he said when they reached the table.

Both his brothers stood, and she smiled. Such manners. "Hope you don't mind if I join you."

"By all means," Kade said. "Besides, you're prettier to look at than that ugly mug standing beside you."

She didn't mistake that he was teasing his brother and not flirting with her. "Well, I just met his girlfriend, who he thinks is the prettiest girl in all the land." She sat, and the three bothers did after her, with Parker taking the chair next to her. "She said he's her favorite Church brother."

"Ah, you've met the infamous Miss Mabel," Tristan said. "Don't tell my baby brother, but I'm her favorite."

Kade snorted. "Dream on, bro, she loves me best."

"She's…um, interesting? She accused me of spying on her."

All three chuckled. "*Interesting* is an understatement," Tristan said. "Get Parker to tell you the UFO story and how our mayor, who is her nephew, came to be part alien."

Huh? "Like an outer space alien?"

Parker nodded. "Yes, and you'll need to make a visit to Marsville's UFO museum."

"Is that the Beam Me Up place you mentioned the other day?" A UFO Museum? She so had to go there.

"No, Beam Me Up is a honky-tonk bar in town," Parker said.

A pretty woman came to the table. "Good afternoon, Church brothers and…" She looked at Willow.

"Katie, this is Willow Landry." Parker lifted his chin toward the woman. "Willow, this lovely lady is Katie, the owner of the Kitchen, and you won't find better food in town."

He really was a silver-tongued devil, Willow thought when Katie beamed. "It's a pleasure to meet you, Katie."

"Likewise. What can I get y'all to drink?"

The guys all ordered sweet tea and she asked for a water with lemon. The menu included the standard things you'd expect from a diner and then there were a few unusual dishes. She loved to experiment, and an applewood bacon, tart Granny Smith apple, and Gruyère cheese on toasted sourdough caught her eye. That sounded delicious.

Katie returned with their drinks, took their orders, and after she headed for the kitchen, Parker said, "Any updates, Tris?"

"Not really. My and Skye's people are keeping an eye out for our suspect, including driving down backroads and checking out places someone might camp. One of Skye's deputies found a recent campsite, but it's been cleared out. Maybe he's moved on."

"One can hope, but my gut says he's still around. I wish I could remember that man's name from my second show. I know we don't know if it's him, but I can't think of anyone else who'd leave a photo with a message to me."

"Someone left you a photo with a message?" That couldn't be good. Parker shrugged as if it wasn't a big deal, but it sure sounded like a big deal to her.

"You find him, call me," Kade said. "I'll have a little word with him. He won't be setting any more fires."

As innocent as those words seemed, the sound of danger in them had her studying the middle brother. There was an air of *don't mess with me or you'll be sorry* about him. It was the first time since meeting him that he came across as a little scary. "Why? What would you say?"

"He probably wouldn't say anything, just death-eye stare at our firebug until he ran for his life, never to be seen again," Parker said. "Kade spent the last ten years in the Army Special Forces. He knows how to hide bodies."

When her gaze flew to Kade, he smiled, and it was the kind of smile that told her she never wanted to make him an enemy. The first book she wrote—which was collecting dust and before she discovered she was meant to write middle grade fantasy books—had been a Navy SEAL romance. It was terrible, but when writing it, she'd fallen down the rabbit hole in researching those Special Forces guys. They were badass bad.

"Remind me not to get on your bad side," she said… mostly joking.

Parker leaned his shoulder against hers. "Don't worry, I'll protect you."

"Here's your lunches, people." Katie arrived at their table with two plates balanced on each arm. "Need anything else?" she asked after setting their lunches in front of them.

"I think we're good, Katie," Parker said.

"Oh, my God, this is amazing." Willow closed her eyes as the flavors of the sandwich burst in her mouth.

Parker chuckled. "Told ya."

"You close to being ready for your show?" Kade asked as he dug into his lunch.

"Getting there," Parker said.

She glanced at him. "What show's that?"

Noises sounded in stereo, some kind of alert filling the air, and both Parker and Tristan pulled out radios she didn't know they had on them.

"Multiple vehicles on fire at Lonnie's Used Cars," a voice said over the radios.

Parker stood. "Sorry, gotta go."

"Me, too," Tristan said.

Willow put her hand on Parker's arm. "Be careful, okay."

"Always am." He leaned down and put his mouth next to her ear. "I'll be over later tonight to hear your answer."

Then he was gone.

Chapter Eighteen

"Daddy, do you think Miss Willow is pretty?"

There was only one answer to Everly's question, and he gave it. "She sure is." To divert her from where he knew this was going, he said, "Have you decided who all you want to invite to your birthday party?"

"Yes!"

He curled around his baby girl in her bed as she ticked off a long list of names, people he'd already invited. How was she turning six already? He didn't want her to grow up and leave the nest where he couldn't protect her, but it was happening faster than he was ready for.

"I told Miss Willow today, and she said she'd be there with bells on." She yawned, then forced sleepy eyes open. "I want to wear bells on my birthday, too, Daddy." Then her eyes closed.

He gave her a few minutes, then eased out of her bed, showered, and being hopeful, he grabbed some condoms and shoved them in his pocket. He could hardly believe how quickly he'd gone from his determination to avoid his new neighbor to being all-in on having a secret fling with her.

It was because of the way she'd listened to him, how she'd been angry on his behalf because of what had happened, and then she'd hugged him. Although not all that often, he'd been with women since Simone, and not one of them had hugged him for the sole purpose of giving him comfort. That Willow had...well, it touched him in a way he hadn't expected. She hadn't done it with the intention of kissing him, he knew that. It had just been the kindness that lived in her. He'd seen it in the way she was with Everly and the other members of his family.

He'd soaked up her hug like a man walking out of an ice storm into the sunshine. She'd known what he needed even when he hadn't. That a comfort hug had morphed into his mouth on hers hadn't been something either one of them had meant to happen, but he was a firefighter and he recognized fire when he touched it. And he'd sure as hell come close to igniting in a ball of fire. What did they say about a moth being drawn to flames? Well, he was that moth.

Even with the explosive chemistry between them, he wouldn't now be crossing his yard to hers—the baby monitor in his hand—if he didn't trust her, and he did.

"You could've stayed in bed with Everly," he told Ember as she walked next to him. She looked up at him as if to say, "Are you serious? You're going to see my new favorite friend, and you're not leaving me behind." He chuckled at the whimsical thoughts he'd attributed to a dog, but as soon as he'd left his and Everly's rooms, apparently knowing where he was going, Ember had appeared. "Guess she put a spell on you, too."

The lady who was keeping him from what he should be doing right now—painting in his studio—was sitting in her swing under her fairy lights, and as he had the previous night, he paused to paint a Willow canvas in his mind.

Tonight she wore her signature cowboy boots, the tiny denim cutoffs that had almost caused him to run into his neighbor's mailbox, and a T-shirt that said *I'm a writer. Be nice to me or I'll kill you off.* Her hair was pulled up in a high ponytail that he itched to wrap his fist around.

Her eyes were focused on her laptop, and at hearing his footsteps, she held up a finger without looking at him. It was the same thing he did if Everly or one of his brothers interrupted him and he needed a minute or two to reach a stopping point on a painting. Silently he set the baby monitor on the porch rail, then sat on the other end of the swing and waited.

A folded afghan was on the floor at her feet, and Ember curled up on it. There was that kindness that was Willow, having a comfortable bed ready for his dog. Typing faster than he'd ever be able to, she toed off a boot without pausing and buried her toes in Ember's fur. His gaze fell on those toes, her toenails bubble gum pink tonight. Colors were his jam, and while he waited for her to get to a stopping point, he debated which was sexier, the lime green or bubble gum pink.

Five minutes passed before she closed the lid on her laptop. "Sorry. The solution for a plot hole popped into my head, and I had to get it down before I lost it."

"Not a problem." When she smiled at him, his heart did that funny bouncing thing. "How are you?" *Seriously, dude. That's the best you can do?* He had no game.

"I'm fine. How are you?"

Amusement was in her eyes, and he realized she was teasing him. Just like that, he relaxed. "I'm fine, too." Was it too soon to ask what she'd decided?

"Before we get to why you're here, I have some questions not related to my answer."

"Let's hear them." So they could get to the good part…he hoped it was going to be good.

"First one, was the fire today a bad one?"

"Someone set three of Lonnie's used cars on fire. They were in his back lot, and unfortunately there aren't any cameras back there and no one saw anything. But they were intentionally set."

"So, you think your arsonist did it?"

"My gut says yes. Next question." Arsonists were hard to catch, and it made him angry that there was one in his town. He just hoped they caught the person before someone got hurt. But he didn't want to talk about it, not now and not here with her.

"Kade asked you if you were going to be ready for your show. What show?"

"I have a show at a gallery in New York in a few months."

"Okay. Wow. That's cool."

He was going to have to tell her who he was, especially since she knew who Park C was. But he didn't want to, not tonight. He wanted her to say yes to Parker Church, who was not famous in the art world.

"We got interrupted when you were giving me a tour, and I didn't get to see any of your art."

"You can come over tomorrow. I'll call you after I get home."

"Can't wait. You must be good if you have a show at a New York gallery."

She was going to be in for a surprise. "I do okay. Next question."

"Tristan said to get you to tell me the UFO story."

"It's a humdinger. You got any beer?"

"Sure do. Be right back."

He'd expected to show up, get an answer, and then react accordingly...either leave or take her straight to bed. Instead, he was about to have a beer with her and tell her the most ridiculous story imaginable. A story the fantasy writer in her was going to love. Strangely, he wasn't disappointed that he wasn't learning the color of her sheets this very minute.

His nerves had been crackling as he'd walked over, both with anticipation and anxiety. Should he go through with it? There were good reasons not to, Everly being at the top of that list. He wanted to go through with it, possible consequences be damned. Would he be able to guard his heart? He would, damn it. It was simple...mind over matter. He knew his weakness now, so he'd be able to avoid that pitfall.

All those thoughts had tumbled around in his mind from the moment he'd walked out the door of his house, baby monitor in hand, and then, somehow, she'd calmed him with her bubble gum toenails, her kindness to his dog, and her soft, musical voice as she'd asked her questions that had nothing to do with why he was here.

She returned, one cowboy boot on and one off, and handed him one of the beers she held. "Why are you smiling?"

"You." He glanced down at her feet. "You're walking lopsided."

"Easier than putting it back on and then taking it off again." She returned to her place on the swing. "So, UFOs?"

"You're going to love this story. Before the town was

called Marsville, it was Foothills because obviously, we're in the foothills of the Blue Ridge Mountains. Then a long time ago, Miss Mabel's twin sister, Mavis, eloped with her boyfriend when she was seventeen. He was from the wrong side of the tracks, and her parents had forbidden her to see him. Miss Mabel, to cover the couple's elopement, told everyone that a UFO had landed in their backyard and an alien had snatched Mavis away right in front of her eyes."

"No one believed her, right?"

"You'd think, but there had been reports of UFOs all over the world around that time, and it helped that a local man had reported seeing a UFO only a few weeks before. That's probably what gave Miss Mabel the idea. Also, most of the town worked for the Mackel family in one way or another, so even if they didn't believe it, they weren't about to admit it."

"Did anyone hear from Mavis again?"

"Ah, this is where the story gets even more interesting. A few years later, Mavis showed up with a little boy in tow. The twins claimed, and Miss Mabel still does to this day, that the baby was half alien, which means that our mayor, Luther, as his son, is one fourth Martian." He grinned when her mouth opened and closed like a fish. "Wasn't expecting that, were you?"

"This is the best story I've ever heard in my life. Please, please, take me to your leader. I need to see this part Martian for myself."

He laughed at her silliness, and as he did, a feeling of contentment settled over him, the likes of which he couldn't remember ever feeling. "It's a date." As soon as the words were out of his mouth, he realized what he'd said, but before he could explain them away, she shook her finger at him.

"Oh, no you don't. You're about to panic over a few innocent words, and I'm not having it."

"No?" A picture of her bossing him in the bedroom flashed in his mind, and he decided he'd be good with that.

"I know you didn't mean a *date* date."

She toed off her other boot, then brought her legs up on the swing and stretched out until her feet were almost touching his thigh, putting those bubble gum toes and her long legs right in his line of sight. How was he supposed to not look his fill?

He put his hand on her ankle. "Is this okay?"

"For you to touch me?"

He nodded.

"I was hoping you would."

"So, it's a yes, then? The answer to last night's question?"

A soft smile appeared on her face. "It's a yes."

"Thank you." He wanted to say so much more, but he couldn't find the words to express the joy bursting inside him. Now that he was allowed to touch her, that was all he wanted to do. Her legs felt like silk under his palm as he slid his hand up her calf to her knee.

"One more thing before we get wild and tear our clothes off," she said.

"Is that what we're going to do?"

"A girl can hope. But first, I wanted to tell you that Everly invited me to her birthday party. I told her I'd come. Is that okay?"

"Of course. She told me she asked and that you'll

be there with bells on. Now she wants to wear bells on her birthday, too."

She laughed. "I keep forgetting that kids take things literally. Now I have to go buy some bells. I'll get some for her, too. What about you? You want bells?"

"I want you."

Chapter Nineteen

Willow had never been this aroused in her life. The way he said he wanted her—his voice low and growly—almost sounded as if his life depended on it. And the way his fingers felt on her skin as he trailed them up her leg… She was ready to tear off her clothes right here on her porch for all the neighbors to see.

"Let's go inside," she said.

He stood, grabbed the baby monitor, then held out his hand.

She put her hand in his. "Is Everly okay alone in your house?" Was a baby monitor good enough for him to be gone?

"Kade and Harper are home, but if she wakes up, I want to know. Once she's asleep, though, she never wakes up until morning."

"Okay, good. The house is a mess from all the construction, so—"

"Don't care. All we need is a bed."

"That's good because I've got one of those."

She'd had her contractor haul out her uncle's bed because she just couldn't bring herself to sleep on the ancient mattress. The new bed was a king, and she'd ordered new sheets, pillows, and a comforter for it. She was glad she had now. The main bedroom was the only room in the house that wasn't torn apart. They were saving it and the attached bath remodel for last.

Ember had followed them in, and when they reached the bedroom, she walked the perimeter of the room, checking things out, then went to the blanket Willow had placed on the floor earlier in case the dog came with him tonight.

"You want something else to drink?" She'd moved the microwave and a mini fridge into the bedroom since the kitchen was down to the bare bones.

"All I want is you."

"What a coincidence. I want you, too."

He moved to the side of the bed. "Come here, Willow." When she was standing in front of him, he traced the words on her T-shirt with his finger. "Promise not to kill me off?"

"As long as you're nice to me." Because the words were over her breasts, the trail of his finger across her shirt sent a delicious shiver through her. The smile on his face said that he knew exactly what he was doing to her.

"Is that really what you want? Just nice?" He flattened his palm just above the curve of her breast.

"No, nice is boring. I want awesome."

"That's the answer I was hoping for. Can I undress you now?"

"Yes, please." A hundred times yes.

"Lift your arms. Let's get this shirt off so I can see you."

She held up her arms, and he pulled the T-shirt up and over her head, then dropped it on the floor. Bared to him made her feel a little shy and a whole lot turned on.

"No bra. If I'd known that, I would have copped a feel."

His grin reminded her of a mischievous boy up to no good.

He lowered his hands to the button on her jean shorts, and while he lowered the zipper, he kept his eyes locked on hers. A man had never undressed her before, and she liked it, especially the way his brown eyes darkened to the color of espresso as he lowered his gaze.

"You're beautiful, Willow."

He was staring at her breasts, and amused, she smiled. "You're such a man."

"Were you in doubt?" He dropped to his knees, taking her shorts and panties down with him. With his face inches from her sex, he lifted those desire-filled eyes to hers.

"What are you doing down there?" Okay, she had a clue since his warm breath was caressing her most private place, and it wasn't that she didn't like it. She did. It was that he was doing everything differently from anything she'd ever experienced.

"I'm smelling your arousal. You make my mouth water."

She was still on her feet, and he was still fully clothed, and she had nothing to compare to that and to the things he was making her feel. Austin had been her first and she his, and they'd explored and learned together. There had been one hookup in her life between Austin and Brady that had barely been tolerable and the reason she'd never tried that again. Brady had been more experienced than Austin, but he'd never made her feel the way Parker Church did.

"I can't wait to taste you." His hands were gentle as

he trailed his fingers up her legs, and when his hands reached her bottom, he placed a soft kiss low on her belly, then stood. "But not yet."

"Oh." With nothing but words and his warm breath, he had her aching to have his mouth on her, and by the amused gleam in his eyes, he knew it.

He wrapped his hand around her neck, spread his fingers over her skin, and brought her mouth to his. As he kissed her, he curled her ponytail around his hand as he pressed his body against hers, and the scrape of his clothes against her naked flesh was arousing, but she wanted them off. She tugged on his shirt, and he lifted his head.

"I showed you mine, now show me yours."

He laughed and then tapped her nose. "I like you, Willow Landry."

"Well, that's good to know since we're about to do the dirty. Liking me is required for that." She grinned when that got a big smile from him, and heaven help her. Parker Church was hot even when he was being Mr. Grouchy Pants, but when he smiled, his hot meter was off the chart. That smile could melt a girl's panties off…well, if the girl had any on.

When he pulled his T-shirt over his head, she wasn't disappointed. He wasn't as muscled as his brothers, especially Kade, but big muscles had never been her thing. His shoulders were broad, but the rest of him was leaner, more of a runner's body without an ounce of fat on him. It was the kind of body she liked on a man.

She lifted her hand and traced the tattoo on his chest, right over his heart. The name Everly was in a curved half circle under a ladybug. "I like this."

"Ev gets a kick out of seeing her name on my chest. Unfortunately, she wants my name on hers."

"Aww. Your daughter's precious."

"Yes, she is, but she's not what I want to talk about right now."

"Same. I want to talk about why you still have pants on." She should probably feel weird being naked while he wasn't, but she'd always been comfortable in her own skin. She didn't have a bombshell body and was on the side of thin with small boobs, but whatever. She liked her body. Even though Parker hadn't touched her breasts yet, his gaze kept straying to them, so it seemed he liked what he saw.

"I don't know why I still have my pants on." He unbuttoned his jeans, then pushed them and his boxer briefs down and stepped out of them. "All better?"

"So much better." She took a step back. "I'm just going to look you over, see what I'm getting, okay?"

He held out his arms as he grinned. "Yeah, okay. Have at it."

Lordy, she liked him. She'd never had an encounter like this, a no-strings-attached fling that included laughter and the feeling that what was in her mind could come right out her mouth without worrying that his ego would be offended.

With Brady, she'd had to measure every word, every thought, to keep from bruising his fragile ego. Why had she put up with him for so long? *Stop thinking about that jerk.* Great advice, especially when a smoking hot firefighter was watching her with both amusement and heat in his eyes.

"Have you looked your fill yet?"

Seriously? Not even. She sighed dramatically. "I guess."

He smirked as he dropped his arms. "And you're satisfied with what you're getting?"

She shrugged. "Eh, you'll do." She loved this playful banter between them, loved the way his mouth quirked when he was amused.

"Little liar." He trailed a finger down the valley of her breasts. "Your eyes are eating me up, and you're practically drooling."

All true. "Big head much?"

He outright laughed. "Now you're making it too easy."

She'd fed him that line, curious to see what he'd do with it, and what she got was his body wrapped around hers, her back to his chest. He put his hands on her hips and pulled her to him so that his erection was pressed against her bottom, then he lowered his mouth to her ear. "So, tell me what you have against big heads."

"Not a damn thing."

"That's what I thought." He trailed his hands up her stomach to her breasts, cupped them, then flicked his thumbs over her nipples, and while he played with her breasts, he nuzzled her neck. When he scraped his teeth over her skin, she shivered. "Like that, do you?"

"Mmm." She arched against him and secretly smiled when a shudder traveled through him. "I want you in me, Parker."

"Yes." He stepped away from her, picked up his jeans, and pulled out condoms.

While he was doing that, she climbed into the bed. She widened her eyes when he dropped three on her night table. "Planning on being here a while?"

"Until you fall asleep on me." The mattress dipped when he kneeled next to her on the bed. He put his hand on her stomach and made circles with his thumb. "I've wanted you since the first time I saw you sitting on your porch wearing your straw hat and cowboy boots."

"You could have fooled me. I thought you didn't like me."

"I didn't want to like you. I told myself I could ignore you, and I definitely didn't plan on ending up in your bed." His gaze skimmed over her body, then he lifted his eyes to hers. "Yet here I am."

"That's because I'm irresistible." She smiled to show him she was teasing, but she was learning that Parker Church, unlike a lot of men, didn't hesitate to share his honest feelings. That was refreshing.

"Yes, you are."

"Same could be said of you." If he hadn't been, her manless vacation plan wouldn't have flown out the window without a single regret.

"Lift your head up." When she did, he reached behind her and pulled the band out of her hair, then he combed his fingers through it. "Your hair is amazing."

"Thank you." He couldn't know what that meant to her. Growing up, both her mother and Cynthia had done their best to try and get her to load it down with product to tame the wildness. It had taken her a long time to learn to like her hair in its natural state.

"Welcome." He crawled over her, settled between her thighs, and supporting himself with his elbows, he kissed her. She opened to him, and the touch of her tongue against his sent tingles racing through her. She could get addicted to kissing Parker Church.

"So many places I want my mouth on you, Willow," he said after he lifted his head and stared into her eyes. "But right now, I need to be inside you." His gaze shifted away from hers. "If that's what you want, too."

"Yes, please. I do want that." There was something in his voice that she couldn't place, vulnerability maybe? What would make this man uncertain? He was beautiful, talented, and kind when he wasn't being grouchy. When he rose to his knees to put a condom on, whatever she was thinking was forgotten.

"Oh, my," she murmured.

He stopped with the condom half-on, lifted his gaze to hers, and grinned. "Still satisfied with what you're getting?"

Oh, yeah. She grinned back at him. "You'll still do." They were keeping the mood light, and she appreciated that. This was an agreed upon fling, no deep feelings for each other involved.

Once the condom was on, he put his hands on her legs, right above her knees. The smile on his face faded away as his gaze traveled over her, starting from where his hands were, then with a pause on her sex before continuing up, pausing again on her breasts. By the time he reached her face, his espresso eyes were even darker, and heat shimmered in them. Had a man ever looked at her as if she was the most delicious thing he'd ever seen, as if he could eat her up?

"Beautiful girl," he said, almost whispering, as he lowered his body over hers.

Beautiful boy. Instead of speaking the words, she reached down to guide him into her, smiling to herself when he hissed out a breath when she wrapped her hand around him. And as he filled her, moved inside her, kissed her mouth, her neck, her breasts, being with him felt right. She closed her eyes and breathed him in, inhaling the spicy smell of man and musk and sex. His scent was an aphrodisiac.

His hands roamed over her, touching her, claiming her, and she claimed him back as she explored him, her hands growing warm from his body heat. She dragged her fingers down his abs, then up his chest to his shoulders. Strands of his hair had escaped his ponytail, and she reached behind his head and pulled the band off. His shoulder-length hair fell around his face as he made love to her.

Her gaze locked on his beautiful lips, and she lifted a finger to their pillowy softness. He sucked her finger into his mouth and swirled his tongue around it, and she felt like even her bones were melting. When the pressure building inside her became uncontainable, she clenched her core muscles around him, wrenching a hiss and an "Ah, fuck, Willow" out of him, and she let go. He followed her with one last deep thrust.

"Wow," she gasped when she could catch her breath.

His face was buried against her neck, and his chuckle vibrated over her skin. "*Wow*'s a good word." He kissed the sensitive spot just below her ear, then rolled away. "Be right back."

"I'll be right here." When she smiled at him, his eyes shifted away. Uh-oh. Was this where it was going to get awkward?

Chapter Twenty

Parker disposed of the condom, then stared at himself in the bathroom mirror. He wanted to go paint a hundred canvases, each one of Willow. Willow in bed, her hair wild and tousled from his hands digging through it. Willow looking at her lover with desire-filled eyes. Willow nude, her long legs tangled in satin sheets. Willow's bubble gum toes. He lowered his chin to his chest and closed his eyes. This was not happening. He was not falling for someone…again. He willed it so, and so it would be.

What had just happened between them had been incredible, yes. Near the end he had felt as if they'd transcended just having sex and traveled into something magical. Just because he'd never experienced anything like it, not even with Simone, didn't have to mean he was falling for her.

He wanted to get back in that bed with her and do it all over again.

Reason enough not to do exactly that. They'd talked about it, had agreed on what this was, but did she really understand the rules? He needed to make sure she did, so he returned to the bed, but instead of climbing in like he wanted to, he sat on the edge next to her legs.

"I need to say something, and please don't take this wrong."

"Okay."

She smiled, and his mind camera-clicked a mental picture of her beautiful smile for future reference, because he might tell himself he wasn't going to fill a canvas with anything Willow, but he knew he was lying to himself.

Even so, he had to say the words that would probably hurt her but would protect him, and in the long run protect her, too. "Don't expect more from me than I have to give."

She put her hand on his arm. "I don't expect anything from you, fireman, except for more amazing orgasms."

"Firefighter." Her grin said she was teasing him. His gaze shifted to the two unused condoms on her side table. As much as he wanted to crawl back in bed with her and wrap his body around hers, he needed to distance himself from the temptation of Willow Landry until he had his emotions under control.

"I seriously need to spend time in my studio before my show sneaks up on me and I'm not ready." Not a lie. She watched him dress, and he wished she'd say something. Did she want him to go? He should be glad she wasn't asking him to stay, and he shouldn't be disappointed that she didn't.

When he was dressed, he stepped next to the bed, leaned down, and brushed his lips over hers. "Sweet dreams, beautiful girl."

Four days later, Parker had finished two canvases. He'd never painted that fast, but the need to paint burned through his body faster than an out-of-control wildfire.

To keep from filling canvas after canvas with Willow in all the ways he saw her, imagined her, he made a list of things to paint, then started with the first one, and then the second. At the rate he was going, he'd have more than the twenty canvases he needed for his show. He seriously needed to sleep, but sleep had been elusive.

The arsonist had left him alone, as had Willow. She hadn't appeared, wearing her cowboy boots, her denim shorts, her flowery dress, or her floppy straw hat, and he should be thankful for that. The arsonist's absence he was thankful for, Willow's not so much.

He hadn't called her the following day for her tour of his studio. He should have—he'd wanted to—but he was afraid that the minute she walked in, he'd lock the door and worship her the night through. He needed time to process, to set his mind straight before his heart decided to give itself to her without his permission. So he hadn't called.

He missed her.

Andrew was taking Everly over to Willow's in the afternoons because he couldn't say no to his daughter when she begged him to let her go see Willow. Parker had come close to taking her himself, but he'd managed to resist. The more time that passed since the night he couldn't stop thinking about, the harder it was to decide what to do. Go see her? Accept that their time together was a one-off since she hadn't reached out to him?

The hardest part about keeping Willow out of his thoughts was Everly with her Miss Willow this and Miss Willow that. The two of them were working on another story, this one about a magical cat (Jellybean being the inspiration) and his three dog friends (sweet Ember, who could put out fires by barking at them, silly Duke, whose job was apparently to make his friends laugh, and Fuzz, who wore a cape that repelled evil magic). The four set out on a journey to save the world from...

"From what, Daddy?" Everly said, as he drove her to school. "I have to tell Miss Willow when I see her today."

It had taken her all the way to school to tell him the story they had so far. He glanced behind him to where Everly was sitting in her car seat. "From the wicked toads that steal all the fun from children." See what Miss Willow could do with that.

His daughter looked at him as if he'd lost his mind.

When Parker arrived at the station, it was to find their newest recruit, Carlton Fendley, muttering with his head in Engine One's equipment compartment. "Looking for something, Carlton?"

"Where would I find the hose stretcher, Chief?"

Parker kept his smile off his face as he remembered when he'd been pranked as a newbie with that one. He'd searched for hours for something that didn't exist. "Last time I saw it, it was..." He stared up at the ceiling as if thinking. "Hmm, I don't remember now."

"What does it even look like?"

Parker took pity on him. "There isn't such a thing. They're pranking you."

Carlton laughed. "I was beginning to suspect that."

"Glad you can laugh," Parker said. "You're going to fit right in. Watch for them to short-sheet your bed next." Or put a rubber snake in it, but for that one, he'd let the guys have their fun.

The speakers located inside and outside the station blared with the tone for a fire. "Marsville Dispatch to Marsville Fire Department. Respond to a fire at Burrell's on 1701 Mountain View Road. Structure fire."

The bay doors opened. The address for the fire was at Tommy Burrell's junkyard where there were piles of tires, probably dating back from the days of the first cars on the road since the place had been in the Burrell family for four generations.

The two MFD engines left the station, sirens blaring. There hadn't been a call for a bus, but as always, an ambulance followed. Parker let Ember into his chief's SUV, then jumped in. When he pulled up behind the engines, it was to see the junkyard's shack ablaze. The shack served as an office and a place for Tommy to sleep when his wife kicked him and his hound dog out of the house, which happened at least once a month.

He rolled down the windows for Ember, then exited the car, knowing she would stay until he came for her. Spotting Tommy sitting on the hood of one of his junk cars as he watched his firefighters lay hoses, Parker walked over to him. Tommy's bloodhound Bubba sat on the hood next to him, and on the ground in front of them was a fire extinguisher.

"You okay, Tommy?"

"I tried to put it out, Chief."

They both stared at the shack that was going to be a total loss. "What happened?"

"Don't know. I was sleeping, and Bubba woke me up barking and pawing my face." He wrapped his arm around the dog. "Saved my life, he did."

"You spent the night here?" He wouldn't know if it was arson until he and Ember could do their search, but if it was, the arsonist would have thought the building was empty.

Tommy grunted. "The missus was having one of her spells."

"Did you hear anything, notice any strangers around lately?"

Tommy squinted his eyes at Parker. "Meanin' what? You think somebody did this a'purpose? Nah, the wiring was bad. Been fixin' to do something about that."

He'd probably been *fixin'* to do something about it for years. Not that Parker wanted Tommy to lose his home away from home, but he hoped it was the wiring and not arson. "I'm going to have Josie come check you out, make sure you don't have smoke inhalation," Parker said when Tommy coughed.

After sending his EMT to Tommy, Parker went to his car to get Ember. It hadn't taken much to put the fire out since the shack wasn't any bigger than a shipping container, but it was, unfortunately, burned to the ground.

"Time to go to work, Ember." He hooked her leash to her collar. It would be a while before the shack's foundation was cool enough for her to walk on, so he checked the perimeter of the building, and when he came back to where they'd started, he widened the circle. Halfway around, Ember stopped and lifted her nose in the air.

"What is it, girl?" He let her have her lead.

She pulled him to one of the junk cars sitting up on cement blocks. The car was a seventies era Pinto with the doors missing. She stopped at the driver's side back door, sat, and looked up at him, giving him an alert. "Good girl." He kneeled next to her and held out a treat, which she lifted from his palm with a delicate sweep of her tongue.

Without touching anything, he leaned into the car. There was a pile of rags on the floor, and the smell of gasoline was strong. On the seat was an envelope with his name on it. "Shit," he muttered. He'd almost decided that the arsonist had moved on. He was still here, and the man was playing games. Parker glanced around, but he didn't have the feeling he was being watched.

He called Skylar, since Burrell's was in her jurisdiction. "You need to come to Burrell's and send a CSI out here."

"Tristan and I are already on the way, and you're on Speaker, so he's calling for a CSI now. We're seven minutes out."

"Okay, I'll meet you at the entrance." After disconnecting, he radioed Greg.

"You got me, Chief."

"I'm on the east side of the building. Send Carlton this way."

"Copy."

When Carlton jogged up to him, Parker said, "Stand here until I return. Do not touch anything on the outside or inside of the car. Do not let anyone else come near it."

Carlton glanced at the Pinto with wide eyes. "Is it a crime scene, sir?"

"Yes. I'll be back shortly."

"I got this, Chief," Carlton said.

Parker chuckled as he and Ember went to meet his brother and Skylar. Had he looked that young and wide-eyed as a recruit? His firefighters were rolling up the hoses, and he paused next to Greg. "It's going to be arson, so keep everyone away now that the fire's out."

"This is getting old, Chief."

"Couldn't agree more." The junkyard was in an isolated area, so there weren't any spectators or witnesses. Also, the man Willow had seen couldn't be their arsonist because he didn't have a car. The fires were too spread out for someone to walk to. The odds weren't good that they'd catch their firebug, but if this continued, someone was going to get hurt, and today it had almost been Tommy. Bubba was the hero of the day.

Tristan and Skylar arrived, and he filled them in. "There's an envelope in the Pinto with my name on it but I haven't touched it." Another car pulled up next to Tristan's SUV. "Here's our CSI now."

When Maurisa joined them, Parker filled her in as they walked to the car. Ember alerted again when they reached the Pinto, and he gave her a few more treats. "We need to see what's inside the envelope but were waiting on you to do your thing," he told Maurisa. He nodded at Carlton. "You can join the crew now."

After Carlton jogged off, Maurisa snapped on gloves. He, Tristan, and Skylar stood by while she took pictures of the inside of the car to document the scene. Once that was done, she bagged the rags soaked with gasoline, then picked up the envelope by its corner.

She glanced at Parker. "It's got your name on it. Let's see what it says." She slid a finger under the flap, removed the sheet of paper, and held it up for them to read.

Fire shines a light in the darkness, but fire burns all, consumes all. Beautiful, beautiful, arousing fire. Are you having fun yet, Parker? I am…so much fun!

"Dear God," Parker said.

"Finish up here, Maurisa." Tristan put his hand on Parker's shoulder. "Let's take a walk."

Parker swallowed hard against the bile in his throat.

He hadn't wanted to believe the fires were directed at him, but he couldn't deny it now.

"You okay?" Tristan said after he, Parker, and Skylar were alone.

"No, I'm not okay." What had he done to draw the attention of a person who found fires arousing and fun?

Chapter Twenty-One

"Don't expect more from me than I have to give." Had she asked for more? Willow wished she was wearing her cowboy boots so she could stomp her feet like a child throwing a tantrum while making a lot of noise. Parker obviously regretted their time together, considering he'd ghosted her. Four days had passed since she'd had the best sex of her life and nothing. Nada. Not a word from him.

If she were prone to being an insecure person, she'd be blaming herself. She'd be asking herself if she'd been terrible in bed. She wasn't. It had been good between them. She hadn't imagined that. When he hadn't called her for the tour the next day, she'd almost gone over anyway, but had managed to stop herself. A girl had to have some pride.

The lights in his studio had burned into early mornings each night. If he wasn't interested in continuing their fling, no problem. What she didn't appreciate was being ghosted without knowing why. She'd thought they were on the way to being friends, with or without any sex involved. Guess not.

At least he was letting Everly come over in the afternoons. Willow was having a blast with the little girl.

What a creative mind Everly had. Even if no one outside of her family would see her illustrations, Willow considered herself blessed to be in the presence of such talent. What she wouldn't give to be around in ten or so years to see her develop that talent into something spectacular.

She glanced at the bedside clock. It was only ten, and although she'd been trying to read until she was sleepy, she finally gave up as she couldn't concentrate because a certain someone kept invading her thoughts. She was considerably ahead in her word count goals and had thought to take the night off and read a book for a change.

Funny how spending time with Everly had stirred her creative juices on her own story. Her daily word count had almost doubled, and if that kept up, she'd finish the book a few weeks early. Since sleep was being evasive, she might as well write some more.

Thirty minutes later and almost four hundred new words on the page, her phone chimed with a text from Parker.

Tour of my studio?

He wanted to do that now? She should tell him no, considering he'd ghosted her for four days, but her curiosity wasn't to be ignored.

Give me 20. Need to get dressed.

No you don't (Winking emoji)

She snorted. The man was a conundrum. He could

go from grouchy to sweet, to rude, to teasing faster than she could blink her eyes. It was enough to make one dizzy. Still, he fascinated her, and she really wanted to see his art, so she slipped on a sundress and a light sweater, then slid her feet into a pair of flip-flops before pulling her hair up into a ponytail. She'd already cleaned her face and put on moisturizer, so only a little lip gloss would have to do.

The studio door was open, so she walked in. Parker was standing in front of an easel, a paintbrush in his hand. She walked up next to him but didn't say anything. He was the one who'd ignored her for four days, so he could be the one to talk.

"Oh, wow," she gushed, her intention not to speak first forgotten when her gaze landed on the canvas.

An old man, his age-lined face full of character, and his watery blue eyes filled with longing, sat in front of a window in a blue-and-yellow plaid chair, the kind you'd see at your great-grandmother's house. A blue afghan covered his knees and on one hand was a baseball glove, cracked with age. The scene outside the window was of a group of tween boys playing baseball in the street.

Parker didn't have to tell her that the man was remembering being a boy, and the yearning to have those days back was there on his face and in his eyes. The painting was breathtaking, and tears stung her eyes for the man who couldn't play ball anymore.

"Is this someone you know?" She glanced up at him to see that he was watching her.

"Norwood Cooper. My high school baseball coach's grandfather. He came to every practice game and always had his glove with him, ready to catch any foul balls that came his way. He played high school and college base-ball with that glove. He died a few months ago."

"It's a beautiful tribute to him. Does your show have a theme?"

"It does. Scenes Through a Window, and this one's titled *Bottom of the Ninth*."

"The end of his life," she murmured.

"Yeah." His eyes lit with pleasure. "You get it."

"I want to cry for a man I've never met. Is that weird?"

"No, that's art." He stepped back and studied the painting. "If it touches you like that, it means I've done my job."

She'd never felt like crying because of a painting before, so it definitely touched her. The painting was a reminder not to make assumptions. Art wasn't just a hobby for him as she'd assumed when his daughter had told him her father was an artist. He was a brilliant art-ist. As her gaze roamed over the painting, the signature at the bottom right caught her attention, and she gasped. "Oh, my God, you're Park C?"

"Guilty."

When she looked at him with what she was sure was an expression of shock, he shrugged. Why hadn't he told her?

"It's not something I advertise," he said, reading her mind. "Very few people around here know. Most couldn't give a fig and would just as soon have an Elvis on velvet over anything I've painted. It's just that I don't want or need people poking into my life."

"Your secret's safe with me." When she'd admired the painting in his dining room, he barely knew her, so she understood why he hadn't said anything. But just wow. Her mother would freak out if she knew Willow was standing next to Park C.

"Do you have other pieces I can see?" She still had a bone to pick with him for ghosting her the way he had, but that could wait. Who he was…she just couldn't wrap her mind around it.

"I thought you'd ask that, but before I show you, I…" He stared at the floor for a moment, then lifted his gaze to hers. "It's not important."

"No, you have something on your mind, so you should say it."

"I'm going to sound like a douche, but okay. I'm still Parker, and that's how I want you to see me. Not as some famous person you treat differently. That's one reason I don't tell anyone around here. I'm just me."

No, he wasn't just Parker. He was someone special, but she got it. "I understand. I'm not as famous in the book world as you are in the art world, but people can be weird. I've had people treat me differently when they find out I'm an author, and it can be awkward. So, show me some of your other pieces."

"They're over here."

She followed him to the back of the studio, where two paintings were on easels. The first one was of a boy leaning on a windowsill, staring out at a storm. The fury of the storm was so palpable that she could almost feel the electricity in the air and smell the rain. In the distance, splitting the threatening black clouds and bolts of lightning, a ray of sunshine promised that a better day was coming. Where the painting of the old man was sad and touching, this one offered a young boy hope.

"What's this one called?"

"*Liberated.*"

She waited for him to explain, but when he didn't, she turned to the second painting. Skylar and Harper stood at a window looking out at a snow-covered landscape. Brilliant red birds perched on an evergreen tree, a beautiful contrast to the stark white of the snow. Behind the ladies, a mantel was decorated for Christmas, and Jellybean snoozed in front of a fire. The painting made her feel happy inside, and she smiled.

"That one's *Christmas at Home*."

"Your art really is incredible, Parker. Thank you for sharing it with me."

"Sure."

"How many pieces do you have to have for your show?"

"Twenty. I'm almost there." He stuffed his hands in his pockets. "I owe you an apology."

Yes, he did. "For?" It was impossible to second-guess this man, so she wanted to hear from him why he thought he owed her an apology.

"For disappearing on you. I shouldn't have done that."

"Why did you?"

Chapter Twenty-Two

"Because… You want something to drink?" He'd hoped that she'd accept his apology without wanting to know the reason for his behavior. Not that he blamed her for wanting to understand.

"Sure."

"Wine, beer, water, or a soda? I can make coffee if you'd rather have that."

"How about a beer?"

"I have some great craft beers that I pick up whenever I'm in Asheville." That reminded him that he'd never gotten around to calling Andrea. He took two beers out of his mini fridge, and as he handed Willow one, he knew he wouldn't be making that call.

With her flowery sundress, flip-flops, her hair up in a ponytail, and her face devoid of makeup, Willow made him think of a fresh-faced college girl. A very pretty one. In his painting frenzy, he'd started *Willow in the Moonlight*. He needed to finish it, but that was it. No more Willow paintings.

"Let's go sit on the deck." The only place to sit in his studio was the daybed or his and Everly's stools. The daybed was out, at least until they talked. He grabbed the throw from it.

"So many stars," she said, looking up as they walked across the yard. "I've always lived in the city, where there was too much light to see the night sky like this."

He lifted his gaze to the sky. "It helps that the moon is only a sliver." When they reached the deck, he let her decide where to sit, at the table or in the rocking chairs. She chose a rocker. When she was seated, he slipped the throw over her shoulders. Although it was late spring, it still got chilly at night.

"Thanks." She rested her head on the back of the rocker. "This is nice, but I like my swing better." She shifted her gaze to him. "So…"

"Yeah, so." He should've planned what he was going to say.

"If you've changed your mind about having a fling, that's fine, but respect me enough to tell me instead of disappearing."

He really was a jerk. "I haven't changed my mind. I just needed a little time."

"To do what?"

"Think, but I should have told you that. It wasn't anything to do with you. It's me."

"Ah, the old 'it's not you, it's me.' Sorry, but that's not working for me. Want to try again?"

It was a clichéd excuse, and she was right to call him out on it. He also liked that she had, that she was demanding he respect her. How truthful was he going to be? What did he have to lose by being honest with her? *Nothing.* She was leaving as soon as her house was sold, so she wasn't expecting a future with him.

Besides, if they moved forward with seeing each other while she was here, and he wanted to, she needed to be aware of his weakness. And he wanted to talk to someone about it, but it wasn't something he was comfortable discussing with his brothers. He sensed that he could talk about it with her and not be judged.

"You're thinking mighty hard over there," she said.

"I was trying to decide how honest to be with you." He turned his head toward her. "I look at you, and I want to paint you."

"Although I'm flattered and would feel really special if you did, I don't understand why that's a problem."

What would she say if she knew he already had? "That's how it starts for me. It happened with my girlfriends in high school and then Simone. But with you, the need to paint you burns like a fire inside me."

"You must have felt that fire with Simone."

"That's the thing. Not like this."

"What are you saying?"

"That I fall in love. Often and easily. It's not a desirable trait."

She stopped rocking as she frowned. "Are you saying you're in love with me?"

"No, but after we were together, I was ready to fall in love with you. The old me would have jumped right in, happily handing you my heart on a silver platter without thinking of the consequences, even after the consequences of loving Simone. That's why I needed time. I can't explain it, but being with you, inside you, was more than anything I've ever experienced before. I left you, thinking that I couldn't let it happen again."

"Not that we are, nor do we want to be, but what's wrong with being in love?"

And this was where it got embarrassing, but he'd decided to be honest with her. "It never works out for me. My first girlfriend broke up with me because I was too needy. That was in the ninth grade. The next one said I didn't need her. I did, but I was trying not to be needy. The third one accused me of smothering her. That was probably true and the reason I turned a blind eye to Simone's faults. I didn't want to smother her. I can't seem to get it right, so I've taken falling in love off my life goals." He sounded ridiculously pathetic even to his own ears. "And now I have Everly to think about, so she gave me even more reason to change."

"Why are you telling me all this?"

"Because I want to keep seeing you while you're here, but I'm not going to fall in love with you."

"Okay."

"Why are you smiling?" That wasn't the reaction he was expecting.

"Because you're adorable."

"No, I'm not." *Adorable* was for little girls and kittens.

"Oh, yeah, you are." She set her beer on the table next to her, then stood, came to him, and sat on his lap. "I don't want you to fall in love with me, and I promise not to fall in love with you. We good now?"

"I guess we are."

"Great. You can kiss me."

"I have a better idea. Hold on." He slipped his arms under her legs and stood.

She laughed as he carried her back to his studio and that daybed he'd avoided earlier. He had been sure that she'd run for the hills after his information overload, but here she was, laughing as he locked the studio door behind them.

He wasn't going to fall in love, she wasn't going to

fall in love, she hadn't run away, and he'd been smart enough to put a daybed in his studio. Go him!

The next morning, an alert sounded at the station for a fire, then the dispatcher's voice came over the speakers and on Parker's phone. The location was a residence, one Parker and every Marsville firefighter knew well, and collective groans filled the air.

"It's the newbie's turn to go up the tree," Greg said, coming up behind Parker.

"What the fu—"

"Carlton," Greg said. "Don't finish that. You know how the chief feels about cursing when we're on duty."

"But, Cap, there's something squishy in my boots."

"Figure it out when we get back."

"Bananas?" Parker asked.

Greg chuckled. "Yep."

"How about telling the guys that they've played enough jokes on Carlton."

"Already told them when I caught them putting the bananas in his boots."

There was no reason to go out on this call, but if he didn't, Mrs. Stubble would call her dear friend Miss Mabel and complain that the fire chief wasn't doing his job. Miss Mabel would then use that as an excuse to show up at the station and stick her nose into things.

He followed the ladder truck as it left the station for the same cat, same tree at least a dozen times now call. Parker was of the opinion that Mrs. Stubble purposely let the cat out—probably even had it trained to go up the tree so she could flirt with the "sexy firemen"—her words, not his.

He stopped behind the ladder truck, indulged in

a long sigh, then told Ember to stay in the car. After rolling the windows down halfway, he headed for the handsy elderly woman who was already testing the firmness of Greg's ass. As soon as he stepped next to them, Greg bailed. Not that Parker blamed him.

"Mrs. Stubble, you really have to keep Josephine inside."

"I don't know how she escapes, Parker. It's so distressing to see her up there."

Uh-huh. Knowing what was coming next, he prepared to catch her when she fell against him.

"Oh, dear. I feel faint."

The scene never varied. He wrapped an arm around her back and supported her as they watched Carlton climb up the ladder. More than once in the past, Parker had been tempted not to catch her when she claimed to feel faint just to see if she'd really fall to the ground. But these calls to save her cat were the highlight of her day, so he always played along.

As soon as Carlton reached Josephine, the cat would race down the tree. Since this was Carlton's first Josephine rescue, the crew were taking bets on the newbie's reaction.

"Five dollars on Josephine climbing higher when that boy reaches her," Mrs. Stubble said. "She's petrified."

Petrified his ass. The cat was loving this as much as her owner.

Said owner's eyes were on Carlton's rear as he climbed the ladder. "That boy has a nice tush."

Parker snorted a laugh. "You're a naughty girl, Mrs. Stubble."

"I may be old, but my eyes still work. Besides, what's

the fun of being boring? Take it from me, life is meant
to be more fun than a barrel of monkeys."

Margarite Wyler had been a Rockette before she met
Larson Stubble, fell in love, and married him. She'd always been a bit wicked and up for fun. It had only gotten worse since Mr. Stubble died. Theirs had been a true
love story, and she missed him and was lonely, which
was why Parker put up with her shenanigans.

Carlton reached the cat, extended his hand to get
it, and screamed when it flew from the branch it was
perched on to a lower one. As expected, Josephine
climbed down the trunk, and after reaching the ground,
she ambled to the open door of the house and disappeared inside.

"Did I kill it? Did I kill it?" Carlton shouted, refusing to look.

"I was sure she'd climb higher," Mrs. Stubble said,
then pulled a five-dollar bill from her bra and handed
it to Parker.

Parker snorted. Eric won for betting that Carlton
would scream like a girl. Mrs. Stubble was waiting for
Carlton when he reached the ground, and Parker and
the guys exchanged grins, knowing what was coming.

"My hero," Mrs. Stubble said as she threw herself
against Carlton's chest.

"Ahh…" Carlton's face flushed red as his help-me-
out-here gaze locked with Parker's.

Parker handed Eric the five dollars, then pried Mrs.
Stubble away from Carlton. Greg rounded up the crew
and they escaped before they each got a hug. "Try to
keep Josephine in the house, okay?" Which she would do
until she got bored again and needed her firefighter fix.

"You know I try. She's just so sneaky." Her hand slid down his ass.

Much like you, Mrs. Stubble. "Enjoy the rest of your day and keep Josephine inside." He eased away from her grabby hand. "You just sit over there and be smug," he told Ember after he got in the car. "You didn't get your ass fondled."

The rest of the day was quiet, and he was able to catch up on paperwork and then, to keep from thinking of Willow, he completed one of the modules in the online fire science course he was taking. To some, fire was fascinating, thrillingly dangerous, and sexually stimulating. Many arsonists were driven by anger at their life and at the world around them. Getting attention was another motivation. Which of those applied to their firebug?

Parker respected fire, but nothing made him happier than to see a fire extinguished. He didn't get wanting to destroy the landscape or someone's home. Other than a thin description, they had nothing.

It was frustrating and worrisome. His biggest fear was that someone was going to get hurt before they caught the arsonist or he moved on. There hadn't been anyone posting on Miss Mabel's Facebook page that they were out of town, but what if they set a trap? Found a place they could lure the man to? He'd talk to Tristan and Skylar, get their opinion, but it was worth considering.

He shut down the computer, made the rounds to check on his crew, then loaded Ember in the SUV and headed home. Willow wasn't on her porch, and her car wasn't in the driveway when he passed her house. He didn't think she was out on a date, but they hadn't talked about being exclusive while she was here. Would she agree to that? Not that he was putting any kind of claim on her, but he wasn't going to see anyone else while she was still here.

After dinner, he and Everly spent a few hours in the studio until it was her bedtime. His gaze kept straying to the daybed, and he'd never look at it again without seeing her in it, her hair spread over the pillow, and her smile as she watched him undress. He wanted her in it again, and after he got Everly to bed, he'd text her to see if she wanted to come over.

"Love you, ladybug," he said, then kissed his daughter's forehead.

"I love you more than the whole wide world, Daddy. I love Miss Willow, too."

He forced a smile. "Go to sleep. Sweet dreams." As he left her room, he couldn't help asking himself if he was making a mistake letting her spend time with Willow. Willow wasn't staying in Marsville, and Everly was going to be crushed when she left.

"How's the painting going for your show?" Kade asked, glancing over his shoulder when Parker walked into the kitchen.

"Sorry, what?" He didn't want to stop Everly from spending time with Willow, but was it wise? And if he didn't allow it, how would he explain it to both of them? Even if she didn't agree, Willow would probably understand, but Everly? No, not at all.

"I asked how it's going with your painting? Where's your mind?"

"Do you think it's a good idea for Everly to get attached to Willow since she'll be moving as soon as she sells her house?"

Kade and Harper were at the sink, cleaning up the dinner dishes, and they both turned. "That's a legitimate concern, I guess," Harper said. "Won't be easy since Willow's right next door, and you know Everly. If she wants to see Willow, she'll figure out a way."

Without doubt she would. "I just don't want to see her get hurt, and she will. She told me she loves Willow."

"Does she know Willow's not planning to stay?" Kade asked.

"I don't think so, or she would have said something." Harper wiped her hands on a dish towel, then dropped it on the counter. "I think Everly needs to know so that it doesn't come as a surprise. At least then she can get used to the idea."

"Should I tell her, or should it come from Willow?" Everly did need to know, and maybe if she did, she wouldn't feel betrayed when Willow left.

"You and Willow need to talk about it first, then the two of you can decide who should tell her and how," Harper said. "However, my feeling is that she needs to hear it from Willow."

"That's a good idea. I'll—" His phone blared an alert.

"Marsville Dispatch to Marsville Fire Department. Respond to a tree on fire at 24 Deep Creek Road."

Parker frowned. "That's Mrs. Stubble's address. We were just there this morning, rescuing her cat from the tree again."

"I'll send a text to Andrew, let him know Harper and I are here," Kade said.

"Thanks."

Ember raced past him to the door. Harper chuckled. "I can't believe she heard that alert all the way from Everly's room."

"Apparently she has excellent hearing. Catch you later."

When he arrived at Mrs. Stubbles's, Josephine's tree was fully engulfed, and the crew were pulling the hoses to it. He rolled down the windows for Ember. "Stay."

"Oh, Parker," Mrs. Stubble wailed when she saw him. She fell into his arms, and this time her anguish was real. "Josephine's tree is burning up."

"I see that. How did it happen?"

She gripped his shirt. "I don't know. I looked out the window, and it was just on fire. How does a tree just catch fire? It wasn't lightning or anything."

No, a tree didn't just catch on fire all by itself. The back of his neck prickled. He scanned around him. Neighbors were out in force, but all their eyes were on the tree. Someone was watching him, though.

"Greg," he called. When his captain, reached them, he pried Mrs. Stubble's fingers from his shirt. "Get someone to stay with her."

"Why don't we go sit on your porch, Mrs. Stubble," Greg said, leading her away.

Parker retrieved Ember from the SUV. He first went to the closest group of people. While he questioned them, Ember sniffed them for accelerants. Finding nothing interesting, she sat next to his leg. No one had seen anything suspicious, so he moved on to the next group. The entire time he talked to them, he tried to sense who was watching and from where.

"Chief," Greg said, coming up next to him. He leaned toward Parker's ear. "You need to come see this."

No one in this group had seen anyone near the tree, and as Parker walked with Greg back to Mrs. Stubble's, the feeling of being watched faded away. The arsonist was here, or had been, but where had he watched from?

While he'd been talking to the spectators, his firefighters had put out the fire. Parker's gaze took in the blackened tree. "I don't know much about trees. Think it can come back from this?"

Greg shrugged. "Don't know. She'll need someone who knows about trees to come take a look. At the very least, it'll need a good trimming."

"Like Mrs. Stubble said, a tree doesn't catch on fire all by itself. Have a couple of the guys go around the neighborhood tomorrow to see who has doorbell cameras. Maybe someone caught something that'll help us find out who's doing this."

"Will do. A little warning, Chief. You're not going to like what you're about to see."

Greg was right. He didn't like it at all.

Chapter Twenty-Three

The engines and crew returned to the station, and Mrs. Stubble went inside her house with a neighbor friend. Parker had called his brother, and Tristan and Maurisa arrived on the scene.

"You know that it's not the man Willow saw," Parker said to Tristan as they waited for Maurisa to take photos. "To get around to the different locations of the fires, our arsonist would need a car, and that man didn't have one."

Tristan nodded. "Yeah, I was already thinking that."

"I think we have one of those rare cases where the arsonist is a female." A red piece of tin cut in the shape of a heart had been pinned to the tree with a wicked-looking dagger. Parker couldn't see a man doing that and then setting the tree on fire. Considering the envelope with his name on it they'd found at Tommy's, this message was meant for him, too.

"Someone's not happy with you, baby brother," Tristan said. "If you dated, I'd say you broke some woman's heart, but you don't date."

"I haven't broken anyone's heart, so I don't have a name for you." When he'd first seen the dagger stabbed into the heart, the only person he could think of who was unbalanced enough to play games like this was

Simone. But why would she? While waiting for Tristan and his CSI to arrive, he'd called Benoit. His old friend had confirmed that Simone was still in France, which was a tremendous relief. Someone was obviously angry because of him, but who and why?

"Well, think hard. Whoever she is, you know her or at least have met her."

Parker wanted to deny he was the reason for any of this, but his brother was right. He eyed the tree. "It's going to break Mrs. Stubble's heart if the tree's a total loss. How's she and Josephine supposed to get their firefighter fix?" If the tree was a loss, he'd find someone who could replace it with another full-grown one.

His brother chuckled. "Only you would worry about Mrs. Stubble not getting to grab ass to make her day. I don't suppose you've ever seen that dagger before?"

"That's the one and only dagger I've ever seen in my life." The knife was ornate and evil looking, like something a villain in a horror movie would wield. "It looks expensive. Think you can trace it back to the store it came from?"

"I'm sure as hell going to try."

"You know, Kade's boss or his brother at Talon Security might be able to help you with that." Chase and Nick Talon had resources that a police department didn't.

"Good idea." Tristan took out his phone. "I'll take some pictures that Kade can send them."

While Tristan was getting photos of the dagger, Parker tried to think of who hated him this much, and his mind drew a blank. The only woman he'd seen more than once since returning from France was Andrea, and she would never do something like this, nor did she have a reason to.

So who?

* * *

After getting Everly to bed, Parker went to his studio to paint. Well, that was the plan. For the first time since getting his desire to paint back, he was blocked. He stared at the blank canvas, and... Nothing.

He grabbed his phone and the baby monitor. When he reached his front yard, he stopped. He couldn't just barge over to Willow's because he felt like it. Also, he should stop lying to himself. He didn't just feel like seeing her, he needed to. And that was him falling in love. No, that was the old him. The new him turned around to go back to the studio. He wasn't blocked. It was just the shitty day that was messing with him, and he didn't need to see Willow.

Not two steps across his yard, his phone chimed with a text.

Were you coming over to see me, or are you just ambling around in your yard?

He read the text and laughed.

Full disclosure. Haven't a clue. Been a bad day.

Come tell me about it.

There was nothing he wanted to do more. He didn't bother responding, just turned around and went to her. She was on her swing, her laptop resting on her legs... her long, sexy legs, which his eyes immediately landed on, and his artist eye wondered if a canvas with nothing but legs that ended with their feet in cowboy boots would be too weird to paint.

He stopped in front of her. "I need to stop wanting to paint you." Damn his wayward mouth. But that beautiful smile of hers at hearing his confession had him sitting down next to her—right next to her so that their bodies were touching—even though his brain was ringing warning bells. He ignored them.

"I already told you, you can paint me whenever you want." She leaned against him. "Even nude if you want, but that one you'd have to give to me so no one saw it but me and you."

Like he'd let anyone else see her nude. "I should have brought my sketchbook and charcoal." That was how he'd do a nude of her, in shades of gray and white.

She put her hand on his arm. "I'm sorry you had a bad day. I had a great one. Want to come see my new stove and fridge? I'm dying to test the oven."

"You haven't had dinner?" It was pretty late.

"I didn't know Buddy was installing the appliances today, so when he did, I stopped at the Kitchen for a bowl of soup and Katie's amazing bacon, apple, and Gruyère sandwich for dinner. Then I went shopping for the ingredients to make my favorite cookies. Want to help me make them?"

He couldn't think of anything he'd rather do. Turned out she was serious about cookies. They made four batches, one for now, one for him to take home, and two for what she called her writing fuel.

"Taste," she said, holding out a cookie from the first batch, still warm from the oven.

"Mmm, that's really good." He'd turned up his nose when she said her favorite cookies were oatmeal chocolate cherry. It wasn't a combination he would have thought to try.

"Told ya."

What he really liked about baking cookies was all the laughing and kissing they'd done. He'd needed that, both the kisses and the laughter.

"Let's take them out to the porch. Would you rather have coffee or a beer with them?"

"Coffee. I'll make it while you divvy up the batches."

"Great. Coffee's in the pantry until the kitchen's finished. There's a box of assorted flavored pods. I'll take a chocolate one. Mugs are in the cabinet above the coffeepot."

He found the box and choose a dark roast for himself. Her cabinets were in, but the granite hadn't been installed, so plywood was serving as temporary countertops. "I like your cabinet style and colors." The upper cabinets were cream color with glass doors, and the kitchen island cabinets were cobalt blue. It was a great contrast.

"Thanks. I fell down a rabbit hole, looking at kitchen colors and what would fit a Victorian-style house. The granite will be here next week, and I can't wait to see it all come together."

And as soon as the house was finished, she'd put it up for sale and leave. That was what he wanted, or thought he had. He wasn't in such a hurry anymore for her to leave. They carried their coffee mugs and a container of cookies out to the porch.

"Tell me about your bad day," she said when they were seated on the swing.

"Someone set fire to Josephine's tree."

"Who's Josephine?"

"A cat."

She stilled with a cookie halfway to her mouth. "Huh?"

He grinned. "Thought that would get your attention."

"A cat has a tree? Does it live in the tree?"

"No, Josephine only goes up the tree so her owner has a reason to call the fire department, which then gives Mrs. Stubble, Josephine's owner, the opportunity to feel up the firefighters." He should have waited for her to swallow the drink of coffee she'd just taken because she spewed it. He laughed, and while he was laughing, the image of a finished canvas flashed in front of his eyes. "I need to go paint."

"Right now?"

"Yes. Why don't you come over? Bring your laptop and the cookies. You can write while I paint."

"Okay."

The piece was wonderfully whimsical, and as he painted, he kept stealing glances at Willow. She'd made herself at home on the daybed and was typing away as fast as he was putting paint on the canvas. That feeling of contentment he'd felt with her before settled over him. She was going to leave, so there wasn't any harm in imagining what it would be like if she stayed and there were more nights like this, where he painted and she wrote, two artists doing their thing together. It was not to be, but he liked having her here. If he was unblocked because of her, great, but it didn't mean anything.

A few hours later, he glanced at the clock on the wall, surprised to see that so much time had passed. He hadn't put on any music because he didn't know if she needed silence to write, and it was so quiet that he glanced over at her to see if she'd fallen asleep. But she was still typing away.

As if she sensed him watching her, she looked up and smiled. "I need some fuel. Time for a cookie break."

"How late do you usually write?" It was almost midnight, and he'd go another hour or two.

"Sometimes until two or three in the morning if I'm on a roll like I am now."

Good. He liked having her here. "Want something to drink? Coffee, water?"

"Water's fine. Can I see what you're painting?"

"Sure." He got two bottles of water, took the caps off, handed her one, then followed her over to his easel. "I need to add the layers, but you can tell what it is." Whimsical wasn't his usual style, and he was curious to see her reaction.

"Oh," she said, then laughed. "Is this Josephine in her tree and her cop-a-feel owner?"

"Well, they were the inspiration." A fire engine was parked next to a tree, and a firefighter was at the top of the ladder, his hand reaching for the tuxedo cat perched on a branch. On the ground, a firefighter and a petite white-haired lady were standing next to each other as they watched. The view of them was from behind, and the elderly woman had a handful of the man's butt. The painting had a cartoonish feel.

"This is fabulous, Parker. It makes me smile."

"Thanks. Listen, I've been thinking. What if we had two copies of your and Everly's book made? One for you to give her for her birthday, and one for you to keep?"

Her eyes lit up. "Oh, I'd love that. Are you sure you're okay with it, though?"

"As long as you promise there will only be two copies…make that three. One for me, too. And you'll have to wait until after her birthday party to give it to her, so no one else is around. And instead of her name as the illustrator, make it Ladybug."

"That's a great idea. Let's make it hardcover so it's super special."

"Can we get that done in time for her birthday?"

"I have a friend who makes hardcovers of their favorite books as gifts to her family and friends. She showed me once how she did it, and it's pretty cool. I think if I get the story and illustrations scanned and formatted in the next two days, she'll be able to bind them with covers in time. I'll call her first thing in the morning."

"Great. I'll pay whatever to make it happen."

"Nope, the present's from me. I'll cover the cost. Speaking of her birthday, that reminds me. I need to find bells for me and her."

"You're something else, you know that?" She really was. He softly kissed her. "Back to work."

She returned to the daybed, and he picked up his brush and palette. As he began to layer paint on the canvas, he thought about her and how she was everything he could possibly want if he was looking for a serious relationship. Not only was he attracted to her—more than he'd ever been attracted to any other woman—but his daughter loved her.

Even if he wanted something more, she had a dream, and she was going to leave.

Chapter Twenty-Four

Things were moving along faster than Willow wanted. The house renovation was a week ahead of schedule, and the first ten chapters of her book had been sent to her agent to read, and she'd finished four more since. Only seven chapters left to go, and the first draft would be done. Buddy and his crew were making progress on the house faster than she'd expected, and she'd be able to put the house up for sale sooner than she'd planned. She wasn't ready to think about leaving.

And why is that? Well, duh… Parker. Also, Everly. The little girl had stolen her heart, and it was going to hurt to leave them both when the time came. Her nights were spent in Parker's studio, her writing and him painting. Sometimes their cookie breaks led to making love on the daybed, and sometimes they worked until their eyes were gritty and burned. Then he'd kiss her, and she'd go home to sleep alone while he went to his own bed.

She was doing her best to guard her heart, but she feared it was a losing battle. Even though she wasn't ready to leave Parker and Everly, it was probably best that it was sooner rather than later. Not that she was trying very hard to distance herself from the two of them.

Everly said she needed a dress "so bad" for her birth-day party, so Willow offered to take her shopping. Parker accepted and told her to try Fanny's, the boutique that Willow had noticed on her first tour of downtown.

When she and Everly arrived, Fanny's eyes lit up at seeing Everly, and she showed them her small assort-ment of little girl dresses.

"This one, Miss Willow."

Willow removed the dress Everly was tugging on from the fixture. The dress with a square neckline was pale pink with an overskirt of lavender tulle. "You like this one?"

"I love it so much!" Everly exclaimed.

"Well, let's try it on." Most of the children's clothing in the store was for girls Everly's size, and Willow had a suspicion that the reason for that was Everly herself.

"Do you like it, Miss Willow?" Everly said as she pirouetted in front of the three-way mirror.

Willow nodded. "I think it's perfect for your birth-day party." A dress for a princess.

"I need to show it to Miss Fanny." She skipped out of the dressing room. "Miss Fanny, look at my birthday dress."

Willow followed Everly to the middle of the store, where Fanny was talking to a pretty woman with long black hair. The woman was holding a pale blue sweater in front of her chest. The sweater matched the wom-an's eyes.

"I think I'll take this one," the woman said. Then she smiled at Everly. "Well, aren't you pretty in that dress." She kneeled in front of Everly. "Is it for a special occa-sion?"

Everly backed up a step. "I'm not allowed to talk to strangers."

"Aren't you the sweetest thing? My name is Cassandra. See, now I'm not a stranger. What's your name, honey?"

Willow glanced at Fanny, who was frowning. The woman was entirely too friendly to a little girl she didn't know. Willow put her hand on Everly's shoulder. "Sweetie, let's go change out of your dress so we can take it home." She purposely didn't use Everly's name. When they came out of the dressing room, the woman was gone. Willow took the dress to the register, and when she handed Fanny her credit card, Fanny refused to take it. "Parker called and said to put it on his account." Fanny gave her a curious look. "He also said for you to pick out a dress for the birthday party."

"Oh, I'm good." She hadn't even thought about what she was going to wear tomorrow, but one of her sundresses would be fine.

"He said you'd say that. He also said that I'm to lock the door and not let you out until you find something you like."

Willow glanced at the door. "You're making that up."

"Nope. Try to leave if you don't believe me. Or you could just go in dressing room two where there are a few items to try on that I think you'll like."

It wasn't fair for Parker to steal another piece of her heart. No man had ever bought a dress for her before, and why did that make her smile like a fool?

Fanny waved a hand. "Go on with you. But Everly and I want to see each thing you try on." She winked at Everly. "Don't we?"

Everly clapped her hands. "Oh, yes. But she needs a pink one like mine, Miss Fanny."

"Well, I don't have one like yours in a big girl size, but there is something pink for her to try on." Fanny put her hands on Everly's shoulders. "We're waiting."

"Okay. Going." She was curious to see what Fanny thought she'd like. There were three outfits hanging in the dressing room, and the first one was a sundress with blue and yellow flowers. Since she loved sundresses, she was sure she'd choose it.

It was pretty and fit well, and when she modeled it for her audience, Everly and Fanny gave her a thumbs-up. The second outfit was a sleeveless pale blue blouse paired with a soft blue-and-white-striped cotton skirt. She liked the outfit, but not as much as the sundress. Her fashion advisors agreed.

She almost didn't bother with the third outfit, but decided to give it a try, even though it wasn't her style. "Well then," she murmured when she stood in front of the three-way mirror.

The dusty rose wrap dress with a V-neck that showed a hint of cleavage fit her perfectly. She loved the soft material, the way the skirt flared, and the above-the-knee hem. The sleeves were elbow length, which she liked.

"Miss Willow, are you coming out?" Everly yelled.

Willow smiled. She was pretty sure Everly was going to pick this one because it was a shade of pink. She walked out, her smile growing at the way Everly's mouth formed a big O.

"You have to get that one, Miss Willow. It's so pretty, and it's pink. We'll look like princesses." She looked up at Fanny. "Tell her to get that one."

"Get that one, Willow." Fanny smiled and winked.

"This one it is. What color shoes would go best with it?"

"I'm glad you asked." Fanny reached behind her and picked up a pair of strappy nude sandals. "These would be perfect. I'm guessing you're about a size seven?"

"You're good at guessing sizes."

"Honey, I've been at this a long time."

Fanny was right—the shoes were perfect for the dress, and once both dresses were wrapped in tissue, and they were ready to go, Willow thanked her.

"I'm not the one you need to thank."

Willow laughed when Fanny winked. "We'll be sure to thank Parker, too."

Everly tugged on her hand. "Why are we thanking my daddy?"

"Because your daddy's a very nice man for buying us dresses to wear on your birthday."

"Then you should kiss him. He'd like that."

Fanny's keen eyes landed on Willow, and she grinned. "From the mouth of babes."

"Um… Well, I guess we better go." She could feel that she was blushing, clearly giving away the fact that if she hadn't already kissed Parker, she wanted to.

"I'll see you both at the party," Fanny called to them as they left.

Willow waved, then hustled Everly out the door. She'd received an alert on her phone that her package had arrived. "I have a surprise for you, an early birthday present," she told Everly as they were driving home.

"Oh, goody! I love presents."

"Me, too." Willow glanced behind her at Everly in the car seat, the one Willow had bought especially so

Everly could ride in her car. "Are you excited for your birthday party?"

"Yes!" Everly threw her hands in the air and held up six fingers. "I'll be six years old, Miss Willow. That means I can go to the big kids' school. I'm so excited 'cause I'm not a baby anymore."

Lord, she loved this girl and her exuberance for life. *I'm going to miss you, ladybug, when I leave.* She and Parker had agreed that they'd sit Everly down after her birthday party and tell her that Willow would be moving soon. Willow wasn't looking forward to that conversation.

The small package was waiting for them on the porch when they arrived home, and Everly picked it up. "Is this my present?"

"It's a present for both of us."

"Can I open it?"

"Yes, as soon as we get inside." She got the door unlocked, and inside, set the shopping bag on her gorgeous new granite countertop. The house was turning out to be awesome. She could easily be happy here if she didn't have a dream of living on the beach. Lately, the idea of leaving made her sad, so she pushed the thought away.

She found a pair of scissors, cut the tape on the box, then handed it to Everly. "Go for it."

"Oh, bracelets." Everly picked them up. "One for me and one for you?"

"Yes, with bells."

Everly laughed. "I told my daddy I wanted to wear bells to my birthday party like you."

"I know. He told me."

Suddenly, Everly flew at her, wrapped her arms

around Willow's waist, and hugged her. "Thank you, Miss Willow. I love you so much."

Willow's eyes filled with tears. "I love you, too, sweetie." How was she supposed to walk away from this little girl? From her father?

The birthday party started at four and was being held at the community center that Parker had apparently paid to have built and then had donated to the town. Willow had driven by it but hadn't been inside. She was looking forward to seeing it.

Everly had asked her to come over and help her get dressed. "I can help you," Parker said when Everly had asked Willow to.

"No, you're a boy. Boys don't know how to get pretty."

Willow disagreed. She thought Parker was pretty darn gorgeous. With her new dress and sandals on, she walked next door. Parker was sitting on the porch, and when he stood, she blew out a breath. She'd seen him in sweats when he was painting, in jeans and a T-shirt, in his fire chief's uniform, but she'd never seen him in dress pants and a button-up. The pants were charcoal gray, the shirt a dusty rose with sleeves he'd rolled up.

Beautiful, beautiful boy.

He hadn't seen her dress, so he couldn't have known they'd match. He must have chosen the shirt to match Everly's dress, but the three of them color coordinated was going to make them look like she and Parker were a couple. His gaze stayed on her as she walked up the steps, then stopped in front of him. Should she offer to change her dress so they didn't seem to be sending a message that they were together?

"Beautiful girl." He reached up and curled a lock of her hair around his finger.

"Thank you." Jeez, she sounded breathless. "And thank you for the dress, but do you want me to change into something else?"

Puzzlement filled his eyes. "Why? You're perfect just the way you are."

She touched his shirt. "You, Everly, and I match. People are going to talk."

"I don't care." He lowered his mouth to hers, just a quick brush of his lips over hers. "You better go in and help Everly. She's having her first ever fit of nerves because of a party. Harper's here and offered to help her get dressed, but the little brat stomped her foot and said that was Miss Willow's job. Makes me dread the teenage years if this is a preview."

Willow laughed. "Be afraid, very afraid."

He shuddered. "Trust me, I am."

"Guess I better go in. Where's her room?"

"Come with me." He took her hand.

She wasn't sure they were a secret anymore, not with his buying her a dress—cluing Fanny in—holding her hand as they passed Kade and Harper on the way to Everly's room, and going to his daughter's birthday party wearing matching colors.

What had changed since they'd agreed that they'd keep their fling a secret?

Chapter Twenty-Five

The entire town had turned out for Everly's birthday. Parker would have preferred something low-key. Cake and ice cream at home with just family. Well, and Willow, of course. That was what they'd done in years past, but to his daughter, turning six meant she wasn't a baby anymore. She was a big girl now, and she'd wanted to invite all the other "big girls and boys" so they would all be her friends when she started first grade.

It wasn't like she didn't already know them from kindergarten, but there was no talking her out of it. He'd finally caved under one condition. No birthday presents at this party. There was no way he was going to stand back and allow the entire town to load her up. She'd get her birthday gifts from the family later tonight at home.

She hadn't been happy about that, nor had she understood why she couldn't get presents from everyone on her birthday. Then Willow had come up with an idea that had made Everly squeal with excitement. On the invitations and by word of mouth, the word was spread that in lieu of a birthday present, there would be a jar at the party where everyone could drop a dollar bill in, and the proceeds would be donated to the local no-kill animal shelter. The part that excited Everly was that she'd be the one who'd get to take the money they collected to the shelter and give it to them. So, thanks to Willow, a win-win for all.

Since he was the fire chief and Tristan the police chief, they couldn't selectively invite people, so it had been an open invitation to all, resulting in a packed community center and the town's matriarch standing in front of him with something clearly on her mind.

"You're looking especially pretty tonight, Miss Mabel." He shouldn't have told her she looked good in orange. And wearing a fascinator in Marsville, especially to a six-year-old's birthday party? A bit over-the-top. Yet he was strangely fond of the woman.

"I already told her she's especially lovely tonight," Kade said.

"As did I as soon as she arrived." Tristan smirked. "Before either of you two clowns got around to it."

Miss Mabel giggled. "Silver tongues, the lot of you." She leaned toward them. "Don't tell anyone, but you three boys are my favorite people."

They already knew that, and if they were together when they came across her, it was a game to try to best each other with the compliments.

She glanced to where Willow stood with Skylar and Harper. "What's that spy to you, Parker?"

"Spy?" Kade said, perking up.

Parker rolled his eyes. "Stand down, soldier. Nothing for you to see here. Willow took some pictures of Miss Mabel's car to send to her father, who also has a classic Caddy." He winked at Miss Mabel. "She's a friend is all. You're still my favorite lady." But Willow wasn't just a friend. She was something more. Exactly what he wasn't sure.

After Miss Mabel wandered away, they moved to a table and turned their attention to Everly. "I can't believe she's six already," Kade said. "Just so you know, baby brother, I'm going to scare the bejesus out of any boy that comes near her until she's twenty-six."

Tristan nodded. "And I'll help."

"You won't hear me saying no to that." Parker bumped fists with his brothers, drinking coffee and wishing it was a beer.

The kids were having a blast playing a version of pin the tail on the donkey. Playing the part of a donkey was Earl's goat, and a blindfolded child had to drop a ring of flowers over Billy's head. Willow, Skylar, and Harper were in the middle of the chaos, also having a blast as they tried to basically herd cats in the guise of children and a goat.

"Aunt Harper!" Everly yelled. "You have to blindfolded Nigel next, 'cause Jeremy got in front of him, but it's not his turn."

His brothers chuckled. "Bossy little thing," Kade said.

"I think women call that being assertive." Parker smiled, though. His daughter definitely had a bossy streak. And yes, Harper had achieved aunt status after showing up yesterday with an engagement ring on her finger.

"Either of you set a wedding date yet?" he asked.

"Harper wants to elope," Kade said. "She doesn't want a big to-do, and I'm all for that."

"Like to Vegas?" He could see Kade and Harper doing that.

"Yeah. She thinks it would be a riot to get married by an Elvis impersonator, especially if he'll sing 'Hound

Dog' but change it to 'Horn Dog' as she's walking down the aisle and looking at me."

Parker laughed. "That would be perfect for you two."

"Are you serious about eloping?" Tristan asked.

"We are. It's what Harper wants, and I couldn't be happier about that. It's just a question of when we can both get time off. We're already taking a week for Parker's New York show, so sometime later in the year."

"Can Skye and I elope with you?" Tristan said.

Kade nodded. "You bet. We'll party down."

"I'll come as the best man to both of you." And try not to be envious.

"Or you could find someone to marry, and we'll make it a family affair," Kade said.

"Not getting married." Yet his gaze sought out Willow. She'd be a beautiful bride.

"If your reason for that is Everly, you know she'd be all-in if it was Willow," Tristan said.

Yes, his daughter had made her feelings known, but he had two good reasons for not letting himself even think about a future with Willow. She had a dream of living at the beach and was leaving soon. The other reason…he couldn't trust himself. Had he really been in love with any of his past girlfriends? He didn't think so. After every relationship had ended, along with the regret had been a bit of relief. So even if he came to think he was in love with her, how could he know for sure?

If he didn't have his daughter, he might be willing to try, but he did have her, and it was one thing to have his heart broken, but Ev's? Just no.

His phone chimed an alert. "Marsville Fire Department, respond to a car fire at 610 Dogwood Lane. Repeat, car fire at 610 Dogwood Lane."

"The hell," he and his brothers said together as they stood, all of them recognizing the address.

Parker put his hand on Kade's arm. "You stay here and keep an eye on our girls." The address was Willow's house, so the car had to be her beloved Sunshine. "Don't say anything to Willow. When I know what's going on, I'll come back."

Willow had ridden to the community center with him, Everly, and Ember. Fuzz was here with Tristan, but Duke had been left at home since the goofball couldn't be trusted not to eat the cake or find some other mischief to get into. Recognizing the alert, Ember was at the end of her leash, ready to go. Fuzz, who was never on a leash because he never left Tristan's side unless it was to go with Skylar, looked up at Tristan with his ears straight up, as if understanding it was time to go to work. Parker walked out of the building with Tristan and their dogs.

Since he'd planned to let Greg cover for him tonight if there were any fire calls, he'd driven the Hellcat. "I'll follow you." He split off from Tristan and headed to his car. He'd had blue lights installed when he'd bought the car, and he lit them up. Tristan lit up his lights and siren on his police SUV, and Parker followed him home.

Willow's car was a total loss. Parker stood next to Tristan as they waited for his firefighters to roll up the hoses. "She's going to be crushed. She loved that car."

"Going on your theory now that a woman is behind this, then I'm thinking our unsub knows about Willow and doesn't like you spending time with her."

"Shit." Not that the same hadn't occurred to him standing here, but shit. Hearing his brother put it into words made it real. He scrubbed his hand through his hair, wincing when he ripped a few strands out of his ponytail band.

"If that's true, that we have a jealous woman on our hands, she's going to escalate if we don't catch her soon." Tristan slung his arm around Parker's shoulders. "Think hard, brother. You've met this woman somewhere. I don't think she's from around here, so think about women you've met at your conferences. You can probably eliminate your art shows since your last one was two years ago."

"This makes me so angry that I can't think right now. I have to tell Willow about her car, and then there's Ev's private party with the family tonight. I don't want to ruin that for her. But I'll start making a list later." And did this mean he had to stop seeing Willow? For her safety, he should.

"Tristan and Skylar are taking Everly with them," Parker told Willow when he returned to the community center to find the birthday party was winding down. He'd sent Ember home with his brother, too. After the fire was extinguished, Ember had alerted on an accelerant. No surprise there.

"Everly was looking for you when it was time to cut her cake. Skylar said you and Tristan got called out to a fire."

"We did. I was sorry to miss her cake cutting." Especially because of the reason.

She slid her arm around his as they walked to his car. "I took lots of pictures for you."

Before her car had been destroyed because of him, he would have loved that she felt comfortable doing that, but now he scanned the people around them, wondering if someone who apparently thought he'd wronged her was watching them. Was he putting Willow in more danger just by walking with her? He should swear off women for the rest of his life. Obviously, the universe didn't think he was meant to be in love. Funny that, since he was a boy who'd always wanted to love and be loved back.

He closed the passenger door after she was seated, then as he rounded the hood, he debated when and how to tell her that Sunshine was basically a large piece of burnt toast sitting in her driveway. Now? Take her somewhere else to tell her? He had to drop that bomb on her before she saw her car.

"What's going on, Parker?" she said, seconds after he buckled his seat belt. "You're acting weird."

Okay then, telling her now was the answer. He unbuckled his seat belt, then shifted to face her. He blew out a breath. How was he supposed to tell her that some vindictive woman he'd apparently wronged had set fire to her car? That he was bad news to be around?

If his little girl wasn't home waiting for him so she could open her presents, he'd drive Willow somewhere far away. Somewhere without a risk of her being hurt because of him. But that wasn't a viable option. He had no choice. He had to tell her, and then he had to tell her they couldn't see each other anymore. If something happened to her because of him, he'd never forgive himself.

So he answered her question. "Someone set Sunshine on fire, and I think it's my fault."

Chapter Twenty-Six

"What?" Willow couldn't comprehend what Parker was saying, and when he repeated it, she stared at him. "Why would someone set my car on fire because of you? How bad is the damage? You got it put out and Sunshine just needs a little bodywork, right?"

He wrapped his hand around hers. "I'm sorry. There's nothing left to save."

"My beach car." She sucked her bottom lip between her teeth to keep it from trembling. Sunshine was insured, of course, but she was attached to her car. She didn't want a different one.

"I'll buy you another one."

"No, you will not. It's insured. I just don't understand why someone would burn up my car or why you say it's your fault."

He sighed. "We think now that our arsonist is a woman, someone I've met before, and apparently slighted somehow."

"Seriously? That's...beyond comprehension. Wouldn't you remember doing something to someone to cause her to do this? And why would she burn up my car if she's out to get you?"

"The only reason I can think of would be that she doesn't want me to spend time with you."

"She's watching us?" She thought of all the times sitting on her swing. They'd kissed a lot on that swing. "What about when we were in your studio at night?" That was a horrifying thought, that some deranged woman had been watching them. He'd always dimmed the lights when they made love on the daybed, but had someone been outside, looking in at them?

"We have to assume so, but not while we were in the studio. We have too many dogs that would have alerted to a stranger being in the yard. I know she's been at some of the fire scenes. I've felt like I was being watched several times."

"Are you sure it's a woman and someone you've met?" She couldn't imagine what Parker could possibly do to cause anyone to burn homes and cars up. He was just too nice. He was the sweetest of the three brothers, and it just wasn't in him to do something to a woman that deserved some kind of warped revenge.

"No, but it's the only thing that makes sense." He squeezed her hand. "It's the last thing I want, but until we catch her, we can't see each other. I won't risk you getting hurt."

She turned her face away and stared out the window so he wouldn't see the tears pooling in her eyes. It wasn't fair that some faceless person got to decide when her time with Parker was over. She wasn't ready to walk away from him.

"I'm not sure I'm okay with letting someone dictate my life." She squeezed her eyes shut, willing her tears away, and then she turned back to him.

"Willow—"

"No, I'm serious. I hear what you're saying, but I'm already on her radar apparently, so screw her. She doesn't get to tell me what I can and can't do. Are you willing to give up that easily?" She wasn't looking for some kind of commitment from him. There was an expiration date on their time together, but she wanted him to say that he wasn't ready either for that date to be today.

"It's just that the thought of something happening to you scares me."

"We can be discreet. No more making out while sitting on my swing."

"Damn, I love kissing you on that swing." He let go of her hand, then tugged on a lock of her hair. "The family's waiting for us to finish Ev's birthday, so let's go do that. Then we'll talk about what happens between us."

When they were on the road, he took her hand and placed it on his thigh. "I had your car towed to the police lot. If you want to see it, I'll have Skylar take you there tomorrow."

"I don't think I do. I hate this so much." She wanted Sunshine back, not to mention the hassle it was going to be in dealing with her insurance company.

"Me, too. We're doing everything we can to catch this person. For tonight, try to enjoy the rest of Ev's birthday. She's going to love your present more than anything her family is giving her."

For Everly, she'd smile. As they drove past her house, she couldn't help glancing at her driveway. There was a big blackened spot where Sunshine should be parked. "Oh," she whispered.

"Hey, eyes on me." He dropped his hand over hers. "We'll be sad tomorrow, okay?"

"Yeah, okay." She could wait a day to be sad, and he said he'd be sad with her, which kind of made her happy.

He parked his car in the garage, then moved her hand back to her lap. "Don't move."

"Why?" But he was already out of the car and didn't hear her. As he walked around the car's hood, she grabbed her phone and took a picture of him. She made a mental note to get one of Everly, too. When she was at her beach condo, she'd be able to bring up the photos and remember the two special people who'd made a home in her heart.

After opening her door, he held out his hand to help her out. "Such a gentleman," she said as she rose to stand next to him.

"No, I'm not. A gentleman wouldn't do this." He put his hands on her hips and backed her up to the car door, then pressed his body against hers. "Or this." His mouth crashed down on hers.

Yes, this was what she needed. She wrapped her arms around his neck and lost herself in the feel of him, the taste of him. How was she supposed to give this up before she was ready to?

He trailed kisses across her cheek and then put his mouth next to her ear. "Let's run away."

If only. "And disappoint the birthday girl? No can do."

"Yeah, there is that." He kissed her one more time, then took her hand. "Come. Everyone's waiting for us."

He didn't let go of her hand as they walked into the house. His brothers and their fiancées didn't seem surprised, so she guessed they knew Parker had been spending time with her. Everly, though, her gaze went straight to their hands, and a big grin crossed her face.

"Are you Daddy's girlfriend now, Miss Willow?"

"Um…" She looked at Parker. That was his question to answer.

"Miss Willow is our special friend. Mine and yours." He let go of Willow, then picked up Everly. "Did I tell you how pretty the birthday girl is?" He nuzzled her neck, making her giggle.

Nice diversion, Daddy. A pain sliced through Willow's heart that she'd be leaving soon, and Parker and Everly would be nothing more than a fond memory.

"Can I open my presents now? I waited all day, Daddy, and I didn't even beg."

"But you're begging now?"

"Yes!" She put her hands on his cheeks and stared into his eyes. "Say yes."

"I don't know. Let me think about it."

"Daddy!"

"Say yes, Daddy, before she bursts my eardrums," Kade said.

"Yes."

"Goody!" She wiggled to get down.

Willow followed everyone into the formal dining room. A section of the cake from the party was on the middle of the table, and on the sideboard was coffee, bottles of wine, and a bucket of iced-down beer and sodas. Presents were piled at one end of the dining room table, and the chair in front of them had balloons floating above it.

Everly ran straight to the chair. The rest of the family took seats, leaving the two to the right of Everly for Willow and Parker. Without waiting, Everly tore into the presents, and exclaimed in her loud voice over each thing—new clothes, art supplies, Disney movie DVDs, and a necklace with a heart locket from Parker.

"Look at the back," Parker said.

"Ohhh, a ladybug." Everly turned the locket to show everyone the ladybug etched on the back. "Thank you, Daddy. I love it so much." She'd opened all the presents that were on the table, and she spread her arms wide. "Thank you, aunts and uncles. I love everything."

Parker leaned his chair back and opened the sideboard door. "You have one more present, ladybug." He pulled out a wrapped box and set it down in front of her. "It's from Willow."

"You got me something, Miss Willow?"

"I did." Willow thought she might be more excited than Everly. It wasn't as good as being able to send her story and Everly's illustrations to her agent, but it was close. As if he understood her anticipation to see his daughter's reaction, Parker reached under the table and squeezed her knee. She glanced at him and smiled, and oh, the way his eyes softened as he looked back at her made her feel all melty inside.

"Ooooooh," Everly said, almost whispering after she unwrapped the book and saw the cover. "Our book?" She picked it up, then her gaze flew to Willow's. "I know the word *Ladybug*, but what's the rest of it say?"

Willow pointed to the top line. "This is the title of our book. *The Pink Dragon.* Under that is Ladybug as the illustrator, and then my name as the author." If it was a published book, Everly's name would have gone under hers, but this was Everly's birthday present, and she got top billing. "Look through it." Her friend had done a beautiful job on the cover. She'd chosen a dusty rose for the cover and hot pink for the title and their names.

The family left their chairs and crowded behind Everly as she turned the pages. Willow smiled at Parker as the two of them stayed seated. They'd decided not to show the book to anyone before Everly saw it.

Tristan put his hands on Everly's shoulders. "You have your own book. That's great, Ev."

"I'm so happy." She glanced up. "Will you read it to me, Miss Willow?"

"Sure." As if Everly didn't almost know it by heart.

"I want to hear the story, too," Harper said.

Skylar raised her hand. "And me."

That was how Willow found herself seated in the living room with the Church family surrounding her as she read the story. Everly was on one side of her and Parker on the other. As she turned the pages, Everly would tell her to stop so she could show everyone her illustration for the page they were on and explain the drawing.

"And that's how Serafina got to be in the tournament forever and ever," Everly exclaimed after Willow read the last word.

Willow sat back and observed the family praise Everly and her illustrations, and she loved how supportive they were of the little girl. Having never lived up to her mother's expectations, and being a disappointment in her career choice, she'd never experienced that kind of encouragement, except sometimes from her poet father when his mind wasn't in the clouds. At least she understood her father since she was much like him.

"Thank you," Parker quietly said. "She'll always treasure that book."

"And I'll always treasure writing it with her."

He smiled, then brushed a lock of hair stuck to Everly's cheek. "Ladybug, you've had a long day, and it's almost bedtime."

"But, Daddy, I still have to eat my cake. I was too busy at my party to have any."

"A small slice. You can have more tomorrow."

Everyone moved back to the dining room, and the guys went for a beer. Skylar and Harper wanted wine, and Willow poured a cup of coffee for herself. She needed to write later, and the caffeine would help keep her awake.

"Yum, so good," Everly said after taking a bite of the chocolate cake. "I have a question, Daddy. If somebody tells you their name, are they still a stranger or can you talk to them?"

"We talked about this. Just because someone tells you their name doesn't mean they're not still a stranger. It's only okay to talk to them if someone you trust introduces you to them."

"I told the lady I couldn't talk to strangers, but she told me her name and said she wasn't a stranger anymore."

"Oh, my God," Willow said. Every adult in the room focused on her. How could she have forgotten about that woman, especially after Parker told her they suspected the arsonist was a female?

"What woman?" Parker said.

"The woman at Miss Fanny's." Everly pointed her fork at Willow. "You remember, the lady when we were buying my birthday dress. She talked to me, and I told her I couldn't talk to strangers, so she told me her name." She lifted her gaze to the ceiling. "But I don't remember it now."

"Cassandra," Willow said. Had Everly been that close to the woman starting the fires? It was more likely that the woman just thought Everly was adorable, which she was. But, what if? Willow's stomach churned at the thought.

"Yes! That's it," Everly yelled.

Parker slid his half-eaten cake to the side. "Harper, would you mind taking over bedtime duties tonight?"

"I was just thinking how much I'd love to." Harper pushed her chair back.

"But, Daddy, I'm not sleepy."

Harper stood and held out her hand to Everly. "Come on, sweetie. Bring your book, and after your bath, I'll read it to you."

"Oh, goody." She jumped out of her chair. "Let's go, Aunt Harper." She was halfway out of the room when she stopped and ran back to Parker. "I love you, Daddy. I had the best birthday ever." She went to Willow next. "I love you, too, Miss Willow. Thank you so much for my book." She then made the rounds to her uncles and other aunt, telling each that she loved them and thanking them for her presents.

Once Everly was finally out of the room, Willow resisted squirming when four pairs of eyes focused on her. She'd never thought of these people before as intimidating, but they were that now. Did they blame her for letting a stranger talk to Everly? She met Parker's gaze. "I'm sorry. I should have told you about the woman, but with the birthday party and all, I forgot about her. Do you think she's the woman you're looking for?"

Chapter Twenty-Seven

"Hey." Parker put his hand over Willow's. She was upset, thinking she'd done something wrong. "You didn't know until a few hours ago that we thought the arsonist was a woman. You have nothing to be sorry about. Tell us about this Cassandra person. Exactly what did she do and say?"

While Everly had been opening presents, he'd thought of the woman he'd hooked up with at his last conference. She had ended up being a problem, and he'd planned to tell Tristan about her, but her name wasn't Cassandra. He'd never met a Cassandra.

"She was in Fanny's shop when Everly and I came out of the dressing room," Willow said. "She was holding up a blue sweater, and I remember thinking that it matched her eyes, and that she should buy it. I don't recall her exact words, but she told Everly she was pretty, and she kneeled in front of Everly and asked her name. That was when Everly said she wasn't allowed to talk to strangers, so the woman said her name was Cassandra and that now she wasn't a stranger. I was uncomfortable with how friendly she was being to a little girl she didn't know, so I took Everly back to the dressing room. When we came back out, the woman was gone."

"Everly never told the woman her name?" Tristan asked.

"No. She did exactly what she was supposed to. I think Fanny was uncomfortable with her, too, because she frowned when the woman kneeled to talk to Everly."

"I'll talk to Fanny first thing in the morning," Skylar said. "See what she remembers and if the woman used a credit card."

Kade leaned his elbows on the table, his eyes on Parker. "Do you know a Cassandra?"

"The name's not even remotely familiar. But what if that's not her real name?" He glanced at Willow. "Blue eyes, and what else did she look like?"

"She was a few inches shorter than me, and on the thin side. Shoulder-length black hair, and I mean true black, which is unusual."

"Could it have been a wig?" Skylar asked.

"I guess it could have been. I didn't pay that much attention to her hair, other than thinking how black it was. Sorry."

Tristan tapped his fingers on the table. "Do you think you could draw her from Willow's description?"

"Good question." Parker had never done anything like that before, but why not? "It's definitely worth a try." He touched Willow's arm. "Let's go to my studio and do that now."

"Okay."

Harper came back into the room. "She's asleep. What did I miss?"

Parker stood. "They can catch you up. Willow and I are going to go play police artist."

She blinked at him. "Is that some kind of kinky new game?"

Kade laughed. "Yeah, and we'll play it later tonight. Come here, sugar honey lips." He patted his lap.

"You should run for the hills from that one," he told Harper.

"It's an option," she said, then got a goofy smile on her face as she headed for Kade.

Parker took Willow's hand and pulled her up. "Let's go do our thing, Miss Willow."

Thirty minutes later, he handed her his sketchbook. "This her?" They were sitting side by side on the daybed, and instead of quizzing her on the woman's features for the past half hour, he would have rather spent that time making love to her. He didn't want to stop spending time with her, but someone had burned up her car because of him. Although they weren't entirely sure about that as the reason, it had to be. Why else target her?

"I think so." She handed him back the sketch pad. "I wish I'd paid more attention."

"You didn't know you needed to." He hadn't taken in the entirety of the sketch while he'd been drawing as she gave him the details of what she remembered of the woman, but as he studied it now, he frowned. The face was familiar. Skylar had asked if the black hair might have been a wig, and he visualized that face with blond hair. "Eff me." It was her.

"What?"

He'd give anything if he didn't have to tell Willow he knew the woman and how. Her name wasn't Cassandra. "Hang on a sec." He called Tristan. "Leave the dogs in Ev's room to keep an eye on her, and bring everyone to the studio." Without waiting for a reply, he disconnected, then got up and turned on the baby monitor. He was only going to tell this story once, and even that was going to be embarrassing.

While they waited for the others, he took Willow's hand and brought it to his lips. After placing a kiss on her palm, he said, "Please don't judge me."

"You know her?"

"Unfortunately, yes. Just remember that I met her before I knew there was a you."

"I'd never judge you, Parker. I had a life before you, too."

Which he refused to think about. Willow with another man was a visualization he didn't want to see. What did that mean? Was he doing it again, falling in love? And was he maybe okay with that? Willow loved Everly, and Everly loved Willow. That wasn't something he had to worry about, except his daughter was going to be hurt when Willow moved away. Would Willow give up her dream to live on the beach for him and Everly? He supposed the bigger question was if Willow could fall in love with him? If not, she'd have no reason to stay.

His family arrived, and he waited for them to settle. Skylar and Harper joined Willow on the daybed, Kade sat on the floor at Harper's feet, and Tristan leaned against the wall. No one said anything as they waited for him to speak, and he'd rather be anywhere but here, even cleaning the toilets at the station.

Everyone still had on the clothes they'd worn to the birthday party, and he wished he'd changed into jeans or his sweats. He stuffed his hands into his pockets. There was no easy way to say it, so he blurted it all out. "Her name's Crystal. At least, that's the name she used when I met her. I never asked her last name." He glanced at his brothers. "I met her four months ago at that fire science workshop in Atlanta that three other fire chiefs and I organized. I went down to the bar for a beer and something to eat the night I checked into the hotel. She was already there and was by herself. We talked, I bought her a drink, and..." His gaze fell on Willow. If only he could ask her to leave for this part.

She smiled. "It's okay, Parker. Like you said, that was before you knew there was a me."

"Yeah, but I wish now I had known there was going to be a you." He huffed a breath. "Anyway, things progressed as you'd expect. The next morning I hinted that I had to go to work, and it was time for her to leave. She refused to take the hint. Said she'd just hang out in the room while I was gone. She wanted to know what time my workshop was over, and what we were going to do that night. I told her I didn't date, and that she couldn't stay in my room. She wanted my phone so she could put her number in, and when I refused to hand it over, she wrote hers on a piece of paper. Told me to call her as soon as I was free. I thought, yeah, whatever, just go. As soon as she left, I dropped her number in the trash." He glanced at Willow again. "By then, I was regretting leaving that bar with her."

"Was that the last time you saw her?" Tristan asked.

"I wish. You know what they say about hindsight, but I should have been more forceful in telling her we wouldn't have a repeat. I went to my workshop, and when we broke for lunch, the other fire chiefs and I planned to meet in the hotel's restaurant. Of the other three, one was a woman, Maribel Jennings, who is happily married and has two kids. Mari and I arrived first and were seated. While we were waiting for the other two, Crystal walked up to the table, picked up my glass of water, and dumped it over my head."

"Holy moly!" Harper exclaimed.

"Tell me about it. Crystal accused me of cheating on her with Mari, and to make things worse, the other two chiefs had walked up behind her and saw the whole thing."

"My God," Willow said. "I would have died of embarrassment."

"I wanted the floor to open up and swallow me. Unfortunately, it didn't. I escorted Crystal out of the hotel, told her I never wanted to see her again, and went back inside. Since my shirt was wet, I went to my room to change, then had a power bar and a cup of coffee for lunch before returning for the afternoon session."

"And now she turns up here?" Tristan said.

"Oh, that wasn't the last of her there. My fellow fire chiefs didn't mention anything about the incident, so it was awkward. I couldn't decide if I should try to explain, but what could I say? I slept with a stranger, and now she was stalking me? Then, not five minutes into the afternoon workshop, Crystal slips in the door and sits at one of the tables. She smiled and fluttered her fingers at me as if nothing had happened. It was bizarre."

"And I thought I had some wild hookup stories," Kade muttered.

Harper thumped his head. "We do not want to hear about you hooking up with anyone but me, buster."

"Duly noted, snuggle bunny."

It was so weird to hear his hardcore warrior brother come up with those silly names for Harper. He'd also never thought to see Kade ever fall head over heels for a woman, but he had. Tristan had fallen hard for Skylar, too. After the past six years of telling himself he was happy being single, Parker now admitted he wasn't. He wanted what they had, and he wanted it with Willow.

"What'd you do?" Willow asked.

It was a relief that she was taking all this in stride and not looking at him as if he was a disgusting male. "My first reaction was to tell her she couldn't stay, but she'd proven that she had no problem causing a scene, and there were twenty-five participants at the workshop. There were three other fire chiefs who could carry on without me, so I called for a short coffee break. I told the other instructors that I didn't know the woman other than her first name, but that it would probably be best if I removed myself. Let them think what they wanted, but I'm sure they figured it out. They agreed, and I slipped out the back of the room, went upstairs, packed my bag, and came home. End of story. Or so I thought."

"And now she's here," Tristan said.

"Seems so. My full name, along with the other fire chiefs', was on a whiteboard at the front of the room, as was the name of each of our firehouses. She didn't even have to do any research to learn my last name and where I lived." He picked up the sketch he'd done and handed it to Tristan. "She's a blonde, so the black hair is definitely a wig. Who knows what other color wigs she might use, so I'll do another drawing of her with both blond and brunette hair." That was all of it, and he was exhausted. It had been a long day and telling his embarrassing story had drained him.

Willow, sitting between Skylar and Harper, linked her hands through theirs and pulled them up with her. "You guys have all you need for now, right?"

She understood he needed them gone, and he gave her

a grateful smile. Apparently his family also understood that Willow was what he needed right now, and they filed out after the girls gave him a hug and his brothers squeezed his shoulder.

When it was just him and Willow, she pulled him down to the daybed with her. "That was hard, wasn't it?"

He slid his fingers around hers. "I'm sorry you had to hear all that." Did she think less of him?

She tsked. "Stop it. You were single. There shouldn't have been a damn thing wrong with hooking up when you were a single man and never expecting it to be with a wack-a-doodle."

He laughed, which was rather amazing after how embarrassed he'd just felt. "Wack-a-doodle, huh?"

"You have a better description?" She pulled the bottom of her dress up her thighs, then swung her leg over his legs and straddled him.

"Nothing even close to that." He stared into eyes that he wanted to look into for the rest of his life. "Hey, you."

She smiled as she stared back at him. "Hey. Here's the plan. For tonight, I'm in charge, and I'm going to make you forget all about wack-a-doodle. You good with that?"

"As Everly would say, I couldn't be more gooder." He reached for the remote and dimmed the lights.

"Such a way with words," she said, then kissed him. "Now hush."

Chapter Twenty-Eight

Willow was going to make her guy forget all about that woman. She kept her eyes locked on Parker's as she unbuttoned his shirt. When he tried to help her, she brushed his hands away. "What part of 'I'm in charge' do you not understand?"

"My bad."

Oh, that sexy grin of his. Made a girl all hot and bothered. "Off," she said after the last button was undone. She leaned away so he could remove his shirt. Her gaze roamed over his chest. The view was spectacular, and she licked her lips as she considered where her mouth should go first.

"Here." She nipped at the skin below his ear, then sucked his earlobe between her teeth, smiling to herself when a shiver traveled through him.

She then moved to his chest, and when she swirled her tongue around his nipple, he groaned. When he lifted his hands to her hips, she pushed them away again. "Your job is just to sit there and enjoy."

"Trust me, I'm enjoying."

While she explored his chest with her tongue, she slid her hands down his stomach to his belt, and when that was unbuckled, she lowered the zipper on his pants.

His boxer briefs were tented, and she slipped her hand inside and wrapped her fingers around his erection. "You feel like velvet."

"What I feel like is a cannon that's about to go boom."

"You're just saying that. I've barely touched you." She squeezed her hand and laughed when he growled. "You sound like a grouchy cat."

"A grouchy cat that's going to bite you if you stop doing that."

His eyes were hooded and almost black and staring at her as if nothing mattered more to him than her. She admonished herself for wishing that was true. She couldn't think there was anything in that look on his face than that he was a man who was into her in the moment. She didn't want anything more than that from him, so all was good.

Liar.

Was she lying to herself? Maybe. Probably. But this was what it was. A moment in time with the best man—in so many ways—that she'd ever known and would likely ever know. She wanted to make sure he never forgot her, and to get to what she wanted to do, she tugged on the waist of his pants. "Up." When he lifted, she pulled his pants and briefs down, and when they reached his knees, he kicked them the rest of the way down and off.

"I need your dress gone, Willow."

"All in good time. First, I have to do this." She dropped her knees to the floor, lowered her mouth, and wrapped her lips around him. He whispered her name, sounding as if he treasured her, and when he dug his fingers into her hair, she didn't brush them away. His taste, his scent, the sounds coming from low in his throat sent heat spiraling through her.

"Enough," he growled, then pulled her up. "I'm taking over."

A minute later, he had her out of her dress and her panties off. "Like magic," she said. "One second I have clothes on and in the blink of an eye, I don't."

"Is that a complaint?" He pulled her over him so that she was straddling him again.

"No, sir, not from me."

He reached over to the side table, picked up a condom, opened it, then handed it to her. "Put it on me."

This bossy side of him was new, and she liked it. Heat turned his eyes dark as he watched her put the condom on. When it was rolled on him, she put her hands on his shoulders, then lowered herself down on him. She'd always liked sex, but sex with Parker was beyond anything she'd ever experienced. The way he filled her, the intimacy of it, his eyes locked on hers… it was intense.

He put his hand behind her head and pulled her to him, then as they kissed, he tangled one hand in her hair while his other one cupped her breast. If this was the last time she'd be with him, she didn't want it to end. Something felt different between them tonight, a gentleness mixed with sadness, as if they both knew their time was up.

"I don't want the night to be over." He flipped her so that she was under him. As he supported himself on his elbows, he brushed his thumbs over her cheeks and stared down at her. "Beautiful girl."

Beautiful boy. She memorized the way his eyes turned soft as he looked at her. Those soft eyes said that he had feelings for her, as she did for him. Maybe more than either of them expected, but he wasn't wanting a forever, and her dream—a home on the beach—was in her future. But for tonight, he was hers.

Two days later, Willow was in the garage, sorting through the junk her uncle had crammed in it, most of it going in the construction crew's trash bin, when a car turned into her driveway, a yellow convertible Beetle. Obviously, she was hallucinating, and she blinked. Nope, it was still there.

Another car pulled in behind the Volkswagen. A man exited the Beetle, and she walked toward him. "Can I help you?"

"Sure. You can take these." He held out a set of keys.

"I don't understand."

"Well, it's simple. You'll need the keys to drive your new car. All the paperwork's in the glove compartment."

"My new car?"

"Ma'am, all I know is I was given your address and paid to deliver the car to you."

"By who?"

"The dealer in Charlotte." He lifted a chin toward the car behind the Beetle. "My ride back's waiting."

He tossed the keys toward her, and reflexively she caught them, then frowned as the man got in the other car and they drove away. She'd planned to rent a car until her insurance check came and she could replace Sunshine but hadn't gotten around to it yet. How and why was another Sunshine magically sitting in her driveway?

She retrieved the paperwork and frowned again at seeing the car was paid for in cash. There was only one person she could think of who might be behind it, so she texted him.

You know why there's a new car sitting in my driveway?

Parker: Maybe

You can't just buy me a car

Parker: Huh. Good thing I didn't know that

Her phone rang, Parker's name on the screen. "Parker Church, you can't buy me a car."

"Too late. I already did. Besides, it's used, not new, since they stopped making Beetles a few years ago. I was lucky to find one in great shape with low mileage and…yellow."

"You said *yellow* like you had a bad taste in your mouth."

"No comment."

"Yellow's a great color, but seriously, you can't give me a car."

He sighed. "Accept it so I'll feel better. It's my fault yours was burned up."

"You're not the one who poured gasoline on it and lit a match to it. Look, I appreciate the gesture. It was a really sweet thing to do, and I'm not going to return it to the dealer since I need a car, but when I get the insurance check for Sunshine, I'll pay you back."

"Why can't I give you a gift?"

"An acceptable gift would be flowers or a box of cookies from Sweet Tooth, not a freaking car!"

"Fine."

And in that "fine" she heard his message…he had no intention of letting her pay him back. Well, they'd just see about that.

Later that night, she was sitting up in bed, her laptop resting on her legs, but not getting much writing done. She blamed Parker for that. She missed him, missed sitting on his daybed and writing while he painted. Missed the way he'd lean his head around the side of his easel and give her heated looks.

In spite of her declared Man Hiatus, she was falling for one. It wasn't what she wanted. She had a plan, and it didn't include falling in love, especially with a man who claimed to fall in love at the drop of a hat. Even if he said he was falling in love with her, too, how could she trust he really was? She should probably consider leaving sooner than she'd planned.

Her phone chimed with a text.

Parker: Come to the studio

Not sure that's a good idea

Parker: It's a great idea. Please

She should refuse, but she couldn't resist being with him again. It would be for the last time. Okay.

Parker: *heart emoji*

She'd put on a camisole and boy shorts after her shower, and she debated changing. "Nah." Whatever she wore wasn't going to stay on long, so why bother changing? She slipped her feet into flip-flops, grabbed her laptop, and went to him.

Parker was waiting at the door for her, and as soon as she stepped inside, he pulled her to him and kissed her. "I missed you," he said when he let her go.

What happened to *they couldn't be together*? But she missed him, too, so she didn't ask. "Are you painting?"

"I am."

"Good. Go paint while I write." When she reached the daybed, she stopped and stared at the vase of wild-flowers and the box of cookies from Sweet Tooth. She laughed, then looked over her shoulder at him to see he was watching her. "How about I keep the flowers and cookies, and you keep the car."

He smiled as he shook his head. "Nope, everything is all yours. Now go write so I can get this done."

"Stubborn man," she muttered.

"I heard that."

"Just speaking the truth." He disappeared behind his easel, and she settled down to write. A little later, she felt eyes on her and glanced up. Parker was peeking around the canvas, and he winked, then disappeared from view. She was going to miss these nights with him when she left.

Willow dreaded the talk that was about to happen. She'd left Parker at dawn to come home and sleep for a few hours. Even though she'd been up most of the night and her body ached in all the right places for the best of reasons, sleep eluded her, so she gave up and went down to her new kitchen to bake some cookies.

Parker was bringing Everly over after lunch so they could tell her that Willow would be selling the house and moving away. That was probably going to happen sooner than she'd thought. Buddy and his crew were ahead of schedule, and the first draft on her book was done, also ahead of schedule, and she'd started the next one. She'd probably be able to put the house up for sale in a few weeks.

She slid the tray of cookies into the oven, then she leaned back against the counter and took in her beautiful new kitchen. It wasn't on a level with Parker's, but she was happy with how it had turned out. She loved the glass doors on the cabinets, the gray-and-white swirled granite, stainless steel appliances, light gray farm sink, and wood floors. If she was keeping the house, she'd have added more color, but she wasn't, so no use thinking about it.

The downstairs remodel was finished, as was the upstairs except for her bedroom and bath. The crew would start on that tomorrow, so after Parker and Everly left, she'd move to the bedroom down here.

Her phone chimed with a text. We're headed over.

She wanted to text Parker back and tell him not to. If he didn't bring Everly over, she wouldn't have to break her favorite little girl's heart, because that was what she was about to do. She left her phone on the counter and walked out to her porch to wait for them.

"Miss Willow!" Everly ran up to her, and Willow lifted her up. "Miss Willow, I thought of another idea for a story you can tell me, and I can illustrate."

Willow met Parker's eyes over Everly's shoulder, and she wanted to park her butt on the ground and cry. How was she supposed to leave these two? His forced smile, and the sadness that dimmed his eyes hurt her heart.

"A new story?" She slipped her arm under Everly's

bottom and carried her into the house. "I can't wait to hear it. But first, I have cookies in the oven that should almost be done." She'd made her favorite oatmeal chocolate cherry cookies.

"Oh, goody! Cookies!"

Willow thought she should probably have a hearing test done. She buried her nose against Everly's neck, breathing in her little girl scent. Heaven help her, she loved this child, and she loved Everly's father, but that was her secret.

"Kitchen turned out really nice," Parker said after following them in.

"I'm happy with it." She set Everly on the island counter, then made the mistake of glancing at him. His eyes were on her, burning as hot as they had last night, and she smiled. What she really wanted to do was to walk right into his arms. She tore her gaze away from his and tapped Everly's nose. "Sit here while I get the cookies out of the oven, then you can help me put them on a plate."

When she turned back around with the cookie pan, father and daughter were sitting side by side on the counter. The sight of them making themselves at home in her kitchen sent a longing through her the likes of which she'd never felt before. It was so startling that she almost dropped the pan.

"Um…" She had no idea what she meant to say. Parker tilted his head and raised his brows. Then, as if he understood that she'd just had a moment, he gave her one of his soft smiles. Somehow, she managed to return it. "These need to cool off for a few minutes." Should they tell Everly now or after they had cookies?

"Are those the ones with the cherries in them, Miss Willow?"

"They are."

"Oh, goody!" She clapped her hands. "Those are my favorite."

"Now?" Willow mouthed to Parker, and he nodded. They'd talked about how to tell Everly, and she'd said it should be her. Parker had accepted that but said he should be here when she talked to Everly, and she agreed.

"Before we have our cookies, I need to talk to you about something, Everly."

"Is it about our new story, 'cause I have so many ideas."

"No, it's not about that." She stepped in front of the little girl she'd grown to love. She'd had a little speech ready that had sounded good in her head, but no matter how she said she was leaving, Everly wasn't going to understand. "I need to tell you that you're going to see a For Sale sign in my yard soon, and—"

"Are you selling your house 'cause you're moving in with me and my daddy?"

Willow hated seeing that big smile on Everly's face because with her next words, that smile was going to disappear. "No, sweetie, when the house sells, I'll be moving away."

"Away where?"

"I'm not sure yet, but it won't be in Marsville."

"No, Miss Willow, you can't move away. You're supposed to marry my daddy and be my mommy. That's what I want."

"Oh, sweetie…" She glanced at Parker. How long had Everly been thinking that would happen? What was she supposed to say?

He picked up Everly and set her on his lap. "Sometimes we don't get what we want, Ev. Miss Willow only planned to be in this house until it was remodeled, and she could put it up for sale, and it's about time for her to do that."

"No! That's not a good plan. Who's gonna write stories for me to illustrate?" She looked at Willow. "Please, Miss Willow, you can't move away. I won't let you."

Everly's lips were trembling, and tears were welling in her eyes, and it was breaking Willow's heart. "We can FaceTime and do stories and illustrations." She glanced at Parker. Would he be okay with that?

"No! I hate you. I was happy, and you made me not happy."

"Everly Isabella Church, we do not tell people we hate them. Apologize to Miss Willow."

"No." She pushed against Parker's chest. "Put me down, Daddy. I want to go home."

He lowered her to the floor. "Wait for me by the door."

"I feel so awful, and she hates me now," Willow said as she watched Everly run through the living room.

"She'll get over it. I'll talk to her, make her understand. After she's asleep, I'll come over, and we can talk."

What was there to talk about? "Maybe it's for the best this way. A clean break before she and I get even more involved." That was true for Everly's father, too. "And you said it was better if we weren't seen spending time together."

He stepped in front of her and put his hand on her arm. "What are you saying?"

"That it's been fun, but our time is up." Her bottom

lip trembled, and she sucked it between her teeth. She would not cry, not in front of him, anyway.

"Willow," he whispered.

She put her finger over his mouth. "No, don't say anything. Just go." Before she did cry in front of him.

He leaned his forehead against hers. "I'll never forget you." And then he left.

When she heard the door close behind him, her knees gave out, she sank to the floor, and the tears came. She'd fallen in love with him. So much for her vacation from men. Should she have told him she loved him? Would he ask her to stay if he knew?

She might have offered him her heart—the one that hurt so hard right now—if he'd asked her to stay. He hadn't, so tomorrow she'd call a Realtor. The house was close enough to being finished to put it up for sale. Really, there was no reason to stay any longer. Buddy knew what needed to be done and didn't need her here, and a Realtor didn't need her here to sell the house.

It was time to go.

Chapter Twenty-Nine

Parker held his daughter until she cried herself to sleep. He'd tried to explain to her that Willow had never planned to stay, but that she'd always be Ev's friend. Everly wasn't buying it. It was all or nothing with his little girl.

Would Willow stay if he asked her to? He'd wanted to, but his history of thinking he was in love when he really wasn't had waved red flags. He might have if she hadn't put her finger on his lips and told him to go.

He thought he loved her—or was getting there—but he'd thought that about other girls and women too many times. Willow had a dream, and he couldn't ask her to give that up if he wasn't sure if his feelings for her were real.

But if they weren't real, then why did his heart hurt worse than it ever had before, even after Simone's betrayal?

"Keep her safe," he told Ember as he eased his arm from under his little ladybug. He kissed her cheek, then slipped out of her room and went straight to his studio.

They needed to find Crystal/Cassandra. The woman was like a ghost. Other than the day she'd appeared at Fanny's, no one else shown his drawings of her had seen her. Tristan had even sent his officers to different businesses to review their security videos to see if she showed up, and she hadn't. Not even at the grocery store. Where was she eating or getting her food? Where was she staying?

Skylar had talked to Fanny, and the woman calling herself Cassandra hadn't bought the sweater, so there was no credit card on file. Chase Talon had traced the knife they found pinned to the tree to a store in Atlanta. The knife was one of a kind, made by a local who sold his knives to the store. The store owner remembered the knife as one that had been purchased from his store some ten or so years earlier. He'd agreed to search back through his files to see if he could find a record of the purchase.

Bottom line, other than finally knowing what their arsonist looked like, and maybe a first name, they had nothing. Not for lack of trying. Every police officer and sheriff's deputy were searching the motels, vacation cabins, and campsites in the county. So far, no sign of her. Parker had notified the state fire investigator that Marsville had an arsonist, and Tristan had run Parker's sketch through a facial recognition database but hadn't found a match. That told them she'd never been arrested. As soon as they had a last name for her, Nick Talon would do his thing and see if she'd been registered at the hotel during the conference. Kade had gone to the Atlanta hotel with the sketch of her, but neither the bartenders nor other staff recognized her.

It was frustrating and worrisome. Where would she strike next? He'd been keeping an eye on the town's Facebook page, but no one had posted that they'd be out of town. Because the last target had been Willow and her car, Parker feared she was closing in on people close to him. His brothers agreed. What was her end-game? That was the question.

He didn't have answers, so for tonight he shoved his worry to the back of his mind and painted. A few hours later, he stepped away from his easel and frowned at the abstract painting. Abstract wasn't his thing, and he'd never attempted it before, but he recognized his confusion and anger in the dark colors slashed on the canvas. The anger was with himself for not knowing his own mind, for his past behavior and the one-night stand that was now threatening Willow.

He walked to the window and looked up at hers. The light was still on in her bedroom. Was he making the biggest mistake of his life by letting her go without telling her he thought he was falling in love with her? He wanted to go to her, but he had his little girl to think of, and she had to come first. Everly was already hurt, and it would only confuse her if he started seeing Willow again while she was still here and then she left.

After Simone, he'd decided he was done with wanting to be in love. What did that even mean? For him, it had meant nothing more than getting it wrong over and over. It had meant a lot of hurt. You'd think he'd learn. Willow wasn't Simone or any of the others he'd loved. He knew that. It was himself that he didn't trust to know his own damn heart. Was he still that little boy who needed—yearned for—someone to love him?

The light went out in Willow's bedroom window, and with a heavy heart, he turned away. He took the finished canvas to the fireproof room, set it on an easel to dry, and deciding he wasn't in the mood to paint more angry slashes tonight, he headed to bed.

Before he could crawl between the sheets, his phone chimed an alert. "Marsville Fire Department. Respond to a fire at 28 Main Street. Repeat. Fire at 28 Main Street."

Fanny's! Kade, Harper, and Duke were in Charlotte, but Parker only had to wait a few minutes for Andrew to arrive. "Lock the door behind me, set the alarm, and don't answer for anyone while I'm gone," he told Andrew.

"Okay, I won't."

He put his hand on Andrew's shoulder. "I mean it. I don't care who it is or what they say, don't open the door." Assured that Everly was in good hands, he and Ember jumped in the SUV and with lights lit and the siren blaring, he raced to Fanny's.

The firehouse was only two streets over from Fanny's, so his firefighters and engines were already there when he arrived, as were Tristan and Skylar, since their loft was on Main Street, close to Fanny's shop.

He rolled down the windows for Ember, then headed for his brother and Skylar. "Just the dumpster?" he asked as he surveyed the scene. The contents of the dumpster were still smoldering, but there were scorch marks up the back of Fanny's building from the fire. The back door had black soot on it, too. He made a mental note to send his crew out to businesses and order any who had dumpsters backed up to their building to move them away.

"Yeah," Tristan said. "Fortunately, one of my officers out on patrol saw smoke coming up behind Fanny's. If he hadn't seen the smoke, it could have been worse."

"I'll bring Ember in when it's cooled down, but we know the fire's intentional. We need to find this woman before someone gets hurt."

Skylar glanced from Tristan to him. "I keep asking myself what she plans and what she wants."

He nodded. "That's the question, isn't it?"

"Whatever it is, it involves you, brother," Tristan said.

That was obvious by now, and he hated that he'd brought trouble to his town.

Chapter Thirty

"Wake up, honey."

Everly tried to push away the fingers digging into her arm. It wasn't her daddy's fingers. He wouldn't hurt her like that. The hand didn't go away no matter how hard she pushed.

"Up with you," a woman said, pulling her out of bed.

"Who are you?" It was too dark to see, but she thought she'd heard that voice before. She couldn't remember where. "Where's my daddy?"

"Your daddy told me to come get you. He's hurt, and he needs you."

"Daddy's hurt?" How? Her daddy was a strong man. No one could hurt him. "I want my daddy."

"I'm going to take you to him, honey. But first, I need you to drink this."

A glass was pushed into her hand. "What is it?"

"Milk."

"I don't like milk."

"Your daddy said you need to drink it if you want to see him."

Everly wished it wasn't too dark to see the woman's face. But she wanted to see her daddy, so she drank the milk. It was hard because she really didn't like milk.

The woman took the glass from her, then picked her up and carried her out of her room.

Something didn't feel right, and she tried to get down. "I don't know you. I can't talk to you." Her tongue felt like it was bigger than it was supposed to be.

"We have to go," the woman said. She took Everly to a window. "See, your father's studio is on fire. We have to leave now."

Was her daddy in there? "Daddy!" she screamed. She tried to get down, but she was so sleepy.

"Stop it," the woman said, sounding mean.

Everly didn't like this woman, and she had to save her daddy. "Let me go!" She bit the woman on the face when the woman's arms tightened around her.

"Damn it! You little bitch. When you're my daughter, you'll learn to behave."

"I want my daddy." She tried to fight harder, and she tried to stay awake, but her arms were so heavy, and her eyes so sleepy.

"That's right, go to sleep, my precious little girl. Mommy's going to take care of you."

I don't have a mommy, Everly thought as sleep took her.

Unable to fall asleep, Willow went to the kitchen to make a cup of tea. Since she was up, she grabbed her laptop and started on a list of things she needed to do. First was to decide where to go and then find a short-term rental. Would she prefer the Atlantic Ocean or the Gulf? Before she decided to buy, she'd spend some time in a few beach locations in both North Carolina and the Florida Panhandle. She was really lucky in that she could work from anywhere.

As she made her list, she tried not to think of Parker, but her mind apparently had a mind of its own. She thought a few words about Simone that should get her mouth washed out with soap. If not for that woman, Parker might be open to seeing where things could go between them. She got why he was gun-shy, and she especially got that Everly had to come first. She respected him for that last one, but damn it, she'd be a great mother to Everly.

She was going to miss them both, and she was afraid that this ache in her chest wasn't going away anytime soon. All the more reason to leave now and start working on getting over the man and his daughter.

The doorbell rang, and then someone pounded on the door. It was past midnight, and no one should be banging on her door. Was it Parker? Was something wrong? She ran to the door and put her eye to the peephole. What she saw sent her heart to her stomach.

The woman every law enforcement officer in Marsville was looking for stood on her porch holding Everly as if she was no more valuable than a sack of potatoes. Willow so did not want to open the door, but how could she not? This couldn't be good. She bowed her head, took a deep breath as she called up all the courage and bravery that she hoped was inside her, and pulled the door open.

She should have called the police before opening the door, she realized too late, but seeing Everly slung over the dangerous woman's shoulder like a limp rag doll had caused her to act without thinking. Plus, her phone was upstairs in her bedroom, and she wouldn't have taken the time to go get it anyway. Not with Everly being held by a deranged woman.

"Give her to me," Willow demanded, because the best thing was not to let this woman—Cassandra? Crystal?—know she was terrified out of her mind. For herself, yes, but she didn't count, not when a woman who wasn't in her right mind had Everly. Parker's little girl was all that mattered.

The woman lifted Everly from her shoulder and held her out. "She's all yours." After dumping Everly in Willow's arms, she pushed her way inside. The strong smell of gasoline assaulted Willow's nose.

"Get out," Willow said as soon as Everly was safe in her arms. How was Everly sleeping through this?

Cassandra/Crystal laughed. "You're not calling the shots here." She reached behind her, and when her hand appeared again, a gun was in it. "Here's how this is going to work. You're going to write a letter admitting that you've been setting fires."

Willow scowled. "I'm not doing any such thing." Keeping her eyes on the gun, she backed up to the sofa. "I'm going to put her down here." She was banking on the out of sight, out of mind theory, making Everly safer.

"Whatever." The woman waved the gun around. "Then write the damn confession."

The way she was handling the gun made Willow nervous. It could easily go off, being handled like that. After lowering Everly to the cushion, she frowned. Everly wasn't just asleep, she was out cold. Her breathing seemed okay, but Willow wasn't a nurse or doctor. "What did you do to her?"

"Just a little something to make her sleep."

"I'm taking her to a doctor." Willow slid her arms under Everly, then screeched when a gunshot filled the air. She spun. "Are you crazy?"

The woman shrugged. "Not any crazier than most people." She pointed the gun at Everly. "Unless you want me to shoot her, write the damn letter."

"No one will believe it." She moved so that she blocked Everly from the woman.

"Why not? You're new in town, the fires started around the time you arrived. You even burned up your own car to shift suspicion away from you. Clever that." She nodded to herself. "That's good actually. Put that in the letter."

"What's your name?" The blonde, blue-eyed woman was beautiful, but the unholy light in her eyes sent chills up Willow's spine.

"Doesn't matter. We're not going to get chummy."

"Fine, I'll just call you Bitch."

Her face turned red. "You do, and I'll shoot you. You already know it's Cassandra, so stop playing games."

"Well, you said it was Cassandra at Fanny's shop, except I think I'll call you Crystal." She probably shouldn't be baiting the woman, but it was satisfying to see the surprise on her face. "How do you think this is going to end, Crystal?"

"It's simple, really. You're going to confess to the fires, including Parker's studio, which is burning up right now—"

"What?" She took a step to go look out the back door.

Crystal fired another shot at the ceiling. "You're testing my patience."

"At least let me call and report the fire." Her stomach rolled at knowing all of Parker's art was burning up. He'd worked so hard to get ready for his show.

"Oh, I think he'll know soon enough. His burglar alarm was going off when I left. Write the damn let-

ter. Then when I save Parker's daughter from you and
he learns how evil you are, he'll be so grateful that he
found the perfect mother for his daughter."

Dear God. This woman was delusional, and how did
you reason with someone this messed up? Somehow,
she had to get Everly away and safe. If she was writing
a character like Crystal, how would she save the little
girl in the story?

Chapter Thirty-One

The fire was out, and Ember unsurprisingly alerted after sniffing around the dumpster. "She's playing with us, but I feel like we're missing something," Parker said to Tristan and Skylar. Was it simple revenge for his rejecting her? Maybe, but his gut said there was more to it than that.

His phone rang, Kade's name appearing on the screen. "Hey, I'm a little busy right now. Our arsonist set Fanny's dumpster on fire. Can I call you back?"

"Nick has intel on the woman that you need to hear," Kade said.

"I'm with Tristan and Skylar, so I'm putting you on Speaker."

"This is Nick. Chase is also with me and Kade. The shop owner in Atlanta where the knife was purchased found a name for us, and I was able to track down people who know her. Crystal Erickson, lives in Atlanta, twenty-seven years old. She has a backstory I wouldn't wish on anyone. Not that I'm excusing what she's doing, but it explains the person she is today."

"We're listening," Parker said.

"Twelve years ago, her father was the fire chief at a station in Atlanta. For three years during his time in that position, there was an active arsonist that no one could get a bead on. The last fire he set was at an abandoned building. Unfortunately, a homeless family—parents and three children—were living in it, and all died in the fire. And unfortunately for the arsonist, a cop making rounds saw a man leaving the scene. He wasn't able to catch him, but he was able to give a description. It was Matthew Erickson, the fire chief."

"Whoa," Parker said.

"Yeah, it was a shock to everyone because he was well respected. He was brought in for questioning, and he lawyered up. The detectives and arson investigator were able to link him to three of the eighteen fires he was suspected of setting. An arrest warrant was issued, but before they could pick him up, he set fire to his own house, stayed inside with his wife, and they both died. They don't know if the wife stayed with him willingly or was forced to."

"That's one hell of a story," Tristan said.

Parker nodded. "What about the daughter? She wasn't there?"

"No, when the detectives talked to her after, she said that her father had taken her to her grandparents to spend the night. I talked to the lead detective on the case back then, and he said the daughter was inconsolable, that she was more torn up over losing her father than her mother. From the things she told him, she and her mother didn't get along, but her father was everything to her."

"Was she their only child?" Skylar asked.

"Yes, and after losing her parents she lived with her maternal grandparents. I called them, told them that I was doing a background check on Crystal for a job. The grandfather answered, and all he'd say was that she was a sweet girl. A few hours later, the grandmother called me back. Said she had to wait until her husband wasn't around. She wanted to know if I knew where Crystal was. I asked her some simple questions and eased her into telling me about her granddaughter. She made excuses for Crystal, blamed the girl's father, who she never liked, for Crystal, and I'm quoting here, 'not being right in the head.' She said she was afraid of the girl because Crystal was fascinated by fires. Blamed that on the father, too. She also said that Crystal has a thing for firefighters, but her relationships never ended well. She'd even had two restraining orders against her."

"Good God," Parker muttered. He'd never have another hookup. Ever. Crystal was beautiful and had seemed normal and fun when he'd met her in the hotel's bar. "Remind me not to ever let you interrogate me." It was impressive how much Nick had learned.

"My brother has skills that terrify me," Chase said. "He's not allowed anywhere near me and my mind."

Before Parker could comment on that, his phone and Tristan's beeped with an incoming call. "Anything else?"

"Crystal's been missing for a few weeks, and her grandmother's worried about her," Nick said.

"Well, we know where she is, and she should be worried," Parker said. "I can't tell you how much I appreciate what you've learned."

Tristan snatched his phone away. "We gotta go. Our burglar alarm's going off at home."

"Call me back," Kade said.

Not thirty seconds later, his, Tristan's, and Skylar's phones chimed an alert. "Marsville Fire Department, respond to a structure fire at 612 Dogwood Lane. Repeat. Structure fire at 612 Dogwood Lane."

"Shit," Tristan snarled as the three of them raced to their cars.

Their house was on fire! Parker was the first out as Tristan and Skylar had to run down the block to their SUV. He glanced in his rearview mirror to see his two engines pull out behind him. "Call home," he told his Bluetooth. The phone rang and rang. He tried Willow next, and it was the same.

By the time he reached home, his heart was banging against his chest from worrying about Everly. Was she okay? Why wasn't anyone answering their phone? Why had the burglar alarm gone off, and who had reported a fire?

It was a relief not to see his house on fire as he raced down his street, but that was short-lived. When he turned into his driveway, he saw the flames shooting up behind the house. His studio was on fire. He backed out of his driveway so the engines could get as close as possible to the studio. Where was Everly? Andrew?

He ran inside the house, and Ember raced in with him. "Everly! Andrew!" No answer. Maybe they were asleep. Tristan and Skylar followed him in. "I'm going to check Ev's bed. See if you can find Andrew."

She wasn't in her bed. The window was open, the screen on the floor. He leaned out it, and he thought his heart was going to explode at seeing one of the chairs from the deck table under the window. He only took a moment to watch his firefighters drag hoses through the backyard. His studio burning down didn't matter, not when his daughter was missing. "Tristan!" He ran out of the room, searching for his brother. "Tristan!"

"In the library."

"Send out an Amber Alert. Now! She took Everly." Oh, God. His baby was gone.

"Are you sure she's not in the house?" Skylar said as he ran past her.

"She's gone. We have to find her." He came to an abrupt stop in the library at seeing Andrew tied to a chair.

"Talk to us," Tristan said as he cut the plastic ties.

"I'm sorry." Tears ran down Andrew's face. "She had a gun, and I didn't know what to do."

A gun? The woman who took his daughter, his reason for breathing, had a gun? "I... I..." He bent over, put his hands on his knees, and tried to suck air back into his lungs.

Skylar put her hand on the back of his neck. "Breathe, Parker. You have to get it together or you're no good to Everly. We'll find her." She gave him a gentle squeeze, then left.

Right. She was right. He had to get it together and find his baby. He needed to be like Kade—fucking invincible, take-no-prisoners Kade. A warrior who refused to fail. That was who he had to be, so that was who he was. He stood, drew that air he needed into his lungs, and forced himself to focus.

Tristan had cut the ties from Andrew's wrists and ankles, and he kneeled in front of Andrew. He put his hand on Andrew's knee. "There was nothing you could do against someone who had a gun but comply. Tell us what happened from the beginning."

Skylar returned with a glass of water, which she handed to Andrew. The young man drank half of it, then with tears still rolling down his cheeks, told his story. "I don't know where the woman came from."

"Everly's window," Parker said. They didn't have alarms on the windows because when the weather was nice, they'd leave them open overnight. That was going to change. "What happened when you saw her?"

"Tomorrow's laundry day, and since I was here tonight, I decided to get a head start. She came behind me when I was putting clothes in the washing machine. I'm sorry." He swiped at the tears rolling down his cheeks.

"Hey, hey, you have nothing to be sorry for," Parker said, shocked that he wasn't bringing the house down around their heads in a rage that knew no bounds, but he was channeling Kade, who was deceptively calm even when chaos was raining down on him. "Did the woman say anything, give you a message to tell us, maybe tell you where she was going?"

Andrew shook his head. "No. After she tied me up, she walked out the front door with Everly. That's when the burglar alarm went off when she opened the door. I'm so sorry. I was supposed to take care of Everly, and I didn't."

"You said she had a gun. There was nothing you could have done, Andrew." Skylar put her hand on his shoulder while Tristan called his dispatcher, telling her to activate an Amber Alert.

Ember ran into the room, her nose sniffing the floor. She stopped in front of Andrew and alerted. That would make sense if Crystal had gasoline on her hands, then had touched him. Because she expected it, Parker pulled a treat out of his pocket and gave it to her.

He paced a few steps, then back. "We need to split up and—"

Ember trotted out of the library with her nose to the floor again. Parker followed her, hoping that she'd find some clue that would help him locate his little girl. Ember's nose took her to the front door. She stopped, looked up at him, and whined. He opened the door, and she walked out. Was she on Crystal's scent? He wished Duke was here. That dog could find anyone anywhere, but Duke was in Charlotte with Kade and Harper. As long as Crystal had gasoline on her, maybe his dog could find the woman.

"Is she on the scent?" Tristan asked, jogging up next to him.

"Hope to hell she is." Ember was crossing the yard toward Willow's house, and understanding what that meant, Parker wanted to rage at the universe. A woman with Crystal's background and a gun had the two girls he loved? He came to a dead stop. "I love her."

Tristan stopped next to him. "Of course you do. She's your daughter."

"No, I mean I love both of them."

His brother smiled. "That's not news. Everly's a given. As for Willow, everyone could see it in your eyes and the way you looked at her. Come on, let's find your girls. Skylar's with Andrew and coordinating the search with our people."

"Tell me we'll find both of them safe," he said, desperation in his voice.

"Yes, we're going to find them and bring them home."

That was all he cared about, and Tristan had never let him down, so he'd believe his brother. He glanced over his shoulder and no longer saw flames shooting over the roof of his studio. It was probably a total loss, but he didn't care.

Chapter Thirty-Two

Willow heard the sirens, heard the sound of big engines that had to be the fire department trucks. That meant that Parker was there, too. How long would it take him to realize that Everly was missing? Would he think to look for her here?

Crystal was pacing, talking to herself, and waving the gun around as if she'd forgotten she held a lethal weapon in her hand. That wasn't good, and it terrified her that Everly still hadn't woken up. She needed a doctor, and Willow decided she couldn't wait in the hopes that someone would come save them.

In the story running through her mind, the heroine accidently on purpose trips the evil witch, wrestles for the gun, gets it away, and holds the evil villainess at gunpoint until the police arrive. Could she do it without getting herself killed?

She had to time it just right. She studied Crystal's movements, and how she held the gun. Every few steps, Crystal would lower the gun to her side for a few seconds before waving it around again. That was when she needed to act. In the way athletes visualized their next move, Willow did the same, seeing in her mind how it would go down…how she prayed it would.

She stood and took a step toward Crystal when she paced away. Suddenly, Crystal changed her routine of six steps one way, then back. She'd only taken two steps when she spun and Willow froze.

"I thought I wanted to keep Parker's kid. You know, daddy, mommy, and their perfect daughter, one big happy family. But I don't like her. She bit me."

Good for Everly, but where was Crystal going with this? "I'll take her. That way, you'll have Parker all to yourself."

"That won't work. Parker won't give her away. You're going to have to kill her. That's the only way he'll forget about her."

You're out of your freaking mind, lady. And that was what scared Willow the most, how mentally unbalanced this woman was. "I'm not going to kill her. No way."

Crystal waved the gun in the air. "Oh, I know you won't, Miss Goody Two-Shoes, so I'm going to do it for you. Parker will be devastated that you killed his little girl, and I'll be here to comfort him."

"No one will believe you." Her sneak attack plan wasn't going to work. It was going to have to be an all-out frontal assault. It was going to be a risk, and she'd probably get shot, but she had no choice.

"I'm very convincing."

Crystal smiled, and it was a smile that sent fear all the way down to Willow's toes. She couldn't be serious that she'd actually kill an innocent little girl, could she? But that smile gave Willow chills, and as she looked into those eyes that had seemed so pretty at first and now showed no compassion or mercy, what she saw were dead eyes and a woman who could and would kill a child.

"You don't have to do this, Crystal. Parker would hate you for it."

"No, he's going to hate you." She took a few steps toward Everly, lifted the gun, glanced at Willow, and smiled that spine-chilling smile again.

Willow dived for the gun and managed to get her hands around the barrel. They fell to the floor with Willow on top of Crystal. Crystal was surprisingly strong and squirmy. It was like wrestling an octopus. Hoping to gain an advantage, Willow fisted her hand and hit Crystal in her jaw as hard as she could.

The gun went off, and a pain the likes of which Willow had never felt before burned its way through her chest. The gun fell next to them. She rolled off Crystal and managed to push the gun under the sofa. "Crap, that hurt," she muttered. She tried to get up, but her legs refused to cooperate, and she fell back against the sofa.

"You bitch!" Crystal screamed as she pushed up from the floor. "You're going to be sorry because now I'm going to make you suffer."

Willow's vision was growing blurry as she watched Crystal walk to a pile of rags and debris the construction crew had left on the floor. Willow closed her eyes… but as much as she wanted to slip into that peaceful sleep, she couldn't let the darkness take her. She had to save Everly. When she forced her eyes open, it was to see Crystal with a lighter in her hand, and Willow was powerless to stop her from setting the rags on fire.

Tears pooled in her eyes. She'd failed to save Everly.

No! She couldn't fail. Wouldn't. Parker would not lose his precious girl. She closed her eyes again, gathered all the strength she could muster, and willed herself to ignore the pain and burning in her chest. When she opened her eyes, she gasped. The flames—a hungry monster—were shooting up the wall, devouring the decades-old dried-up wallpaper. Unstoppable now.

Crystal stood near the door, watching the fire as if it were the most fascinating thing she'd ever seen. Willow reached under the sofa and wrapped her fingers around the gun. She was going to die today, but Everly was not.

She held the gun up with both her hands and put her finger over the trigger, then pointed it at Crystal. "Take Everly out of here, or I'll shoot you."

Crystal laughed. "The way your arms are shaking, you couldn't hit the side of a barn."

Probably true, but she'd damn well try. "Please, take her out. Parker will love you for saving his daughter." The darkness was closing in, and she had to get Everly out while she still could.

"I don't think so. He'll love me for trying to save his daughter, but with her gone, I won't have to share him with that little brat."

Crystal wasn't going to take Everly with her, and when she took a step toward the door, Willow pulled the trigger. She missed. Crystal was gone, and she'd failed.

"I'm sorry, Parker," she whispered. She gathered the little bit of strength she had left and pulled herself up on the sofa. She gasped for breath from the effort. God, her chest hurt. "Everly, sweetie, please wake up." She pinched Everly's arm, hoping the pain would wake up the little girl. Everly didn't move.

"Okay. Okay, you can do this, Willow." She pulled Everly to the floor with the intention of dragging her out of the house. The black was consuming her, and she'd only made it halfway to the door. She wasn't going to be able to get Everly out. The only thing she could think to do before the darkness took her was cover Everly in the hope that her body would shield Everly from the fire until Parker found them. She wouldn't be alive to see that happen, but hopefully somehow, in the afterlife, she'd know she'd done her job. Maybe it was what she was put on this earth to do.

The last thing she saw was the flames spreading across the floor toward her and Everly.

God, if you're listening, please save this precious little girl.

And then the blackness took her.

Chapter Thirty-Three

"That was a gunshot," Parker said. He and Tristan raced across Willow's yard.

Crystal ran out the door and jumped right into his arms. "Oh, my God, Parker. She shot me." She held out her arm. A trickle of blood dripped down from where a bullet had grazed her, barely breaking the skin.

"Where are they?" He pried her off him. "Where's my daughter and Willow?"

"I'm so sorry. I tried to save our daughter, but she… that woman…" Crystal took a shuddering breath. "I tried, Parker. I really did."

Our daughter? He stamped down the rage boiling up inside him. If he let go, he'd physically hurt a woman for the first time in his life. Ember growled, something she'd never done before, and he glanced down. Ember was in alert position, her eyes slitted and teeth bared as she stared at Crystal. He had to find Everly and Willow, and he pushed Crystal at Tristan. "Get her out of my sight."

He headed for the house, refusing to let his mind go there, to what her words implied. He hadn't lost his daughter. He would know it, would have felt it inside if she was gone. He had to believe that. Then, he stumbled as he ran up the porch steps. Smoke!

"Tris, get my men over here. Now!" Ignoring all his training, he raced inside. "Willow? Everly?" He dropped to the floor, where the air would be cleaner, and started crawling. The smoke was too thick to see, and he formed a mental image of the layout of the house. Where were they?

A groan sounded to his left, and he crawled that way. Old houses were the worst when it came to fires, burning way too fast, and the smoke was so thick that he couldn't see an inch in front of his face. Even though he was keeping his face close to the floor and cleaner air, he coughed as the smoke found its way into his lungs. How long had Willow and Everly been breathing in the smoke? Didn't matter how much damage the smoke might do to his lungs. He had to find his girls.

He crawled a few more feet toward where he'd heard a groan, and then his fingers touched an arm too big to be Everly's. "Willow?" he said, then coughed again. She didn't answer. He slid his hand over her back and pulled her to him. Where was Ev? Where was his baby girl?

"Willow, where's Everly?" His only answer was another groan. He needed to get her out of here, but that would delay him from finding Everly somewhere in a fire that was already eating its way through the bottom floor of Willow's house.

How could he leave Willow to go search for his daughter? The woman he was in love with would die if he did. But how could he not go find his baby girl? No. Just fucking no. Neither one was going to die on his watch.

"Willow. Wake up." He put his finger on the pulse of her neck, the relief at feeling blood still flowing through her vein was beyond anything he'd ever felt. She didn't wake up. He pulled her toward him. "I'll come back for you. I'll get you out of here, Willow. I promise." He had to find his daughter. Willow would understand. There was no doubt about that.

He tore off his T-shirt and covered her face with it so that she was at least breathing filtered air. "I love you," he whispered.

When he put his hand on the other side of her to crawl over her, it came down on a tiny arm. "Everly, thank God." He put his finger on her neck and squeezed his eyes shut at the relief she had a pulse. It appeared that Willow had covered Ev's body with hers to protect her from the fire. How could he ever begin to thank her for that?

Now to get them out of here. The smoke was growing thicker, and he coughed into the crook of his arm in an attempt not to inhale more smoke than he could help back into his lungs. If he could get Everly over his shoulder and then get his arm under Willow's, he could drag—

"Breathe, Chief," Greg said, crawling up next to him and pushing his breathing apparatus onto Parker's face.

Parker gulped in the fresh air, then handed the mask back to Greg. He pulled Everly out from under Willow and handed her to Greg. "Go!"

Blessed water rained down on him as his crew directed a hose over their heads. Greg took off with Everly, and Parker turned Willow onto her back, hooked his arms under hers, and dragged her out. When he reached the door, Tristan and Eric were there, and Tristan scooped her up and took her to the stretcher waiting at the bottom of the porch steps.

"Come on, Chief, we gotta get you checked out," Eric said.

"I need…" He had a coughing fit. "I need to check on—"

"They're both being taken care of, and you can see them after you let Josie take a look at you."

Parker wanted to say that he didn't need checking out, but another coughing fit put a lie to that thought. "Everly?" he asked as he walked with Eric to the ambulance.

"On the way to the hospital on bus one. The sheriff went with her."

That was good, both that she was on the way to the hospital and that Skylar had gone with her so Everly wouldn't be alone. He needed to get to the hospital.

Josie stood at the back of bus two, waiting for him. "Sit, Chief."

He glanced inside. Charlie, another of his paramedics, was leaning over Willow as he worked on her. Before he could ask how she was, Josie pointed at the floor of the ambulance. "Sit." He sat, and she slapped an oxygen mask over his face.

"How is she?" He shifted so he could see inside.

"GSW to the chest and smoke inhalation," Charlie said. "We've requested Statesville send their Life Flight. They've confirmed that they'll meet us at the high school's ball field."

Gunshot wound to her chest? That wasn't good, and was why she'd be going to the hospital in Statesville, which had a trauma center. Horace County had a small sixty-bed hospital, and that was where Everly was on the way to.

"Par… Parker?"

He stood at hearing what sounded like the voice of a lifetime smoker. He handed the oxygen mask to Josie and climbed into the bus. "Hey." He placed his hand over hers. Her shirt had been cut open and Charlie had put an occlusive dressing over the wound, which was on her upper right chest, thankfully not anywhere near her heart. He didn't see any visible burns, so that was good, too.

"Sle...sleeping pill."

"You took a sleeping pill?"

"No. Ev."

It took a moment before it clicked. "She gave Everly a sleeping pill?"

"Yes," she said, then her eyes closed.

Son of a bitch.

"We've got to go, Chief. The chopper will be at the school in a few minutes."

He squeezed her hand, then backed out of the ambulance. "Take good care of her," he told Charlie and Josie.

"You know we will," Josie said as she closed the back doors. She jogged to the front, and a minute later, the ambulance left with lights flashing and the siren blaring. As it disappeared from sight, he felt like she was being torn away from him.

He found his brother standing with Greg. "Where is she? Where's Crystal?"

"In the back of my car. One of my officers is on the way over to transport her to the jail."

"I need to talk to her."

Tristan frowned. "Not sure that's a good idea right now. You're too angry."

"Damn right I am. I almost lost Willow and Everly

today because of her. She gave Ev a sleeping pill, and I need to find out what."

"Come with me."

He glanced at the house. It appeared that the fire was under control and almost out. Another reason to be angry with that woman. She'd ruined all Willow's hard work.

"She's probably not going to tell you," Tristan said. "She's a bit irrational right now."

As they approached, an idea came to him. When Tristan opened the back door, Parker kneeled in front of her. "Hey, honey." It grated to call her that, but he needed to find out what was in Everly's system. "Can you tell me what she gave Everly to make her go to sleep?"

She held up her handcuffed hands. "Can you take these off? I don't know why everyone thinks I'm the bad one. I tried to save our little girl from that horrible woman."

"Our little girl" again. Was this woman really that far gone, or was she slyer than a fox? "Take them off her," he told Tristan, who raised his brows but did as he was asked. Parker forced himself to smile at Crystal. "Better?"

"Oh, yes." She leaned out of the car and threw her arms around him. "My hero. I knew you'd save me."

He'd never hated a woman before, but he did this one. He put his hands on her arms and pulled them away from him. "Crystal, what did you see her give Everly? We need to know so we can file charges against her."

"Yes, she needs to pay for what she did. She gave our precious girl half a sleeping pill."

A few more questions, and he had the name of the

pill and the dosage. "Handcuff her and take her to the jail," he told his brother before turning his back on Crystal. She screamed obscenities at him as he walked away. He somehow managed to refrain from giving her his middle finger.

"Everly's fine, Parker," said Jim Blaine, Everly's doctor, as he listened to her heartbeat. "She has minimal smoke damage, and she should wake up anytime now. I want to keep her on oxygen and under observation tonight just to be safe."

"That would make me feel better." He wasn't taking any chances with his baby girl. He'd checked out okay, nothing worse than a scratchy throat for a day or two.

Jim wrapped his stethoscope back around his neck. "I know you're not going to leave, so I'll have an orderly bring in a cot for you."

"Thanks."

Because he didn't want her to be alone, and he couldn't leave Everly, he'd asked Skylar to stay with Willow. The latest update from Skylar was that the bullet had been removed from her shoulder and there wouldn't be any permanent damage. Because Willow and Everly hadn't been in the fire for long, they had both suffered only minimal smoke inhalation. As much of a relief as that had been, the guilt that Willow had been shot because of him wasn't going to go away soon.

Tristan walked in and stopped on the opposite side of the bed from Parker. "She hasn't woken up yet?" He trailed the back of his hand down Everly's cheek.

"No, but Jim said she should anytime now."

"Thank God," Tristan said. "Skylar said she talked

to you a little while ago, so you're updated on Willow's condition and know she's going to be okay?"

"Yeah, and thank God for that, too." He hadn't had a choice in staying with Everly, but it had torn him up inside that he couldn't go with Willow, that he wasn't by her side right now.

"Did you know that Crystal intended to shoot Everly, and that was why Willow tackled her and how she got shot?"

"No." Willow had taken a bullet to save his daughter? His legs gave out, and he fell heavily in the chair behind him.

"Willow's awake and insisted on giving Skye a statement. Crystal believed that she could blame Willow for the fires and killing Everly, and you would turn to her, to Crystal for comfort."

"That's... I don't even have words for how fucked-up that is." Willow had saved Everly's life, not just from the fire but from being murdered. How could he ever repay her for that?

"It is. I just came from the jail. Crystal's demanding to talk to you. Said you're the only person she'll talk to."

"She can demand all she wants. I have no desire to see or talk to her."

Tristan rounded the bed, then perched on the edge in front of Parker. "Can't say I blame you, but I'm going to ask you to do it." He glanced down at Everly. "Not tonight, but tomorrow after you get our little girl home. Kade and Harper are on their way back, and they can stay with her while you're gone."

"Why should I?" He couldn't be trusted around that woman. "If I get near her, I'll want to wrap my hands around her throat for hurting my girls."

His brother smiled. "You won't, and your girls are going to be just fine."

"Ask me again tomorrow."

"Better yet, just show up at the jail around eleven. I'll meet you there."

"Fine, but I want it on record that I won't be held responsible for my actions when I see her."

"Duly noted. There's one other thing. Your studio is a mess, but it's not a total loss. The front wall's going to need to be replaced because of the fire, and you have water damage to the inside walls and floor. All fixable. The good news, your fireproof room did its job. Zero damage to the canvases stored in it."

"That is good news." His art show wouldn't have to be canceled. "What about Willow's house?"

"From what I can tell, she's going to need a wall replaced and some flooring. Whether the kitchen cabinets and counters are salvageable, I'm not sure. I called Buddy Napier, and he's going to check out the damage and what needs to be done on her house. He said he'll meet you at the studio when you're ready to assess the damage there."

"Thanks. I appreciate it." It sounded like all his art supplies were going to have to be replaced, which meant a trip to Charlotte. Maybe he, Willow, and Everly could make a weekend of it. Yeah, that was a great idea…or was he fooling himself that she'd even want to be near him after what she'd been through because of him?

At eleven the next morning, Parker walked into an interrogation room with Tristan after his brother's captain had read Crystal her rights. Parker wanted to get this over with because as soon as he could get out of here, he was going to the hospital in Statesville to see Willow.

Everly had awakened early this morning, none the worse for wear physically. Because she'd slept through the worst of it—a blessing that—all she remembered was the woman making her drink milk even after she told the mean lady she didn't like milk. Parker had assured her that she'd never see that woman again, nor would she have to drink milk again, and that was good enough for her. She'd asked for extra pickles at breakfast, and grateful she was alive, he'd put the jar in front of her and told her to go to town.

One of Skylar's deputies had found Crystal's rental car parked one street over from Willow's house. Inside was a key to a room at a motel at the Statesville exit off I-40. All her possessions left in the room had been collected, including a journal detailing each fire she'd set in Horace County. Parker's name was in there, too, but Parker had told his brother he didn't want to know what she'd written about him. In fact, as soon as he finished talking to her, he never wanted to hear the name Crystal Erickson again.

Crystal's eyes lit up at seeing him when he walked in. "Parker, I knew you'd come rescue me."

He took a seat across the table from her, and Tristan chose a spot against the wall behind her. His brother had told him where he'd stand in the hope she'd forget he was there.

One wrist was handcuffed to a bar attached to the table, and it gave him immense satisfaction at seeing that. "I was told you asked to talk to me, so here I am." Tristan had coached him on what to say, and it was mostly to not say much of anything, to let her talk.

That worked for him as he had nothing to say to her and wished he was anywhere but here.

"Remember our night together, Parker, how special it was?"

"I remember." That smile and those blue eyes…he'd thought them pretty that night at the bar, but now he saw what he'd missed. Both the smile and the eyes were off, those of a very disturbed woman. Although he couldn't forgive her for what she'd done, he felt sorry for the things he'd learned that had happened to her. No young girl should have had to suffer the way he assumed she had, both at losing a father she loved and learning of his crimes.

She reached across the table with her free hand and rested it over his. "It was kismet, seeing you there. You reminded me so much of my father. He loved me, and I knew you'd love me, too."

"I'm not your father, Crystal."

"But you're like him."

"How?" Tristan mouthed.

"In what way?"

"You love fire the way he did. You see the beauty in it, its pureness, its power, and I wanted to share that with you. My fires were a gift to you."

"You started the fires here as a gift to me?" That was what Tristan wanted, her admission. Could he go now?

"Yes." Her eyes locked on his with an intensity and an unnaturalness that made him want to squirm. "When you watch the smoke when it's white, doesn't it make you think of a bride wearing her wedding gown, dancing for her lover? I'll dance for you, Parker. I'll be your bride, your lover." She leaned toward him. "Like I was for my father," she whispered.

Parker's gaze shot to his brother, whose mouth had flattened into a thin line at hearing Crystal had been sexually abused by her father. This was some serious messed up. "You started the fires for me because—"

"So you'd see me. And you did."

Oh, he saw her all right. He wanted out of here and silently begged his brother to end this. They now had her confession and enough evidence to convict her, if she was even found competent to stand trial. When Tristan nodded that he could leave, Parker pulled his hand away from hers and stood.

"Where are you going?" she screeched.

He paused and looked at her. "I hope you get the help you need." That was all he had to say, and he walked out.

Chapter Thirty-Four

Willow woke up to find Parker sitting next to her hospital bed. She glanced down at his hand wrapped around hers. When she shifted her gaze back to his, he smiled. She was going to miss that smile.

"Hey," he softly said. "How are you feeling?"

"Oh, like I got shot." She was going for levity but wished she could take the words back when guilt flashed on his face and in his eyes.

"I'm sorry."

"For? You didn't shoot me." Her voice sounded really scratchy, like she was in the middle of a bad cold, but she was lucky to be alive, so she could live with a little croakiness. That she only had minor burns that wouldn't even leave a scar on the back of her legs was a true blessing. Her last thought had been that she was going to be burned alive.

"I didn't pull the trigger, but you were shot because of me. Almost died because of me."

"No, I was shot by a woman who is obviously a violent psychopath." Skylar had filled her in on Crystal's background, and she couldn't help pitying the woman. Skylar thought, and Willow agreed, that Crystal had been trying to replace her father.

He squeezed her hand. "You saved my daughter's life. I don't know how to thank you for that."

"You just did. Skylar said Everly's going to be okay, and that's what matters. Does she remember anything?"

"Only that the mean lady made her drink a glass of milk."

"That's good. I'm glad she slept through everything." She lowered her gaze to their linked hands again. "They're releasing me in two days if I don't have a relapse, and—"

"Already?" He frowned. "Maybe I should talk to the doctor."

"Thankfully, the bullet didn't damage any muscles or nerves, and there's no reason for me to stay here. There's no permanent damage to my lungs, and I just have to keep the wound clean and follow up with my doctor. My…um, my father will be here tomorrow. I'm going home to heal, then I'll start checking out beaches. Decide where I want to live."

She'd jumped at her father's offer to fly down and then drive her home to Ohio. The sooner she was gone, the sooner she could get on with the business of healing her broken heart. She hoped salt, sand, and sea would help her with that, but she wasn't sure even her beloved ocean would be enough to get over Parker and missing Everly.

"What if I want you to stay? What if I said I love you?"

"Oh, Parker." Were those tears in his eyes? She knew he cared for her, but how could she trust that he loved her? "You said yourself that you want to be in love, that you fall too easily, and then later realize that you weren't really in love. I know you're grateful that I saved Everly, but gratitude isn't love." And she needed true love, to know that it was real. She didn't have that with him.

Austin had almost destroyed her, and Parker had the power to make what she went through after Austin left her look like child's play. Staying, falling deeper and deeper in love with Parker and Everly and then losing them if he walked away like Austin had…she just couldn't, not unless she knew in her heart and soul that Parker's love was true and lasting.

It was going to be hard enough to leave now, but she had to. She refused to be that devastated girl again. Austin had taught her that lesson well, and she'd meant it when she'd promised herself never again.

"Willow, please don't go." He perched on the edge of the bed. "Stay and see where it goes between us." He brushed away the tears that were streaming down her cheeks with his thumb. "You can't deny there's something between us."

"You're right, I can't," she whispered. "But is it enough? I'm not sure it is." On his side. She would be all-in if only she was sure of him, but she wasn't. If he really did love her, he'd fight for her.

"I…" His expression blanked, and he got up. "If that's how you feel." And then he walked out of the room.

Any hope that he'd fight for her died. If he was willing to give up that easily, then she was right to leave.

Two weeks at home, and Willow was climbing the walls. Her doctor was pleased with how well her gunshot wound was healing. She barely felt it anymore and knew how lucky she was that the bullet hadn't damaged her internally. Physically, she was doing great, considering what she'd been through. Mentally? Well, she was working on that. Mostly, she was doing her best not to think about Parker. That was proving harder than she'd hoped.

As for being back home—she loved her parents but living with them was taxing. Her father babied her, and her mother was...well, she was trying. She might never agree with Willow's choice of a career, but she was accepting that her daughter would never follow in her footsteps and join the academic world, apparently a dream her mother had had of that happening.

They'd had some good late-night talks, and Willow felt closer to her mother than she ever had before, and for that, she was grateful. Even so, it was time to find her beach house and get back to writing her children's books.

She'd been having group conversations and texts with Skylar and Harper these past two weeks, but they'd said little about Parker, and she refused to ask. Twice they'd put Everly on the phone with her because, according to them, Everly missed her "so bad." It was both wonderful and heartbreaking to talk to Everly. She missed Everly *so bad*, too, and she'd cried both times after hanging up with the little girl who kept asking when she was going to come back home.

Parker's art show was this weekend, and Skylar and Harper had asked if she was coming. No, she was not. She longed to, but to what purpose? Seeing him would only hurt, especially since she hadn't heard a word from him. She couldn't get past the fact that he hadn't even tried to fight for her, the proof she needed that he truly did love her. Seemed apparent to her that he didn't.

The doorbell rang, and since she was the only one home at the moment to answer, she sighed. She looked like crap—her hair was a rat's nest, her leggings had a hole in the knee, and her most comfortable T-shirt had a big wine stain right over her left breast. But whatever. She trudged to the door.

"Willow Landry?" a deliveryman asked as he held a large, flat package.

"That's me." She tried to remember if she'd ordered something online.

"Sign here." He thrust a signing machine at her.

Okay, that was weird. She knew she hadn't ordered anything she'd have to sign for. After electronically signing her name, she carried it to the kitchen. Curious, she set to work getting it open. Inside the brown wrapping paper was a wooden frame protecting whatever was inside. She didn't know what it was protecting but sensed that she needed to be careful not to damage the contents.

After she got the wooden frame and another layer of wrapping paper removed, she came to a layer of tissue paper. Taped to the paper was a white envelope with her name on it. What in the world? She pulled the envelope away and set it aside. It could wait. She was too curious to see what was under the tissue.

"Oh," she breathed when a painting was revealed. "Oh." The framed painting was of her, one she hadn't posed for. She was standing in front of an open window, draped in emerald green silk that was billowing in the breeze. Her hair was tousled, her lips bee-stung and damp, and her eyes were soft and filled with desire. She was looking over her shoulder at a man sitting on a chair in the shadows. The man's face was a mere outline, but she knew it was Parker. A bed was behind him, and it was obvious the couple had recently made love.

"Oh, Parker." Was this how he saw her? Beautiful and sexy and a woman he loved? Because he couldn't have painted her like this if he wasn't in love with her. She cried, but it was happy tears this time.

When her tears dried, she opened the envelope. On a piece of stationery were the words *Willow in the Moonlight*. That was it, nothing else. She unfolded another sheet of paper and inside was a plane ticket to New York. Attached to the ticket was a sticky note. *Please come*. Under the words were the address and time for his show on Saturday night. She unfolded the third and last sheet of paper, a printout of reservations for a room at the Four Seasons hotel for three nights.

"Good gosh, Parker. When you go big, you go big." She laughed, feeling all kinds of giddy. Was she going to go? Hell yes.

Willow walked up to the door of the gallery in New York City on Saturday night. She'd arrived the night before and had gone shopping this morning for a dress, since she didn't own anything fancy enough for an art show at a New York gallery. Although her intention was to find a dress, she'd ended up with an emerald green lady's tux. As soon as she'd tried it on, she had to have it. The tux was silk and consisted of just pants, the jacket, and a silver choker that had an emerald green gem-encrusted bow tie. The jacket buttoned low, showing more cleavage than she was used to, but she had a man to seduce. She'd also purchased strappy silver sandal heels and a small silver purse.

She'd considered calling Parker to tell him that she was coming but had decided to surprise him. Besides, he'd be busy today getting ready for his show, and she didn't want to distract him.

Nervous, she smoothed down the jacket. A man in a tux opened the door for her, and another tux-clad man was inside at a table collecting tickets. She didn't have a ticket. Had she missed seeing it in the package Parker sent her?

When she stopped in front of the man, he said, "Willow Landry?"

"Yes, how did you know?"

"Mr. Church showed us your picture. You're to go right in."

"Thank you." Guess when you had an in with the artist, you didn't need a ticket. She scanned the room but didn't see Parker or any of his family. She walked toward the painting closest to her. It was the one he'd shown her. *Bottom of the Ninth.* Even though she'd seen it before, it still touched her so deeply that it brought tears to her eyes.

"You can see how much he wants to be out there playing ball with the boys," said a woman draped in diamonds standing next to her. The woman glanced at her. "Oh, you're her."

"Her?"

"The woman in his paintings."

"Um…" There were more paintings of her?

"How exciting to meet his muse. I'm Rebecca, and you are?"

"Willow." She saw more questions in the woman's eyes, so she excused herself and lost herself in the crowd. Because yes, the gallery was packed, which made her ridiculously happy for Parker. She eased around the walls, not meeting anyone's eyes, as she looked for those other paintings of her.

She wished she was the only one in the gallery so she could stop at each piece and study it, but she wasn't ready to be noticed again. In her search, she came to one that had her stopping. It was the one he'd titled *Liber-*

ated. And she saw what she'd missed the first time she'd seen it. It was a self-portrait of him as a child, and she wanted to wrap that boy in her arms and keep him safe.

"He captures both the despair and hope of a child who feels unloved," a man close to her said to his companion.

Yes, he did, and his talent was amazing. She passed several more of his paintings that she wanted to study later as she continued searching for the ones of her. And then she came to them. The first one was titled *Willow in Sunflowers,* and it stole her breath. She knew she was attractive enough, but he'd made her beautiful as she stood in the middle of a field of sunflowers with a smile on her face, wearing the sundress from the day she'd met him, her straw hat and cowboy boots, and her hair a wild mess blowing behind her. When had he painted it?

The theme of the show was Scenes Through a Window, and unlike the other paintings where the subjects were looking in or out through a window, this one wasn't like that. Instead, he'd hung an actual distressed window in front of the painting. So clever. And so weird that she wanted to go find a field of sunflowers and dance.

Next to the sunflowers painting was one titled *Willow Under Fairy Lights,* and she laughed at seeing it. She was sitting on her swing, wearing shorts and her cowboy boots, and her head was thrown back as she all-out laughed. As she stood in a gallery in New York City, looking at a painting of her time with Parker, she longed to be sitting on that swing again with him next to her.

Where was he?

Chapter Thirty-Five

She's here. Parker leaned against a wall behind Willow, his hands stuffed in his pockets as he watched her stare at *Willow in Sunflowers*. She was always beautiful, but tonight she was stunning. That she'd chosen to wear an emerald green tux was brilliant. The other women here tonight were wearing sparkly cocktail dresses and gowns, which made Willow unique in comparison. And her hair…it was down and wild, just the way he liked it best.

No woman in the room compared to her, and people were noticing her. Recognition lit some of the faces, those who'd seen the two canvases of her and were realizing she was the girl in them. Others, both men and women, were casting glances at her. He glared at a few of the men who were looking at her as if they wanted to eat her up. *Mine.*

She stepped to the next painting, *Willow Under Fairy Lights*. He wished he could see her face as she studied herself on canvas. A waiter walked by with a tray of champagne, and he picked up two flutes.

It felt like dozens of hummingbirds had replaced his heart, it was beating so fast as he approached her. She'd come, and that had to mean something. When she'd told him at the hospital that she was going home in spite of his asking her to stay, he'd been hurt. Like every other woman in his life, she'd left him.

Poor little boy, so unlovable even his mother didn't want him. It sounded ridiculous now, but that was where his mind had gone when she'd left. Yeah, he'd gotten it wrong with every one of his girlfriends, and that mindset had almost cost him the woman he knew in his heart he could get it right with. And what had he done? Walked away from her, leaving her to believe she didn't matter.

Well, she did matter, more than he had the words to express, but his love for her was in his paintings, and he'd thought—hoped and prayed—that she'd see that.

He'd spent the first three days after she was gone refusing to talk to anyone except for Everly. Once he got over himself and could think clearly, he'd thought about the things she'd said, and he was able to see it from her perspective. So he gave them both some time. For him, time to plan how to win her back. For her, time to miss him…he hoped.

She was here, so it must have worked. He stopped next to her. "The girl in that painting owns my heart."

"The boy who painted it owns mine," she said, not looking at him.

So much joy at hearing her say that sent his heart soaring. Then she did look at him and smiled, and it took all his willpower not to scoop her up in his arms and take her somewhere private so he could show her how much he loved and missed her.

Instead, he handed her one of the flutes. "You look stunning tonight, Willow." Her lavender scent washed over him, and he wanted to rub his nose over her skin.

"Thank you. You clean up pretty nicely yourself."

Although Lawrence, the gallery owner, deemed the show a formal affair, Parker figured as the artist he could dress as he pleased. He wore black pants and a white shirt with the sleeves rolled up.

She turned her attention back to the paintings. "It says they're sold."

"They're mine and not for sale, but it's easier to mark them as sold than to argue with someone who wants to buy them anyway."

"You're keeping them?"

He glanced at the one of her sitting in the swing. "Yes." There was no way he'd let some man buy them, put them on his wall, and stare at her. A crowd was forming around them as people realized the subject of the paintings was here, and they were looking at her and trying to listen in on their conversation. He put his hand on her back. "Come with me."

"Where's your family? I thought they were all coming."

"They're upstairs, keeping Everly occupied for me in case you came. Once Ev knows you're here, all bets are off. She missed you." He paused a few beats, then put his mouth next to her ear. "But not as much as me."

He was going to have to mingle, but not yet. He led her down a hallway to Lawrence's office. As soon as he shut the door behind them, he took the champagne from her hand, set their flutes on Lawrence's desk, then backed her up to the wall. "Please tell me I can kiss you."

Without answering, she threw her arms around his neck and pulled his mouth to hers. He'd given up on finding love, and then she had walked into his life.

He'd finally found her, his soul mate, and it was real this time. He kissed her senseless, or maybe it was her kissing him senseless. He didn't know, didn't care. All that mattered was that she'd come back to him.

He pulled away and braced his hands on the wall next to her head. "Why did you come?" He needed to know.

"The painting you sent me." She dropped her arms from his neck, then placed her palm on his cheek. "When I saw it, I knew. You couldn't have painted me like that if you didn't love me. That was all I needed to know. I'm sorry I didn't trust you when you said it in the hospital, but you—"

"Shhh." He put his finger over her lips. "I understand, and you were right to have doubts, considering my history. I think the time apart was good for both of us, but I missed you, Willow. After you left it felt like someone took a rusty knife and cut my heart out."

"Same, but enough talking. Kiss me again."

He grinned. "I can do that." And he did. As much as he didn't want to stop kissing her, he had to. He had an art show happening, and if he didn't make an appearance soon, Lawrence was going to come looking for him.

"I guess you need to get out there," she said when he pulled away.

"Yeah, although I'd rather spirit you off to your hotel room."

"About that. Are you at the Four Seasons, too?"

"No, the family rented an entire brownstone across from Central Park for everyone to stay in together. You can check out of the hotel and stay with us, but I'd rather you keep your room if I'm invited to stay with you. Then we'd have some privacy without them all in our faces. They're leaving tomorrow afternoon and taking Everly with them. We could have a few days here, just the two of us."

"I'd like that, but I do want to see everyone."

"And they're waiting to see you. We'll all go out to dinner after the show, and after that, it will be our time, okay?"

"Very okay."

He didn't want to leave her side, but she'd be too much of a curiosity since her paintings were on view. He should have thought of that before including them. "The family's upstairs, and you can stay with them until the show's over. Everly won't let you out of her sight once she knows you're here."

"I can't wait to see her."

"Well, prepare to be tackled." Everly had told him that she'd talked to Willow on the phone, something his future sisters-in-law had arranged, and he appreciated they'd done that for his little girl.

She chuckled. "If I don't tackle her first."

The upstairs was open, and he glanced up as he led Willow to the stairs. Both his brothers were standing at the railing, and both broke out in grins. He'd worried since sending Willow the invitation that she wouldn't come, and they'd both been positive that she would. Thank God that they'd been right.

"Parker, where've you been?" Lawrence said, stopping them at the foot of the stairs. "You need to be on the floor. People are wanting to talk to the artist."

He wanted to sigh. Yes, he knew he needed to be available to the people who'd come to his show. "Lawrence, I'd like to introduce you to Willow Landry. Willow, this is Lawrence Dubois."

"Dubois Gallery, so your gallery," Willow said. She held out her hand. "It's a pleasure to meet Mr. Dubois."

"And you're the woman in the paintings. Entirely my pleasure, Miss Landry. Please, call me Lawrence."

Parker wanted to knock that male appreciation right off Lawrence's face as the man's gaze skimmed over Willow. Parker glared at his friend. He was a territorial dog, because he wrapped his arm around Willow's back and pulled her next to him. She softly chuckled, letting him know she was onto him.

"I'm taking Willow upstairs to my family, then I'll come down and mingle." He led her away.

"He seems like a nice man." She laughed when he growled. "I think you're jealous, Parker Church."

He didn't know that it was jealousy, but he sure as hell didn't like the way Lawrence looked at her. At the top of the stairs, he pulled Willow to a stop. Everly was sitting at a table drawing in a sketch pad. He kissed Willow's cheek, then said, "Why don't you sneak up behind her?"

"Okay."

He stayed to watch his daughter's reaction when she realized Willow was here.

Willow eased up behind Everly, then put her hands over Ev's eyes. "Guess who?"

Everly froze. "Miss Willow?"

"Yes. Surprise!"

Everly screamed as she shot out of the chair and right into Willow's arms. "Miss Willow. You're here! I missed you so much. Are you coming home? You have to. Say yes. I've been drawing pictures for you."

As words flew out of his daughter's mouth, Willow smiled at him over Everly's head. He smiled back, and now that all was right in his world, he went downstairs to mingle. The sooner he could get this show over with, the sooner he could have his arms around her again.

Parker closed the door to Willow's hotel room and turned the dead bolt. The family dinner had been great, with amazing food and lots of laughter. He loved how well she fit in with the people he loved. They'd all gone back to the brownstone, and it had taken longer than he had patience for to get Everly to go to sleep. She'd refused to let Willow out of her sight.

Finally, he had Willow all to himself. She stood in the middle of the room, looking at him, waiting for him to make his move. He moved. "You have two choices. A shower. With me. Or a shower with me."

She tapped her finger against her lips. "Hmm, I think I'll go with the first choice."

"I was hoping you'd choose that one." He trailed his knuckles down her cleavage. "This outfit is sexy as fuck but take it off." He unbuttoned his shirt, loving the way her eyes followed his fingers as more of his chest was revealed with each button freed. "Willow."

Her gaze shot up to his. "What?"

"Your clothes. Take them off." He let his shirt slide down his arms and to the floor.

"I would if you'd stop distracting me."

"How am I distracting you?" He unbuttoned his pants, then slid down his zipper, and now he was amused and more than a little turned on by the way her eyes were locked on his every move. But his amusement only went so far, since distracting her was keeping her from taking her own clothes off. And he really, really wanted them off.

She huffed. "Because you're almost naked. It's distracting."

He dropped his pants, and her gaze went straight to his groin where his boxer briefs were tented, and he couldn't stop his grin. "Willow, clothes off before I tear them off."

"Don't you dare. I love this outfit."

"I would dare. I want you naked. Now. You have thirty seconds before what you have on isn't fit for anything but the trash."

That threat did the trick, and as soon as she was down to her beautiful naked self, he lost his briefs, scooped her up, and took them to the shower. The thing he decided he loved most about the Four Seasons, there was no end to the warm water. It wasn't until he'd made her come with his mouth, after she'd returned the favor, and after he'd kissed every spot on her body and was ready to bury himself deep inside her that he realized the condoms were in his pants in the other room.

"Condom. Don't have one in here," he said.

"I'm on birth control, and I'm clean."

"So am I. I want inside you right here, right now, but only if you're sure that's okay." He nuzzled her neck.

"I'm sure."

"Thank God." He slid into her wet heat and groaned. "Home. I've found my home, Willow, and it's you."

"Welcome home then, love," she said.

And he was never leaving.

Epilogue

Parker sat on the deck of the beach house he'd bought as a wedding present to Willow. Over the past year, he'd taken her to different beaches for long weekends, and she'd fallen in love with the small town of Mexico Beach, Florida, with the sugar white sand and the crystal clear waters of the Gulf. He hadn't told her they'd been house shopping, and she still didn't know this house was hers. As far as she knew, he'd rented it for a week.

Although it was her wedding present, he intended the house to also be used by his brothers and their soon-to-be wives. By soon-to-be, he meant today at sunset when he and his brothers would marry the women who owned their hearts.

Yep, it was a triple wedding, and they'd told no one that they were eloping. Miss Mabel wasn't going to be happy about that, but a reception was planned for when they returned, which would mollify her. Not that they were doing it specifically for her, but for the brides' families.

Skylar's parents, Harper's father, and Willow's parents and sister would all be at the reception. The decision to elope and have a private triple wedding had been agreed on by all of them when Willow's mother had tried to take over the wedding planning, insisting on an extravagant affair that was worthy of Park C. That was a big no, and fortunately Willow had agreed.

Parker had instantly liked Willow's father, who was, like her, a free spirit. Her mother had made him uncomfortable in the beginning with the way she'd gushed and fluttered over him. After being around her a few times, she'd settled down and was treating him somewhat normally. As for Willow's sister, he was trying to like her. It might take some time.

"When you gonna tell Willow this house is hers?" Kade asked.

"Tonight." He tore his gaze away from Willow in a bikini and grinned at seeing that Kade's eyes were glued to Harper, also in a bikini. He glanced at Tristan, and his grin grew. Tristan's attention was on his bikini-clad almost-wife.

He and his brothers were kicked back on the deck with a beer and munching on the snacks the chef he'd hired for the week had brought out for them. The women and Everly were having a blast playing in the water. They'd given up on trying to build a sandcastle since the dogs thought their job was to tear it down as soon as a castle wall went up. Even somber Ember was letting loose and finding her inner puppy.

They'd talked about a destination wedding, but he, Tristan, and Skylar couldn't all be gone at the same time for two weeks, and he hadn't been agreeable to going to some other country for less than two weeks. So, they'd created their own wedding venue, and as far as he was concerned, this beat any destination wedding they could have had.

"Yo, cuddle bunny," Kade yelled when Harper bent over to pick up a shell. "Looking good there."

She looked between her legs and stuck her tongue out.

Kade laughed. "That woman gets me all hot and bothered without even trying."

"I think we could all say the same about our lady," Tristan said. "I'm thinking Skylar needs a nap so she's not too tired to get married."

Parker snorted. "Nap? Is that what we're calling it these days?" Although he'd love a *nap.* He'd have to get Everly to take an actual nap, though, which she'd fight.

"It occurs to me that you and Willow will have the beach house, and Kade and Harper have the lake cabin," Tristan said. "Skylar and I need a special place."

Parker pointed a thumb behind him at the house. "You know you can come here anytime you want to." Tristan and Skylar had sold their downtown loft and had moved into Willow's house because they wanted to be closer to the rest of the family. It was almost like having a family compound now, and Parker loved the idea of that.

"I do, and we will, and I appreciate it, but the more I think about it, the more I want something special that's ours."

"Like what?"

"Maybe a place in the mountains around Asheville. Something on a good-sized, fast-moving creek."

"Do it," Kade said. "Then we'll have three great places to go. The beach, the lake, and the mountains."

Parker thought back to their early years after their mother had dumped them on her sister's doorstep with nothing more than the clothes on their backs, and then had disappeared from their lives. They'd each dealt with her abandonment in different ways, and they'd come a long way since then, had become men they could be proud of. And now, each of them had found a woman who made them want to be even better men.

Life was good.

After an early chef-prepared dinner, Parker was back on the porch with his brothers. The girls had kicked them out of the house so they could dress. They'd chosen early November for the triple wedding since Florida started cooling down around that time and they wouldn't have sweat dripping down their faces as they got married.

He and his brothers were a colorful bunch. The girls had bought shirts for each of them, lavender for Kade, pale blue for Tristan, and pink for him. They'd refused to let the guys see their dresses, but Parker guessed that the shirts matched their respective bride's dress. They each had been told to wear white pants and no shoes, and Parker loved the idea of getting married barefooted.

Kade looked down at his shirt. "I'm having trouble computing that I'm wearing a lavender shirt and drinking brandy out of an actual snifter. I've never in my life worn anything lavender."

"Lavender's definitely your color, brother," Parker teased. "Shows off your eyes."

"Fuck off."

Parker laughed as he glanced at Tristan. "Kade said a bad word, and he's being mean to me. Make him stop."

"I keep hoping the two of you will grow up someday," Tristan said.

Kade snorted. "Where's the fun in doing that?"

"A toast." Parker held up his snifter. "To putting the past where it belongs. To a future that's better than any one of us thought to dream. To the beautiful women who love us, although I'm not sure why."

"Speak for yourself. Mine loves me because of my big—"

Parker saw that mischievous glint in Kade's eyes the second that Tristan did, and he laughed when Tristan slapped his hand over Kade's mouth.

"Don't finish that," Tristan said.

Kade pushed Tristan's hand away. "I was going to say my big heart."

It was Parker's turn to snort. "You're so full of it, Kade."

"What he said," Tristan said. "I'll finish the toast. To the two men I call my brothers. Even if I could choose different men for the role, I wouldn't. Well, sometimes I would trade Kade, but mostly I'd keep him."

"Hey, I resemble that remark." Kade held his snifter up. "To us, the lost little boys who somehow managed to grow up without going to prison." He glanced at them and winked. "I'm mostly talking about me on that one."

"It was touch and go for a while there," Tristan said.

Parker nodded at that piece of truth. "One last toast. This one's to you, Tris, for stepping up when you were just a boy yourself and raising two messed-up kids. No one could have done it better, brother."

"Amen to that," Kade said, then finished off his brandy. "Isn't it about time to get this show on the road? I'm ready to be a married man."

A little dynamo dressed in pink barreled out the door, followed by three dogs. The brothers laughed at seeing the silk scarves tied around the dogs' necks—a lavender one for Duke, a blue for Fuzz, and Ember wearing a pink one.

"Daddy! Mommy said it's time for us to get married. Is the preacher here yet?" She spun in a circle, searching for a preacher. "Where is he? He's supposed to be here. What if he doesn't come? I'm ready for my mommy to be my real mommy. What—"

"Hey, Ladybug, calm down. It's not quite time to get married, and I promise, he'll be here. Just try to be patient." Parker's heart did that funny bounce thing every time Everly called Willow Mommy. Willow had been promoted to Mommy status the day Parker had put an engagement ring on her finger.

Everly dramatically sighed. "Mommy can't come out 'cause you can't see her until the preacher's here, so I'll go tell her we have to try to be patient." She put her hands on her hips and narrowed her eyes at him. "But I have to tell you, Daddy, it's not easy." She then glared at Tristan and Kade, as if they were also to blame for the wedding not happening when she thought it should. "I'll tell my aunties they have to be patient, too."

"Thanks, kiddo," Kade said. "You look mighty pretty today."

"I know. Mommy said I was the prettiest flower girl in the history of the world." She skipped back inside the house, and the dogs that she'd given the title Flower Girl Helpers followed her in.

Tristan chuckled. "You realize she's the boss of all of us."

"Pretty much has been since I brought her home, yeah?"

His brothers grunted their agreement, and he smiled at hearing the love for his little girl in their grunts.

* * *

The preacher had arrived, along with the photographer, and Parker and his brothers were standing at the edge of the water at sunset. If he wasn't getting married, he'd have an easel set up on the beach so he could paint the brilliant pinks and oranges of the sky. Instead, he took a mental picture for the painting he'd do when he got home.

They were lined up by birth order as instructed, and Parker turned his attention to the house, waiting (impatiently) to see his bride. The glass door slid open, and their barefoot, dressed-in-pink flower girl walked out with her helpers. In her hand was a basket filled with pink, lavender, and blue flower petals.

As she walked along the sand toward them, instead of dropping the petals, she tossed them into the air, laughing when they caught the breeze and floated around her head. Ember and Fuzz walked with dignity beside her while Duke jumped in the air, snapping at the floating flower petals.

"That's my boy," Kade proudly said.

Parker and Tristan chuckled, and Parker thought that his middle brother couldn't have found a dog that matched him any better than Duke.

Then, three visions in pastels appeared and Parker caught his breath, as he was sure his brothers did. Their brides held hands as they walked across the sand. Skylar in blue was at the end facing Tristan, Harper in lavender was in the middle, and Willow was at the other end. Each was beautiful, but it was the one in pink that he locked eyes on. Her hair was down and wild the way he loved it, and her dress was some kind of gauzy material that swirled around her legs in the breeze. The hem was different lengths, and she was barefoot.

If he died this minute, it would be as a happy man. She was smiling as she gazed back at him, and the smile on his face felt like it was the biggest one he'd ever worn. In a few minutes, she would be his wife, and as difficult and soul-destroying certain times of his life had been, he'd do it all over again if that was what it took to reach this point, to have this woman walking toward him, her eyes filled with love.

"She's the most beautiful woman I've ever seen," Tristan said.

Kade nodded. "I know, right?"

"Without a doubt," Parker said, smiling because he knew where his brothers' gazes were, and they were each right. His girl was the prettiest, though, if only by a little bit. Not that he'd say that unless he wanted Kade to put him facedown on the sand.

When Everly reached them, she looked in her basket. "Oh, no. There's not supposed to be any left over. I have to go back and do it again."

He put a hand on top of her head. "No, you're supposed to drop what's left on the sand here for the brides to stand on."

"Oh, goody! I like that." She dumped the basket over. "Now can we get married?"

The preacher chuckled. "Yes, young lady, it's time to get married."

When Willow reached him, he took her hand and squeezed it, then as she had asked him to do—and he'd fallen more deeply in love with her for it—he let go her hand and they put Everly between them, him taking one of his little girl's hands and Willow the other.

Everyone had written their own vows, and when it was his time, he turned and picked up Willow's free hand so that his small family stood connected in a circle. "Willow, I didn't know what love truly was until you came into my life. The first thing I thought after meeting you was that you disturbed me." He smiled when her eyes widened, and then he grinned when Kade snorted. "And by *disturbed*, I mean in a good way, but a way I didn't think I was ready for. I was wrong. You speak to my heart, to my soul. You love Ladybug as much as I do, and—"

"I love Mommy, too, Daddy. Can I talk now?"

He smiled down at his other favorite girl. "I know you do but wait your turn." After allowing his daughter an impatient sigh, he lifted his gaze back to Willow. "As I was about to say, you almost gave your life for her…" His eyes burned, remembering how close he'd come to losing both of them. He cleared his throat. "I have no words that can adequately tell you what that meant to me other than I love you. Deeply. Profoundly. You have my heart always and forever. But don't ever scare me like that again."

"I won't. I promise," she said.

"Is it my turn now?"

He and Willow shared a grin at their daughter's impatience. "No, it's Willow's turn, and then yours."

"I'm already forgetting what I want to say," Everly muttered.

Willow covered her laugh with a cough, then said, "I'll make this quick so our girl doesn't forget everything she wants to say." She squeezed his hand. "I love you, Parker, more than I thought I could ever love a man." She smiled down at Everly. "I love you so much, too, Ev, and I couldn't find a more perfect daughter or book partner if I tried. Thank you for loving me back."

"I do, Mommy, soooo much!" She threw her arms wide. "Now is it my turn?"

Everyone laughed—him, Willow, his brothers, their new wives, the preacher, and the photographer.

"Please, baby brother, say yes so I can get going on my wedding night," Kade said.

"What he said," Tristan said.

The preacher chuckled. "I don't think I've had a more entertaining wedding than this one."

Parker agreed, and wasn't that perfect? Yes, it was. "Go, Everly. Your turn."

"Finally," she grumbled. "I wanted a mommy, so I made a wish when Daddy let me pull apart a chicken wishbone with him and I got the biggest part."

Parker blinked. That was a good two years ago, and she'd been wishing for a mother that long?

"I don't know why you can make a wish on a chicken bone, but I guess you can, because my wish came true, and now you're not Miss Willow anymore. You're my mommy."

Willow's eyes filled with tears, and he let go of her hand so he could brush away the ones falling down her cheeks. She gave him a trembling smile, telling him how touched she was by Everly's words.

"I have some questions, Mommy." Everly held up a finger. "Do I have to take a bath every night? My daddy makes me, but maybe you can tell him I don't have to. Not every single night. And I don't like carrots, but he says they're good for my eyes. I don't want my eyes to look like carrots, and…" She took a deep breath. "This last one's important. I want a baby brother."

Parker grinned as he leaned over Everly's head and whispered to Willow. "I give you my daughter. It's your job now as her mommy to make her eat her carrots." As for a baby brother for Ev, he was all for it.

"You want me to take on that chore, it'll cost you lots of bedroom time," she whispered back.

That was a deal he could live with for the rest of his life. "I'm in. Also, I love you, wife. Thank you for loving me back."

"Loving you back is the easiest thing I've ever done, husband."

He smiled at his beautiful, free-spirited happily ever after.

* * * * *

Acknowledgments

This is where I say a lot of thank-yous.

The first one is always to my readers. Thank you for loving my stories. Thank for your emails telling me that you did, and a super big thank-you for your reviews. Readers are the rock stars in the book world because without you, there would be no reason to write books. True story! I've been at this for ten years, and in those years, I've made many reader friends throughout the world, and I'm so grateful for that. If I could make one wish, it would be that I could meet each one of you.

Next up are the book bloggers, especially Christine from ireadromance. Thank you for talking to your followers about my books. No one can spread the word about a book like you guys. You all are also rock stars!

Sandra's Rowdies…boy, do I love my Rowdies. Y'all are the most awesome and hilarious troublemakers in the world. Thank you for the love and support you give me and my books. Thank you for all the fun!

From my first book and on, I've thanked the following people, my three best author friends. Jenny Holiday—bestie, critique partner, sounding board—thank you for ten years of an awesome friendship. Here's to many, many more. A. E. Jones and Miranda Liasson, my

Lucky 13 Golden Heart sisters, what a journey we've been on since we were finalist in an unpublished authors' contest. I can't tell you how much I look forward to our monthly Zoom call. Thank you for your friendship and the laughter.

Brandy Morrison, thank you for so many things. You were one of my very first book fans, and over the years you became a friend. You also give me Saturdays off in Sandra's Rowdies, and a big hug for that. Someday, we'll meet! I promise. Heather from Maine, my funny friend, thank you for being the world's best beta reader. Love you both.

Kerri Buckley, my Carina Press editor, this is our sixth book together, and it's been a fantastic journey. Thank you for being awesome! Deb Nemeth, my developmental editor, thank you so much for showing me how to make my stories tons and tons better.

To my agent, Courtney Miller-Callihan, it's been fun, hasn't it? Let's keep on having fun. Thank you for being a great agent and believing in me.

Last but never least, my family. Jim, Jeff, and DeAnna, love you all so much! To Jim, thank you for not talking (even when you want to) when I'm writing. Love you, O.

About the Author

Bestselling, award-winning author Sandra Owens lives in the beautiful Blue Ridge Mountains of North Carolina. Her family and friends often question her sanity but have ceased being surprised by what she might get up to next. She's jumped out of a plane, flown in an aerobatic plane while the pilot performed death-defying stunts, gotten into laser gunfights in air combat, and ridden a Harley motorcycle for years. She regrets nothing.

Sandra is a Romance Writers of America Honor Roll member and a 2013 Golden Heart finalist for her contemporary romance *Crazy for Her*. In addition to her contemporary romance and romantic suspense novels, she writes Regency stories. Her books have won many awards, including The Readers' Choice and The Golden Quill.

To find out about other books by Sandra Owens or to be alerted to cover reveals, new releases, and other fun stuff, sign up for her newsletter at bit.ly/2FVUPKS.

Join Sandra's Facebook Reader Group: Sandra's Rowdies: www.Facebook.com/Groups/1827166257533001/

Website: www.Sandra-Owens.com

Connect with Sandra

Facebook: www.Facebook.com/SandraOwensAuthor/

Twitter: www.Twitter.com/SandyOwens1

Instagram: www.Instagram.com/SandraOwensBooks/

*After a bomb injures Navy SEAL Jack Daniels and
his trusty dog, they return home to Asheville, where
he agrees to help a gorgeous local potter train her
rambunctious pup. Nichole Masters is open to some
no-strings distraction, and when danger threatens,
Jack steps in to protect her.*

Keep reading for an excerpt from
Operation K-9 Brothers
by Sandra Owens

Chapter One

"Stupid me. I trusted you," said the voice on the other end of the phone.

Jack Daniels, Whiskey to his SEAL teammates, blinked sleepy eyes at his bedside clock. Three in the morning sucked for getting angry calls from women. What the hell had he done to this one?

"Who's this?" That was the wrong thing to say. Jack held the phone away from his ear in an effort to save his hearing. He didn't recognize the number on the screen. Her voice wasn't familiar either.

"Sweetheart," he said, interrupting her tirade. "You sure you have the right number?" Even though her voice and phone number didn't ring any bells, he couldn't say for sure he wasn't the douchebag—along with some other impressively creative names she was calling him—in question.

Ah hell, now she was crying.

"How could you?" she said, her words slightly slurred. She hung up on him.

After thirty minutes of trying to go back to sleep, Jack let out a long sigh. How could he what? That question was going to bug him until he got an answer. Although her voice hadn't been at all familiar, he'd liked it, even when she'd been calling him names. He grinned. Sewer-sucking slimeball and twatwaffle were good, but his favorite was doggy doo. That one had a nice ring to it.

He got out of bed and padded to the living room where he'd left his laptop. Dakota sighed in resignation before hoisting herself up from her dog bed, her nails clicking on the wood floor as she followed him. She liked her sleep, something he interrupted too often for her taste because of his nightmares. At least they weren't occurring every night anymore. She sat near his leg and peered up at him with worried eyes.

"Not a nightmare this time, girl. We got a mystery on our hands. What do you think of that?"

She knew him inside and out, knew from the tone of his voice that he wasn't weighed down by his memories this time. Once she determined he didn't need her comfort, she made two circles, got her damaged leg under her, then curled up on the floor at his feet, apparently liking her sleep more than mysteries. Jack was intrigued, though, his interest in something flaring for the first time since coming home.

It only took a few minutes to find a name and address attached to her phone number. Nichole Masters, currently living in Asheville. Nope, not ringing even one little bell in his memory bank of female acquaintances or hookups. It was possible he'd forgotten one but not likely. He had a good memory, especially for women, and she had a sexy voice he was sure he wouldn't have forgotten.

Jack stared absently at the half moon framed by the window. Coming to a decision, he nodded. "All right, Nikki girl, you have me curious." As his teammates would tell anyone who asked, get on Whiskey's radar and all bets were off.

He showered, and after staring at himself for a minute in the mirror, he shaved off his beard, seeing his face for the first time in months. He felt naked.

At sunrise Jack made a recon run on one Nichole Masters. Her house was a cute little bungalow near the River Arts District of Asheville, North Carolina. As soon as he downloaded her Facebook profile picture to his phone, he knew that he'd never met her. There was no way he'd forget that face.

He should let it go, but she'd fucking cried, believing he was the cause. That couldn't stand. And yeah, he recognized that his reasoning was skewed. She'd thought he was some other douchebag, but Jack couldn't get her voice out of his head. Then there were her eyes, a warm golden brown. Were they as beautiful in person as they were in the photo? But it was her smile that drew him. It was an honest smile, and he sensed that Nichole Masters was a happy person. That some faceless man had made her cry didn't sit well.

It creeped him out a little that he was stalking her—and it sure as hell would her if she knew—but he needed to learn where she worked. Once he knew that, he'd come up with a plan to meet her in a way that wouldn't freak her out. Besides, he had nothing better to do.

He was on medical leave after getting too up close and personal with an IED. Dakota had saved his life by putting herself in front of him and pushing him back, in all likelihood preventing him from being blown to bits. She'd been severely injured, had almost lost a hind leg. Thank God she had survived, though, and was now recuperating, along with him. He would be returning to his team. She would not. She'd served her time, had saved the lives of many of his brothers, along with his, and had earned her retirement.

But it was preying on his mind. Dakota needed him, but he'd have to leave her behind when he was healed enough to go back. The problem was that he didn't know who to give her to. It had to be someone both he and Dakota trusted, and the only names that came to mind were his teammates. Because he'd given himself a deadline—two more months to get his arm and shoulder in shape—he was running out of time to make a decision.

Since there was a VA hospital in Asheville, he'd come home as soon as he'd been released from Walter Reed Bethesda Medical Center. After a month in the hospital—first in Germany and then at Walter Reed—he'd been ecstatic to leave that place behind. Physical therapy on his arm and shoulder was a bitch, but the sooner he was healed, the sooner he could get back to his team.

The first thing he'd done after getting out of the hospital was to track down Dakota. He almost hadn't recognized her. She'd been curled up in a corner of the kennel, rib bones showing, eyes dull, and fur lackluster. At the sight of him, she'd tried to stand, only to fall over when she put weight on her damaged leg. Since she belonged to the military, he'd had to call in some favors to get her released to him, but he'd been relentless in making that happen. When he'd first brought her home, she had been depressed and lethargic, and Jack thought she'd as much as given up. Thankfully she'd come a long way, and except for her leg, she was back to the dog she'd been before the bomb.

At precisely eight, Nichole Masters appeared, wearing a blue-and-white striped dress and white sandals. Jack blew out a breath as she walked down the steps of her little porch, a mug in one hand and the end of a leash in the other.

She was gorgeous. Her shoulder-length hair was a riot of curls in a fascinating mix of colors—reds, golds, and browns. A man could happily get lost in all that hair. She was tall, which he liked, and a little on the thin side, which he didn't like. Made him want to feed her.

He wasn't close enough to hear what she was saying to the puppy straining at the other end of the leash, but the dog was completely ignoring her. Jack could have told her that the little beast was going to keep winning their test of wills unless and until she positioned herself as the alpha dog in their relationship.

The puppy finally lifted a leg and watered a bush. The woman disappeared back inside with her little friend, and then a few minutes later walked out with a purse over her shoulder and the dog still on his leash.

Jack followed her to the River Arts District. After she parked and exited her car with her dog, he waited a few minutes before heading for the renovated warehouse she'd entered. As soon as he walked in, the aroma of coffee caught his attention and he headed for the small concession stand. While he waited for his order, he scanned the area. Artists on both sides of the aisle were setting up their tables and booths for the day.

It was a mix of arts and crafts. Next to the coffee stand, an older couple had a display of landscape paintings: waterfalls, mountain sunsets, and a few of downtown Asheville. Directly across the aisle was a booth filled with stained-glass pieces.

It was a cool place, one he'd have to come back and investigate when he wasn't on a mission. A puppy bark caught his attention, and coffee in hand, he headed for it. In the middle of the building, he found his target standing in front of a long table loaded with pottery, tangled up in the leash her puppy had wrapped around her legs.

"He taking you prisoner?" Jack said.

She glanced over at him with laughter in those golden-brown eyes, and his heart thump-skipped in his chest. That had never, ever happened before, and he almost turned and walked away. A female-induced twitchy heart wasn't his thing.

Then she leaned precariously, looking like a tree about to topple over. Jack dropped his coffee onto the table next to her and was at her side in time to catch her before she landed face-first on the cement floor. Damn, she smelled good, like vanilla and maybe almonds. Whatever it was, it made his mouth water.

"Um, you can let me go now."

And there was that throaty voice that had kept him awake last night. "Do I have to?" He winked to let her know he was teasing—not really—and then he made sure she was steady on her feet before crouching down in front of the puppy.

"Hey, buddy," he said, putting one hand on the dog's rear end. Jack lifted his gaze to his new fantasy. "What's his name?"

"Rambo."

"Here's the deal, Rambo. When I say sit, you're going to plant your butt on the ground." He pushed down on

Rambo's rear end while pressing the palm of his other hand to the puppy's nose. "Sit." Still keeping his hands on the dog, he had to repeat the command a second time when the little guy tried to climb onto his lap.

Rambo wasn't stupid. He recognized Jack was the alpha and kept his butt glued to the ground this time, although he did wiggle his rear end, all that puppy energy making it impossible to sit completely still. But he kept his gaze on Jack, as if waiting for his next instructions.

"Good boy." Jack gave him a chin scratch as a reward.

"Wow, how did you do that?"

As soon as the puppy heard her voice, he tried to jump up her legs, his tail furiously wagging. She laughed, a musical sound that Jack liked a lot.

"A combination of things. Using my hands to signal what he needs to do for one, but mostly the tone of my voice."

"Can you show me?"

That would be an affirmative. Jack took a moment to rein in his lust before lifting his eyes to hers. "I could help you train him."

He took the end of the leash from her hand and unwound it, freeing her legs. Wasn't his fault if the leash was so tight that his fingers brushed across her skin as he performed his chore. Not that it was a chore in any way, shape, or form. The goose bumps that rose where he touched her pleased him. She wasn't immune to him.

"Are you a professional dog trainer?"

How much truth to tell her? Most of it, just not the stalking part. That was entirely too creepy. He stood, keeping the leash and tightening it so that Rambo had to stay by his legs.

"Jack Daniels," he said, holding out his hand.

She raised a finely arched brow. "For real?"

"Yeah. My parents had a weird sense of humor. My SEAL teammates call me Whiskey, if that works better for you." A lot of people thought SEALs weren't allowed to reveal their identity, but that wasn't true. They just didn't go around advertising the fact. He hoped knowing would make her feel more comfortable with him.

He smiled—impressed that he remembered how—and waited to hear her answer.

Nichole eyed the blond-haired, blue-eyed man who was apparently a dog whisperer. Wow, an honest-to-God SEAL, and he was as hot as the SEAL heroes in her romance books. Maybe even hotter. Definitely hotter.

"Nice to meet you, Jack. I'm Nichole Masters." She held out her hand, and it disappeared inside his massive one. His touch was gentle, but she was sure he could crush her bones if he wanted. His voice sounded vaguely familiar, but she was positive she'd never met him before. Jack Daniels was not a man a girl would forget.

"And you, Nichole." Rambo barked, and Jack let go of her hand. He smiled down at her puppy. "Yes, we haven't forgotten about you, Rambo." He glanced up at her. "That's a big name for the little man to live up to."

"I'm hoping he'll grow into his name. He's a rescue, part German shepherd, part anyone's guess. The vet said maybe some sheltie." Her hand was warm from being in his, her fingers tingling a little from his touch. The last time she'd had tingly anything from touching a man had been with Lane, before he had shown her his true self. But she wasn't going there, not when a hotter-than-hot hero was sharing her breathing space.

He handed her the leash. "Two intelligent dog combinations and very trainable. He'll test you, but he'll also want to please you."

She blinked, trying to catch up with their conversation. She ran his last words through her mind. Right. They were talking about Rambo. "Believe me, he's doing a great job of testing me." She'd never had a dog before, and honestly hadn't had a clue how rambunctious or destructive a puppy could be.

He glanced around. "Maybe this isn't the best place for him. At least not until he's trained."

As if to prove his point, Rambo tangled his leash around her legs again, then stuck his nose under her dress, lifting the hem halfway up her thighs. She bent over to grab the skirt before she flashed not only a hot SEAL but all the strangers around them, whose attention suddenly seemed to be on her.

Rambo dropped to his feet, gave a happy bark, and then tried to run in the opposite direction. With her legs bound together by the leash, preventing her from getting her balance, she toppled forward, her face heading directly for Jack's crotch.

She put her hands out to keep her mouth from landing on the most private part of him, but when she realized that would result in her groping him, she panicked and ended up windmilling her arms. A mere inch before her mouth got entirely too up close and personal with a man she'd only met minutes ago, a pair of hands slid under her arms and lifted her back to her feet. That would have been great if her new position wasn't breast to SEAL chest. An extremely hard chest. Desire spiked through her, adding to her embarrassment. Her cheeks and the back of her neck felt like they were on fire.

"Ah...ah." She realized her arms were sticking out in a pretty good imitation of a scarecrow, so she dropped them to her sides. He kept his hands on her arms, trailed his fingers over her skin, down to her wrists, leaving goose bumps in his wake. She lifted her gaze to his. Lord have mercy, his eyes were a hundred times darker than they had been before she'd smashed her breasts into his chest. She wondered if he would mind if she climbed him like a tree.

A slow—sexy as all get-out—smile curved his lips. "Hello," he murmured.

"Hi," she chirped. *Really, Nichole, you've taken to chirping?* He let go of her and stepped back, then dropped to his knees. Her heart slammed into her rib cage at seeing him in that position while her mind was stuck on the breasts-to-chest thing and her skin tingling from his touch.

As if he could read her thoughts, he lifted his eyes— still a darker blue—and gave her that sexy smile again. "I'm just going to free you."

"Oh." That came out sounding disappointed, and he chuckled. What in the world was wrong with her? She'd never reacted to a man like this before, not this fast and this...well, tingly.

"There, all better," he said once he had her un-wrapped from the leash. He tapped the puppy's nose. "You're a handful of trouble, aren't you?" Rambo tried to lick him. Jack stood and handed her the end of the leash.

"This is the first time I've brought him here with me. I guess I jumped the gun, but he's learned to rec-ognize when I'm leaving and starts to cry. I felt guilty for sticking him in his crate all day. Eventually I want to be able to bring him, but obviously I need to wait until he loses some of his puppy energy."

"That will happen, even faster if he gets some training, but yeah, this isn't a good place for him right now. Too many interesting things and people to check out."

"Live and learn, right?" A couple walked up to her booth. "Um, I need to get to work."

"You have your phone on you?"

"Yes. Do you need to make a call?" Heaven help her, the man really did have a killer smile.

"No. I was going to put my number in it. You know, in case you decide to take me up on my offer to help you train Rambo."

"Oh. Right." He probably thought she was a scatterbrain, but it was entirely his fault for being so sexy that it was hard to think around him.

As if to prove he needed training, her dog was straining at the end of his leash, trying to get the couple's attention with begging yips, hoping for a little petting. "Rambo, no." She pulled him back toward her, and of course, he planted his paws so that she ended up dragging him.

She glanced at Jack, expecting to see disapproval, but the only thing in his eyes was amusement. "Here." She unlocked her phone and handed it to him. "You'll definitely be hearing from me if you can teach him some manners."

"I can."

When he handed her phone back, their fingers brushed against each other, and there was that tingling again.

"Take care, Nichole." He squatted in front of Rambo. "I know you have a lot of energy, buddy, but try to behave for your mistress." Rambo tossed himself onto his back, his tail scraping across the floor.

"I don't think *behave* is in his vocabulary."

Jack glanced up at her as he gave her dog a belly rub. "Part of teaching him that word will be to teach you how to master him."

There was something in the way he said that, in the flash of heat in his eyes, that had her almost fanning her face. "Um, master him, right." *Jeez, Nichole, get your mind out of the gutter.*

That was easier said than done with this man, and when the heat returned to his eyes and one side of his mouth curved up, she knew he knew right where her mind had gone. Again.

She glanced at the couple, who were still browsing. The woman picked up a mug. "I love how you embedded a maple leaf in these. I'll take the set."

"I'll be right with you." She glanced at Jack. "Gotta go." Before something else came out of her mouth… Like *my bed is only a few minutes from here. Want to go play?*

He rose in a slow unfolding of his body that had her eyes tracking every movement and flex of his muscles. Oh, yeah. Sex. On. A. Freakin'. Stick. She'd been burned so badly by her last boyfriend that she'd gone through an I-hate-men stage. That phase might have just ended.

"Hope to hear from you, Nichole," he said before picking up his coffee.

"I think you will," she murmured as she watched him walk away. "And real nice butt, Whiskey," she added.

Her morning had started off as one of the crappiest ever. She'd woken up tired and out of sorts after drinking enough wine to get up the nerve to call Trevor the Bastard Allen at three in the morning and tell him what she thought of him for sabotaging her commission. She'd figured that if she was up at that time of night, stewing over what he'd done, that it was only right for his sleep to be disturbed. The jerk had pretended not to know who she was.

Rambo hadn't helped her mood when she'd found her favorite running shoes chewed up. Her fault for leaving them out, but weren't all the toys she'd showered him with enough? Considering everything the world had rained down on her recently, she deserved a hot SEAL to play with, right? But she refused to appear too eager—because, really, the man probably had eager-to-get-into-his-pants women at his beck and call—so she'd wait a bit to contact him.

Don't miss Operation K-9 Brothers *by Sandra Owens,*
available now wherever ebooks are sold.
www.CarinaPress.com

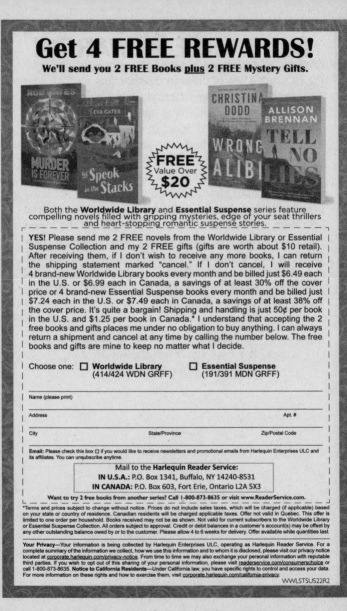

HARLEQUIN
PLUS

Try the best multimedia
subscription service for romance
readers like you!

Read, Watch and Play.

Experience the easiest way to get
the romance content you crave.

Start your **FREE TRIAL** at
<u>www.harlequinplus.com/freetrial</u>.